Faithfully Executed

Also by Michael Bowen:

Can't Miss
Badger Game
Washington Deceased
Fielder's Choice

Faithfully Executed

▲

MICHAEL BOWEN

ST. MARTIN'S PRESS   NEW YORK

Faithfully Executed is a work of fiction. Aside from well-known historical personnages and contemporary political figures referred to in passing by their own names, the characters depicted in the story do not exist and the events described did not take place. They are products of the author's imagination, and any apparent resemblance to actual events or to actual persons, living or dead, is accidental and not intended. There is in fact a major horse show held every year in Kansas City, Missouri, called the American Royal. Unlike the fictional American Royal described in *Faithfully Executed*, however, the actual American Royal takes place in early November.

Design by Judy Dannecker

Library of Congress Cataloging-in-Publication Data

Bowen, Michael, 1951-
    Faithfully executed / Michael Bowen.
        p. cm.
    ISBN 0-312-07018-7
    I. Title.
    PS3552.O864F35   1992
    813'.54—dc20
                                        91-39066
                                         CIP

First Edition: February 1992

10 9 8 7 6 5 4 3 2 1

FOR LENORE WOOLF, WITH GRATITUDE.

"The President shall be Commander in Chief of the Army and Navy of the United States. . . . and he shall have Power to Grant Reprieves and Pardons for Offenses against the United States. . . . He shall from time to time give to the Congress Information of the State of the Union, and recommend to their Consideration such Measures as he shall judge necessary and expedient; . . . [and] he shall take Care that the Laws be faithfully executed. . . ."

—United States Constitution, Article II, sections 2 and 3

Faithfully Executed

CHAPTER ONE

The day before he was supposed to kill Henry Luttwalk, Alex Cunningham tilted at rings. He enjoyed himself.

The chestnut mare responded gamely to the subtle pressure from his knees. The lance's conical guard felt comfortable over his gauntleted hand, its haft natural under his armpit. Eleven times out of twelve he took the mare at full gallop past a gnarled, leafy oak, stabbed out and down at the last moment, and snared the six-inch brass ring dangling from the tree.

The three dozen people who'd gathered to watch him applauded appreciatively at each pass. Mellow September sun turned the northern Virginia countryside emerald. A tangy Blue Ridge scent permeated the gentle breeze wafting over the group.

It was with real regret that Cunningham left around three o'clock to catch his flight and keep the Luttwalk appointment.

Flat, Ginny McNaghten thought. Kansas is supposed to be as flat as a pool table. Everyone in Washington knew that. Where did the hills that had been rolling by and were now crawling past outside the school-bus window come from?

By scrunching down in her seat and looking through the lower half of her window, McNaghten could now just pick out the pinkish red brick wall they were driving toward. Scattered gatherings of people dappled the slope that angled down from the barrier. A group of just over a hundred knelt at the wall's base. Ten yards farther down the slope a slightly larger crowd displayed picket signs in reproachful silence.

A herd of college-aged men wove among these two gatherings and a larger assembly nearer the main gate. All but one of the collegians wore sweatshirts with Greek capital letters on them. The exception was dressed as a bird with blue and red feathers, a gold head, and gold saddle shoes. They shouted derisively at the other groups and flourished beer cans for the benefit of Minicams swarming over the area.

"What's the bird supposed to be?" McNaghten asked.

"Jayhawk."

McNaghten looked blankly at her companion.

"Mythical species adopted as the mascot for the University of Kansas," he explained.

"Oh."

The bus had by now chugged to within thirty feet of the gate that led through the massive wall. McNaghten could read a neat little sign saying "Leavenworth Federal Penitentiary."

> Classes for the masses,
> Not gas for the criminal class!

The speaker's doggerel and the answering acclaim from nearly two hundred surrounding spectators just off the road near the gate easily penetrated the bus full of reporters. The speaker stood on an orange crate and orated through a bullhorn. His group enjoyed the lion's share of the media attention outside the wall. The speaker was running for president of the United States and the election was less than fourteen months away.

"Someone should tell him they're using lethal injection instead of the gas chamber," the reporter from *Rolling Stone* said. He rubbed his palm idly over the Harley-Davidson trademark on his black T-Shirt, down to the words "JAP BIKES SUCK" that undergirded it.

"He knows," the colleague sitting next to McNaghten answered. "He's just taking a little poetic license. Try finding a rhyme for 'lethal injection.' "

" 'Syphilitic infection.' "

"That's racist."

"Bullshit."

"Bullshit my ass. If he were white he'd be president. Right, Ginny?"

"No," McNaghten said. "If he were white he'd be Fred Harris."

Regina V. McNaghten was forty-four years old. Her short, straight hair and her snapping eyes were brown. While she wasn't altogether unattractive, no one would've called her beautiful. Even when something had caught her eye and she was gazing at it with steady attention, she crossed and recrossed her ankles, and her fingers flicked at specks on her lap.

She had been a working reporter since she was nineteen. By thirty-nine she'd been fired six times for insubordination. After the last pink slip she'd started Chesapeake News Service. CNS five years later had one correspondent, one reporter, one secretary, one typist and one full-time staffer, and Regina V. McNaghten was all of them. She made less than a congressional aide. Considerably less.

In the WDAF satellite/sound truck that labored through the gate ahead of the school bus, an assistant producer from Kansas City's NBC affiliate station was trying to get Kenneth Dahl to focus on the diagram she'd drawn.

"We'll be parked right here," she said, using a stiletto-thin pencil point to indicate a small rectangle sketched onto an overview of the visitors' parking lot at Leavenworth.

"Right," Dahl said without looking at the diagram. "As long as the camera can pick up a guard tower and barbed wire and some other prison stuff over my left shoulder."

"It's razor wire, not barbed wire," the assistant producer said.

"I thought razor wire was just a fancy euphemism for barbed wire. Not true?"

"Barbed wire has points. Razor wire just has an edge."

She looked up to see whether Dahl was absorbing any of this. Dahl nodded slowly. He looked deeply and directly into her eyes. He showed perfectly capped, stunningly white teeth in an engaging smile. The assistant producer broke eye contact and glanced back down at the diagram.

Ken Dahl was twenty-six years old. He had golden hair and midnight blue eyes, a melt-in-your-mouth face, and a solidly built frame. He made more than congressmen did. Considerably more.

"You have to be down there and ready to go at 10:35 sharp," the assistant producer said to him. "I'll cue you at 10:37 and we'll have forty-five seconds on the bird. Okay?"

Dahl said nothing. The assistant producer glanced up again. She met the same soulful gaze and the same picture-postcard smile.

"Okay?" she repeated.

"Okay," Dahl said, the slightest hint of condescension coloring his voice. He repeated the deliberate nod. "The timing is fine. My flight back to D.C. isn't until 7:30 tonight."

The assistant producer dropped her pencil and patted Dahl's hand. There was nothing nuanced about her condescension.

"You're back in Kansas, Toto," she said. "I'm not Holly Hunter."

McNaghten killed time in the Leavenworth Visitor Orientation Center figuring out who didn't fit in. The reporters and the TV newspeople—TV newspeople didn't qualify as reporters, in McNaghten's view—stood out like Rotarians at a Vassar reunion. Wisecracking Rotarians. Standing around making macabre jokes, affecting a bored, world-weary cynicism, as if coming all the way to Kansas to watch a man die were just another day at the office.

The guards were obvious too. Especially the ones in plain clothes, warily eyeing everyone else in the room.

The first one she spotted who wasn't a guard or a media type was a portly, round-faced man in late middle age who hurried into the room carrying a black doctor's bag. Before he'd gotten halfway to the well-guarded door on the other side of the room he was surrounded by microphones and notebooks. Dahl, showing energy McNaghten wouldn't have given him credit for, hustled to the front of the crush surrounding the physician and managed seven or eight seconds of close communion with him.

McNaghten waited until the man had worked his way free of the questioners and was signing the register mounted just in front of the door leading to the prison's inner precincts.

"If there's a reprieve," she called across the room then in a piercing contralto, "do you still get paid?"

A slightly befuddled expression on his face, the doctor glanced around in the sudden quiet that followed McNaghten's question.

"No per diem," he shrugged after a moment's hesitation. "Just mileage and expenses."

"I'm innocent, I never killed no one."

This statement, patently and unarguably false, sounded especially pathetic over the closed-circuit television speakers that brought it to McNaghten and her colleagues. Henry Luttwalk, the man who spoke these words, seemed more bewildered than frightened, his eyes vacant, his minimal gestures jerky and distracted. McNaghten figured he had at this moment forty-seven minutes to live.

Henry Luttwalk was white, thirty-eight years old, of average intelligence. He wasn't a member of any racial, ethnic, or other identifiable group enjoying organized protection or perceptible public support. He wasn't suffering from any mental disease or defect. And he was guilty as hell of a hideous crime. He was therefore an ideal candidate for the first legal execution to be carried out by the United States government in more than a generation.

Before he was thirty, Luttwalk had gone to prison twice, once for eighteen months for receiving stolen property and once for four years for hitting a man's left knee with a baseball bat until the knee broke. (The man had failed to repay some money he owed to Luttwalk's boss. The court hadn't considered this a mitigating circumstance.)

On a cold December night not quite two years before the date McNaghten and her colleagues gathered at Leavenworth, Luttwalk had knocked on the door of the lower flat of a duplex in southeast Washington, D.C. A black woman had opened the door as far as the chain would allow, to see who was there. Luttwalk had shot the woman in the face with a .44 Magnum revolver, shredding the protective chain in the process.

Entering the flat, Luttwalk had then hurried to the rear bedroom, where he'd found Terry Hurst, a twenty-two-year-old white male, lying in bed wearing a powder blue T-shirt and nothing else. After pistol-whipping Hurst, breaking his nose and two of his teeth, Luttwalk had dragged and kicked the half-naked young man out of the flat to a wine red Isuzu stretch minivan and forced him into the back.

For at least thirty minutes Luttwalk had driven his victim through Maryland into Virginia, past the Washington-area suburbs, to a semiru-ral area near Fairfax Courthouse. Here he had jerked Hurst from the van, shoved him into the pinewoods off the road, and made him kneel on the frozen, snow-covered ground. Then, according to a persuasive recon-struction based on marks left in the snow and on the ground, Luttwalk had squatted down, raised his revolver to eye level a few inches from Hurst's forehead, and pulled the trigger. An FBI agent the next morning found a piece of Hurst's skull forty-seven feet away.

Unfortunately for Luttwalk, Hurst's bed partner that night hadn't been the woman Luttwalk had killed in the parlor but that woman's fifteen-year-old daughter. She had hidden in a closet until Luttwalk had Hurst out on the street. Then she'd called the police with a mediocre descrip-tion of Luttwalk, an excellent description of the minivan, and three digits from its license plate. A Virginia state trooper finally spotted the minivan just seventeen minutes too late to save Terry Hurst's life.

Reflecting on this story, which she knew by heart, listening to the desultory, almost *pro forma* interview, McNaghten searched the blank, simian face on the screen. She was seeking a frisson of terror, a primordial chill, something you'd hang a man for. She saw nothing.

The pool interview lost momentum and wound down to an anticlimactic end. Reporters began to drift away from the television even before it was over.

McNaghten didn't drift away. The problem with Washington news in her view was that it was dominated by television, whose minions were lazy, stupid, and rich. She was here to cover a story and she was going to cover it.

The sound on the closed-circuit television went off. The picture continued for perhaps thirty seconds. She saw Luttwalk glance over to his left and stand up. Four guards and a man in a three-piece suit whom she recognized as Corky Baldwin, Luttwalk's lawyer, came into view. The guards gathered around Luttwalk and hesitated for a moment. Baldwin stepped forward and gripped Luttwalk's right hand with his own, resting his left hand on Luttwalk's upper arm. He pumped Luttwalk's right hand and then just stood still for a long moment, his face a mask of tightly controlled emotion. He looked into Luttwalk's eyes, and McNaghten wondered if he saw the same emptiness there that she had.

Lime green. The lime green plaster on the walls started about waist level, rising above dark maple woodwork. A plexiglass partition seven feet high divided the room roughly in half, lengthwise. On one side of the partition, twenty-seven men and twelve women—McNaghten had counted them—sat on unpadded folding chairs of dark green metal.

"I think I got some good stuff from the doctor," Dahl, who was sitting next to her, whispered to McNaghten.

"Good for you," McNaghton said, without sounding very impressed.

There were two people in the death chamber, a middle-aged man and a girl in her late teens, that McNaghten hadn't at first been able to place. They sat together, white, middle-class, and somber, at the far end of the front row, as distant from the others as they could get. They certainly weren't reporters. Then, tracking back through her memory of the clippings she'd read and the data she'd warehoused about this story, McNaghten realized that they must be the family of the man Henry Luttwalk had killed.

Something that looked like an operating table, though McNaghten supposed there was some other name for it, dominated the expanse on the other side of the partition. A tray stand stood near the table. On the white cloth that covered the tray lay three syringes and three plastic-cased needles. Hanging about two feet above the tray was a round, tapering bottle filled with clear liquid. An IV tube came from the bottom of the bottle and fell in coils on the tray. Halfway down the IV tube, plugged into either side of it, rubber stoppers, one black and one maroon, marked openings called ports.

At ten minutes of ten Corky Baldwin came into the death chamber on the spectator side of the partition and sat down in the last row. Two men in blue suits, white shirts, and dark ties moved to within a couple of seats of his. The two men were about as inconspicuous as Sherman tanks.

Baldwin was just over six feet tall. His charcoal gray vest strained a little across his thickening middle. His gray hair was thinning, his bushy gray eyebrows weren't. The people McNaghten had talked to said that Baldwin's considerable legal skills could be bought for around four hundred fifty dollars an hour. Yet in the United States District Court for the Eastern District of Virginia, the United States Court of Appeals for the Fourth Circuit, and the United States Supreme Court, Corky Baldwin had defended Henry Luttwalk passionately, doggedly, and apparently without compensation.

What the hell, she thought. It's worth a try. She turned around and leaned over the back of her chair.

"Any shot at all on the habeas action?" she stage-whispered to Baldwin.

For a second she thought he was going to ignore her. Then, a biting smile creasing his otherwise impassive face, he drew a slick, folded fax sheet from his inside coat pocket and handed it to her.

That's interesting, McNaghten thought as she took the page. He must think it'd be useful to have me in his hip-pocket somewhere down the road.

Captioned "United States vs. Luttwalk" and dated that day, the document's text was short. The law, so often awash in mannered prolixity, manages to say really important things with chilling concision: "The Court issued the following order in your case today: 'The petition for a writ of certiorari is denied. The motion for a stay is denied. By the Court: So Ordered.' "

At 9:57 a door at the far end of the room on the business side of the plexiglass partition opened. The silence on the spectator side of the partition deepened. Everyone sat up a little straighter and stiffened a bit.

A balding, ramrod-straight man wearing a lightweight khaki suit came through the door first. Warden, McNaghten guessed. Two unarmed, uniformed guards followed him. Then came someone in a white clinic coat. He pulled a gurney behind him. Luttwalk, lying on the gurney, strapped to it, came into the room head first, seemingly motionless, what they could see of his features—his face was turned away from the plexiglass—even emptier than they had been during the interview.

"How can he just lie there like that?" Dahl whispered. "How could he not turn his head around and drink in every sensation he could in the last few minutes he had?"

"Because he's shot full of thiopental sodium," McNaghten whispered.

"Huh?"

"They stick him with a soporific thirty minutes before they start the lethal injection. Supposed to make the whole thing more humane."

"How do you spell that thiopenal stuff?" Dahl asked.

"Do your own homework," McNaghten said.

Another guy in a clinic coat was at the other end of the gurney. During McNaghten's explanation of thiopental sodium, two more guards, the doctor Dahl said he'd gotten some good stuff from, someone who looked like an all-purpose clergyman, the prison public information officer they'd already met, and a black man wearing a blue dress shirt and dark brown trousers had come in. The black man had a surgical mask over his face.

Perfect, McNaghten thought when she saw the surgical mask. A black hood would've been ghoulish.

The two attendants wheeled the gurney to the far side of the operating table. With practiced, effortless movements they detached the entire bed part of the gurney, lifted it to the operating table and clipped it into place. The black man in the surgical mask stepped to the tray and picked up the IV tube. The public information officer took several steps toward the plexiglass. The warden took an official-looking page out of a mustard-colored civil service routing envelope.

"Michael Rattigan, warden of Leavenworth Federal Penitentiary, will now read the death warrant," the public information officer said.

The warden did so. The warrant said that Luttwalk had been duly tried for and convicted of violating some numbers in the United States Code, had been sentenced to be put to death, and was now to be executed in the manner by law made and provided for. As if this were a sheriff's sale on a mortgage foreclosure. It didn't say that Luttwalk was being killed because he'd brutalized a terrified young man and then blown his head apart after, incidentally, driving him across a couple of state lines.

Everyone in the room seemed to tense. The reporters leaned forward. The two men sitting near Baldwin looked hard at the lawyer. Baldwin stared straight ahead.

Luttwalk lay absolutely still.

The warden waited ten seconds before he nodded at the man in the surgical mask, who had attached the IV tube to one of the syringes on the tray. The masked man took Luttwalk's left arm in his left hand, turned the arm inside upward, hesitated for a long, not very comfortable second, then slipped the needle into a vein in the hollow of the inside of Luttwalk's elbow.

"The procedure officer has started an intravaneous flow consisting at this point of a sterile, saline solution only," the public information officer said.

The procedure officer, as McNaghten now knew to call him, raised a second syringe to the red-stoppered port.

The public information officer mumbled something else ending with "this is not repeat not fatal."

McNaghten stopped listening to him. For one thing, it all seemed wrong to her. Not morally. Aesthetically. An execution should be an execution, not an etiolated bureaucratic exercise. That was part of it.

But there was something else. Something wasn't quite right about the way the guy in the mask was acting as he raised the third syringe. The hint of indecision, the moment of uncertainty before he put the IV needle into Luttwalk's arm—she couldn't put her finger on exactly what had tipped her. But every journalistic nerve end she had was tingling.

Fascinated, intent, she watched the masked procedure officer inject what she knew to be procuronium bromide into the black-stoppered opening. Down the tube, through the needle, into the vein, through Luttwalk's bloodstream to his heart, which the poison was supposed to stop in a big damn hurry. Six minutes after the injection, the man with the doctor's bag stepped up to the table. For several minutes, he felt for Luttwalk's pulse, listened for his heartbeat, checked for respiration, examined the pupils of his eyes, and tested for nerve responses. When he had finished doing all of that, he pronounced Luttwalk dead.

The attendants lifted the body back to the gurney. The execution party followed them through the far door. The reporters started to stir.

"All right," Dahl said. "We've got our story."

You've got yours, McNaghten thought. I just started working on mine.

CHAPTER TWO

"Major Cunningham," Rattigan said to the black man who had by now removed his surgical mask, "I can't believe you're serious."

"I'm serious," Cunningham affirmed. "I'm not much given to humor."

Dr. Frank Dennison had pronounced Luttwalk dead about three minutes before. Rattigan and Cunningham were standing with Leavenworth's public information officer in a tiny office where Rattigan had hastily pulled Cunningham after Cunningham's abrupt demand immediately outside the death chamber that Luttwalk's body be held for an autopsy. The rest of the execution party was waiting uncertainly with Luttwalk's body a few yards down the corridor.

"Autopsies cost money," Rattigan said. "They take time. They require trained personnel. I don't have authority to order something like that in a situation where the procedures don't call for it."

"Then get the authority."

Rattigan crossed his arms over his chest and rocked back a bit on the corner of the desk where he'd perched.

"Major," he said quietly, "this isn't the army and I'm not a second lieutenant. You're not in any position to give me orders."

"I know it's not the army," Cunningham said. "I'm not in the army anymore anyway. But I was in the army once. I was in Vietnam for one year, seven months and twenty-three days. And I was in-country for almost all of that tour."

Cunningham paused for a moment. *I was in-country and you weren't.* He looked at Rattigan to confirm that this comment had produced the moral advantage he expected. It had.

"I've held wounded men," Cunningham continued. "I've held dying men, and I've held dead men. I've held men so hopped up on morphine they might as well've been on another planet. I know the difference between what an arm feels like when it's attached to someone who's alive but unconscious, and what it feels like when it's a piece of dead meat."

"And that's something you can tell based on holding the arm for a few seconds, when a trained physician noticed nothing wrong?"

"The doctor didn't feel the body when I did."

"He sure as hell felt the body when he gave Luttwalk the sleepy-juice," Rattigan snorted. "Are you saying Luttwalk somehow died during the half-hour between then and the time you started the execution?"

"That's what I think."

"Well I think you're wrong."

"Fine. Then an autopsy'll prove I'm wrong."

"It'll open up a can of worms. Media speculation. Everyone wondering why we did it. Even if the autopsy conclusively proves you wrong there'll be some wiseguy claiming it's just a cover-up and there's some dark conspiracy going on. Geraldo Rivera'll still be doing pieces on this ten years from now, just like the Kennedy assassination and the Warren Report."

"The press is on it either way," Cunningham said. "This thing was big news. The networks were here, CNN, *Time* and *Newsweek*, *New York Times*, *Washington Post*. You don't think they're all gonna miss it, do you? They're on it whether you do the autopsy or not. If you don't do the autopsy it looks even more like a cover-up."

"What do you mean 'the press is on it'? The press can't be on anything unless you put them on it."

"That's exactly what—"

A voice over a loudspeaker interrupted Cunningham's reply.

"Warden Rattigan," the voice said. "Please call 4206. Paging Warden Rattigan. Please call 4206."

Rattigan punched the specified numbers into the phone on the desk.

"Rattigan," he said. "What is it?"

"One of the reporters who covered the execution just now, Warden. Regina McNaghten. Wants a comment on the report that something went wrong with the procedure."

Rattigan started to answer, then stopped. Eyes glinting and skeptical, he looked appraisingly at Cunningham. He took two deep breaths. He ran his left hand over his forehead and through his close-cut, salt-and-pepper hair.

"Take a number and say I'll get back to her," he said into the phone. He bolted from the desk, whipped past Cunningham, and stuck his head out into the hall. "Spencer!" he barked.

"Yessir," one of the guards answered.

"Have the body taken to the infirmary and held until further orders."

"Yessir."

"All right," he said then to Cunningham and the public information officer. "Let's go back to my office. I've got to make some phone calls."

At mind-boggling speed the message that something funny was going on with the Luttwalk execution traveled by telephone line and computer circuit throughout the nervous system of the federal government. It raced from the warden's office at Leavenworth Federal Penitentiary to the deputy director of the Bureau of Prisons in Washington, D.C., and from there to the assistant attorney general in charge of the Criminal Division of the Department of Justice and to a senior aide to the deputy attorney general. The information sped almost simultaneously from another phone at Leavenworth, this one held by a man wearing a white shirt and a blue suit, to the FBI field office in Kansas City, Missouri, and from there to FBI headquarters in Washington.

All of this had happened less than five minutes after Rattigan had gotten back to his office. Within fifteen minutes after that the news had reached at least a dozen other government organs, including the Defense Intelligence Agency and the Criminal Investigation Division of the United States Army.

Some of the people who got this information were career employees of the federal government. Their job was to make sure that the permanent government functioned without undue interference from the political hacks that the American people insisted on electing periodically. Other recipients of this data, on the other hand, were political appointees. Their job was to make sure that the people's elected representatives didn't get shafted by the permanent government.

Which was why, twenty-one minutes and thirty-eight seconds after Rattigan got back to his office, the news reached a special assistant to the president of the United States, working in the west wing of the White House.

CHAPTER THREE

Y ou're not going to smoke, are you?" Dahl asked McNaghten
when he saw her open the ashtray on the dashboard.

"Jesus, Ken, nobody smokes anymore," McNaghten answered
distractedly. "Smoking went out sometime in the Carter administration."

She plugged her laptop computer's DC cord into the cigarette lighter
inside the ashtray. Almost immediately, her fingers started dancing over
the laptop's keys.

Dahl and McNaghten were in the Lincoln Town Car that Dahl's
station provided for him, maneuvering out of the main parking lot at
Washington's National Airport. It was after 11 P.M. Since the execution
they'd had a tedious bus trip, two unremarkable meals on the run, a long
wait at KCI Airport, and a plane ride from Kansas City. McNaghten had
spent the waiting time making over forty telephone calls. Dahl had spent
it reading *Sports Illustrated* and wondering whether his station would
repeat his live feed on the evening newscast. Dahl still wasn't sure how
McNaghten had talked him into dropping her off in northwest D.C. on
his way to his own home. Dahl waited until he had the mammoth car
free of the airport's precincts before he risked further conversation.

"What are you typing?"

"Nothing. Just some random thoughts."

What McNaghten was typing at that moment, in fact, was a curious,
telegraphic note about something she'd seen a few minutes before when
Dahl had opened the trunk so that she could put her bag inside. In one

corner of the trunk she'd noticed a red and gold vinyl gym bag with the Redskins logo on it. And peeking out of one unzipped corner she was sure she'd seen the toe of a combat boot and a swatch of camouflage fatigues. She added this to the notes ranging from clearly relevant to so-what that she'd been making since shortly after Luttwalk was wheeled out of the death chamber.

"Can I ask you something, Ginny?"

"You just did."

"Who's Holly Hunter?"

"Actress," McNaghten murmured without looking up. "Played the producer who had the hots for William Hurt in *Broadcast News.*"

"That's right," Dahl said, snapping his fingers. "I couldn't place the name."

"Right," McNaghten said.

"I hope they repeated the feed from Leavenworth," Dahl said then, as if to himself.

"They spent a ton of money getting you out there so you could talk for less than a minute. You can bet they used whatever you sent them as often as they could."

"I hope so. Sometimes I have the feeling they don't really take me seriously as a newsman."

"You can't mean that," McNaghten said, her eyes still riveted to the laptop's screen.

Dahl jerked his head around at the sarcastic tone.

"Keep your eyes on the road," McNaghten instructed him.

"You don't know what it's like," he murmured, shaking his head.

"Like hell I don't."

"That's not what I meant. Look, Ginny, I mean, you're a lot older and more experienced than I am—"

"Thanks a lot."

"But colleague to colleague now. I mean, I'm an electronic journalist and you're a print journalist—"

"I am *not* a 'print journalist,' " McNaghten interrupted him, looking up sharply. "I'm a *reporter.* I dig up stories and I get the lead in the first 'graph. Don't accuse me of committing journalism."

"Okay, okay," Dahl said impatiently. "I'm an electronic *reporter,* you're a print *reporter*—"

"You're not a reporter's left elbow," McNaghten snorted in exasperation. "You're a news-reader. You're a rip-and-read hunk. You don't get stories. You stand in front of a camera looking gorgeous and you read stories that someone else has gotten and someone else has written."

"All right then," Dahl said, confronting this unappealable verdict pluckily and with almost painful earnestness. "Fair enough. What dues do I have to pay? What club do I have to join? What do I have to do to qualify as a reporter?"

"Don't ask that question unless you want me to answer it," McNaghten sighed.

"I'm asking."

"There's nothing you can do," McNaghten said then. "No one as pretty as you can ever expect to be taken seriously in this business."

"Why not?"

"Because no one as pretty as you will ever have to do what it takes—and no one ever does what it takes unless he has to."

THE DAY AFTER
THE EXECUTION

CHAPTER FOUR

Cunningham brought the dark brown colt around in a tight circle and coaxed him at a gentle prance back between the two casual lines of onlookers. Members of the audience commented approvingly on the animal, using words like "flash" and "address" and "true."

"He's quite good with horses," Nathaniel Lever told Richard Michaelson as he turned away from the paddock and began trudging toward a huge, oblong, open-sided tent ten yards away. Lever was a special assistant to the president. "He can add fifty thousand dollars to the syndication value of a stallion just by sitting on top of it while it goes through its paces."

It was three o'clock in the afternoon on the day following Henry Luttwalk's demise. Muted fall sunlight spilled over the gently rolling acres of Lincoln green grassland cut at intervals by white fences. Despite the hour, most of the ten dozen people in the crowd wore tuxedos or evening gowns. Americans, Arabs, Japanese, and Koreans mingled behind Lever and Michaelson, members of the comfortable cosmopolitan fraternity of wealth.

Michaelson followed Lever into the tent. Michaelson wasn't wealthy. He was fifty-eight years old, nearly six-two with a spare frame, eyes so dark brown they looked black, and angular, sculpted features. The pension he'd earned during thirty-five years in the United States Foreign Service and the stipend he now received from the Brookings Institution scarcely counted as pocket change at a gathering like this.

A long table dominating the center of the enclosure groaned under a plentiful buffet. A few latecomers were filing past the table from the opposite end of the tent, discreetly dropping checks into a large, cut-glass bowl as they did so. Michaelson, without paying for the privilege himself, was at Lever's invitation attending a fund-raiser for the party in power at the moment. It was much more understated, much more exclusive, much more upscale than the familiar hundred-dollars-a-plate-for-roast-sirloin-and-green-peas fund-raiser, but the essence was the same: one way or another, the checks had to go in the bowl.

Lever handed Michaelson a china plate, French blue with gold trim, and a small, two-pronged silver fork, and then took one of each for himself. Michaelson loaded his plate with shrimp and cocktail sauce from an ice-filled bowl. Lever took three slabs of pink salmon.

"Lemonade or champagne?" Lever asked.

"Champagne," Michaelson said without hesitation. "Most stereotypes about embassy life aren't accurate, but that one is."

Stemmed goblets of Moet-Hennessy in one hand and food-laden plates in the other, the two men walked from the tent toward an inviting section of fence. A hundred yards to their right loomed an eighteenth-century stone-and-frame house in the uncomplicated Georgian style favored by Virginia's frugal gentry. Lever pointed in the opposite direction, toward a silvery strip barely visible on the horizon.

"Know what that is?" he asked.

"I assume it's the James River, though for all I can actually see of it, it might just as well be the Ohio."

"That's the last speck of tidewater you can see in Virginia. That little dash of pastel blue in the middle of the silver there. From here west is piedmont—horse country."

Michaelson nibbled unhurriedly at sauce-drenched shrimp. Patience wasn't his outstanding virtue, and he assumed that Nathaniel Lever hadn't brought him out here on less than three hours' notice to chat about local geography. But Michaelson hadn't spent three-and-a-half decades in the Foreign Service without learning when to keep his mouth shut.

"We have a problem," Lever said then, abruptly.

"Who's 'we'?"

"The administration. The White House. The party."

"Those are three very different things."

"Not so very different as all that, with an election year coming up."

"What's the problem?" Michaelson asked.

"It's that gent you saw doing the horse work," Lever said.

Michaelson glanced back at the horseman, still showing off the colt.

Just under six feet tall, his build was tight and compact. He was wearing an ordinary white, long-sleeved dress shirt, now sweat stained, a pair of greenish brown twill trousers, and paratroop boots. Maize-colored gauntlets covered his hands. He was black, smooth-skinned, and fuzzy-haired.

"Who is he?"

"Alex Cunningham," Lever answered. "Retired as a major after twenty years in the army. Free-lances as a consultant in the high-priced horse business. Good thing. That was the cover I came up with on the spur of the moment to justify his presence here today."

"Why should he need a cover?"

"His active employment these days also includes eligibility for any jobs that come up for a GS-12/Special Assignments."

"What's a GS-12/Special Assignments?"

"Executioner."

"Literally?"

"Literally. I believe the technical term is procedure officer. If you're going to have capital punishment, you have to make some kind of bureaucratic arrangement for who's going to perform the executions. Especially if you're using lethal injection, which is a little more compli-cated than just pulling a lever or throwing a switch."

"How has he created a problem for you?"

"He was the procedure officer assigned to the execution of Henry Luttwalk at Leavenworth yesterday," Lever said.

"I saw it on the news last night. Because of the local angle a station here actually sent one of its own people out to do an on-scene broadcast. I gathered from the report that the execution went off without a hitch."

"Not quite."

"What do you mean?"

"Cunningham says that he first saw Luttwalk lying on the gurney just before he was taken into the death chamber," Lever said. "He didn't look exactly right, but Cunningham figured that if he were about to spend his last twenty minutes on earth and knew it, he might not look too right either. Then, when he picked Luttwalk's arm up to start the IV, he says the arm just felt like dead weight. No pulse, no feeling of life at all."

"But he must have proceeded anyway," Michaelson said.

"That's right. According to the protocol. Immediately after the execu-tion, however, Major Cunningham insisted that an autopsy be per-formed, and he eventually got his way."

"With what results?"

"The most important initial finding was that there was a very large concentration of procuronium bromide—that's the toxin that was supposed to kill Luttwalk—in the vein just beyond the injection point, indicating that Major Cunningham's injection didn't get any farther into Luttwalk's body than gravity and the hydraulic pressure of the IV could force it," Lever explained. "The physician who explained this to me felt called upon to spell out the key implication: Luttwalk's blood was no longer circulating at the time of the injection."

"In other words," Michaelson said, "Luttwalk was dead before Cunningham put the supposedly lethal needle in."

"Exactly."

"He was still breathing when he was put onto the gurney?"

"Several witnesses independently say yes," Lever answered. "And not very long before that he was talking to a large group of reporters."

"So Luttwalk either killed himself, or was killed by somebody else, a matter of minutes before he was to be legally executed."

"That's the way it looks," Lever said.

"An intriguing stab at the proverbial perfect crime," Michaelson mused. "There'd be no reason to suspect murder, because everyone would quite reasonably assume that the execution accounted for the death. The prison officers might suspect something was wrong, but unless they were absolutely sure, the odds'd be very high that they'd let things proceed and, ah, shroud their doubts in discreet silence."

"That's the way I'd bet," Lever agreed. "Having their highest-profile and most carefully watched inmate killed under their noses wouldn't reflect particularly well on them."

"Especially with a large number of reporters in the immediate vicinity," Michaelson said. "If Major Cunningham hadn't made a snap decision to demand an autopsy, it's almost certain the presumed murder would have gone undetected."

"Hurray for Major Cunningham," Lever commented dryly.

"As it happens, though," Michaelson said, "it was a nice try but it didn't work. Major Cunningham acted on his suspicions. The probability of murder has been established."

"It most certainly has."

"If it was murder," Michaelson continued, "there is a very small number of people who could have committed it. The FBI will investigate them and I'm sure will do so with its customary efficiency and legendary disregard for tact. One of those people will turn out to have had a reason to kill Luttwalk, or suddenly to have come into several thousand dollars that he or she can't explain, or to be extraordinarily suspicious in some other way. From then on it's a matter of routine. Nothing for a senior advisor to the president to get exercised about, Nat."

"There's something else," Lever said. "The man Luttwalk was sentenced to death for killing was a civilian employee at DOD. He worked for the army at the Pentagon as a computer specialist. At the time of his death, his specific assignment related to software security."

" 'Software security,' " Michaelson repeated. "That's the term for measures taken to keep teenage computer prodigies from tapping into the Strategic Air Command codes and ordering preemptive air strikes whenever they get bored?"

"A bit more prosaic, mostly, but that's the general category of concern. An earnest young woman I spoke with about it yesterday talked a lot about 'viruses' and 'worms.' The gist seems to be that there are secret orders you can infiltrate into computer programs without anybody knowing they're there. They lie there for awhile and then when a certain date comes or certain data are entered or something else happens, they start doing very nasty things, like destroying your entire data base or putting three extra zeroes on every check that's cut."

"That does sound quite mischievous from the Pentagon's point of view, even though we're almost pals with the Russians again."

"There's no specific reason to believe that the man's murder was related to his Pentagon work," Lever continued. "The army's Criminal Investigation Division and a couple of people from the Defense Intelligence Agency, however, found ways to be unobtrusively involved in the original investigation."

"And will likewise involve themselves in this one, I take it?" Michaelson asked.

"Your guess is as good as mine."

"I'm beginning to understand," Michaelson said.

"I very much hoped that you would," Lever resumed quietly. "FBI, CID, DIA. We have at least three agencies actively involved. Each employs people who carry guns. Each has turf to protect, parochial interests to safeguard, and a lot of other concerns that aren't necessarily congruent with the interests of the United States."

"Or its president," Michaelson said.

Lever nodded.

"What we need is someone to back things up. Stay in contact with each investigation. Coordinate them. Keep these cowboys from getting out of control. And so forth."

"And so forth?"

"You know what I'm saying. If anything goes wrong make sure the president knows in time to do something about it."

"The assignment seems a bit hypothetical."

"In my experience, it's much easier to deal with problems when they're still hypothetical than when you're shredding documents and getting advice on how to testify before congressional committees."

"Your point," Michaelson conceded. "What resources would this someone have?"

"Major Cunningham to start with. He's anxious to be involved and he can give you a leg up on the army side of it."

"Not only that, but you'd much rather he were on the inside pissing out than on the outside pissing in, to use the vernacular."

"Exactly right. Cunningham's the type who's apt to go to the press if he thinks something he heroically exposed is being covered up or forgotten about."

"So he's really part of the problem rather than part of the solution," Michaelson said. "You're asking me to co-opt him."

"If you like."

"Any unambiguous resources?"

"Need-to-know clearance for all pertinent files, a place to sit in the Old Executive Office Building, and a secretary who knows how to type."

"How much support could I count on, if push came to shove?"

"Enough, if you pick your spots and proceed with finesse."

"Not much, in other words," Michaelson said.

"Dick," Lever said, "I know you're looking for something top rung, and I know you've been banking most of your chips with the other party. I can't promise you anything—"

"Of course you can't. You have a team in place. Why change a hit?"

"—but I can tell you that your contribution will be very much appreciated."

Quiet for a moment, Michaelson looked back toward the James River. He still couldn't make out the patch of pastel blue marking the border between tidewater and piedmont Virginia.

"I know how much 'appreciation' means in Washington," he said. "I can be bought, I suppose, but my price is higher than that."

"Dick, listen, I—"

"I joined the State Department in the early fifties," Michaelson interrupted quietly. "The principal partisan issue then was whether the country was being subverted more rapidly by the department's communists or by its homosexuals—both of which everyone seemed to think the department was harboring in droves. It was not a pleasant time."

"I know," Lever said. "I remember."

"We got through that time by sharing an ethic that made us feel elite. Part of our ethic was that if the president asked you to take a particular job, you didn't have the right to decline. Not the White House. The president. You were exactly like a private being ordered to run up a hill. If the president said he needed you, you couldn't say no."

Lever caught Michaelson's eyes and held them unblinking for a second or two.

"We need you, Dick," he said. "You can't say no."

CHAPTER FIVE

I suppose the leaks have already started?" Michaelson said to Cunningham.

"Something's started. You heard of an outfit called Chesapeake News Service?"

"No."

"They've already got one of their bloodhounds on this thing. Ginny McNaghten. Within fifteen minutes after I put the needle in Luttwalk, she was on the phone to the warden at Leavenworth, asking him about reports that something went wrong with the execution."

"I suppose that instead of saying that nothing had gone wrong he declined to comment?" Michaelson asked.

"Sure."

"Too bad. If she's any kind of reporter at all, that confirmed her suspicions and whetted her appetite. Oh well. Can't be helped."

It was just after 4:30. Michaelson and Cunningham were in the back seat of Lever's Chrysler New Yorker, heading back to Washington. Cunningham had showered and changed. He was now wearing a yellow dress shirt and khaki twill trousers. On a chain around his neck, Michaelson saw an enameled medallion showing the black-horsehead-black-bar-gold-background emblem of the Army's First Air Cavalry Division.

On the seat between them lay a modest stack of papers, the initial array of reports that Lever had gathered for them to look at. On top of the papers, in dark blue little leatherette folders, were the credentials they'd need to get into the Old Executive Office Building and the need-to-know access codes they'd have to have to make documents in three agencies' files pop up on their computer screens.

"While you were showering," Michaelson said, "I had Lever's secretary send out an electronic mail notice of a coordinating committee meeting tomorrow at eleven o'clock. Will you be able to make it?"

"Sure," Cunningham grinned. "I'm on Special Assignments, and this is my assignment. I wouldn't miss it. I hope it's a productive meeting."

"I'm afraid it will be quite unproductive."

"Then why are you having it?"

"We have to start somewhere, I suppose," Michaelson smiled. The smile was professional and just short of chilly.

"What do you want me to do? Other than come to this unproductive meeting?"

"I'm not sure yet."

They rode in silence for a couple of miles. Fat raindrops began to spatter against the windows. Michaelson's eyes were focused on a three-page memo that he'd picked up from the pile, but Cunningham noticed that well over a minute had passed without Michaelson's turning the page.

"Can I ask what you're thinking about?"

"Of course." Michaelson glanced up. "Sorry for woolgathering. I was going over the initial FBI report of the scene-of-crime investigation the day after Hurst's murder."

"Anything wrong with it?"

"Not that I can see. But I couldn't help wondering why the government made a federal case out of Luttwalk's crime in the first place."

"Instead of just letting Virginia nail him for murder, you mean?"

"Yes. Murder alone would've been plenty to deliver Luttwalk from this vale of tears, if that's what they were intent on doing. The Commonwealth of Virginia pays legions of district attorneys who seem to view capital cases as an enjoyable avocation. To prosecute Luttwalk federally, instead of leaving him in state hands, an overworked U.S. attorney had to prove murder plus interstate kidnapping. I'm not a lawyer, but that strikes me as a lot chancier. Why go to the trouble?"

"Good question," Cunningham said.

"And that provokes another question: Why did Luttwalk take the young man he killed on an elaborate excursion through three jurisdictions instead of just killing him in the house where he found him?"

"Okay," Cunningham nodded.

"Which in turn leads to what in a way is the most intriguing question.

The FBI was involved immediately. When did the CID and DIA get into the act?"

"I'll take a stab at finding that out tomorrow morning."

"That should be very helpful," Michaelson said.

"I'm not sure they'll tell me, understand," Cunningham cautioned.

"I'm quite sure they won't. But it should still be very helpful."

"Zen bureaucrat," Cunningham chuckled.

"I beg your pardon?"

"You talk in riddles, like a Zen master. No offense."

"That's marvelous," Michaelson beamed. "I've been searching for a quarter century for a description of how important things really happen in Washington, and I think you've just hit on it. Zen bureaucracy. It's perfect."

"You mind if I ask you something else?" Cunningham said then.

"No, go ahead," Michaelson murmured, his attention focused again on the report.

"We both know why Lever picked me for this job. Why'd he pick you? There must be guys already on his payroll who could chair coordinating committee meetings."

"You're certainly right about that." Michaelson paused. The tricky thing about co-opting someone was deciding exactly how much you had to tell him to make him trust you, without telling him so much that you defeated the purpose of the exercise in the first place. "I suppose the answer lies in defining what the job really is."

"I thought the job was to watch the watchmen, guard the guards, that kind of thing."

"That's the specific part of the instruction," Michaelson agreed. "Then there's the part that Lever covered so eloquently with 'and so forth.' "

"What's that part?"

"Finding out what the three agencies know that they're not telling."

"You mean spying on them?"

"Only as a last resort," Michaelson said. "Most intelligence is much more prosaic. Back in the sixties the government wanted to find out how fast a new weapon system the Pentagon was developing could be duplicated, once the existence of the weapon was revealed. Someone assigned a couple of university scientists, with no access at all to classified data, to compile as much information about the relevant technology as they could solely by looking at published and generally available sources. The scientists did this and submitted their report. The report revealed so much about the weapon system that it was immediately stamped 'Top Secret.' "

Cunningham grinned. "Are you saying Lever hired us to do the bureaucratic equivalent of reading the newspapers?"

"Close," Michaelson nodded. "What we're supposed to do is read between the lines. Force the memos out through the cracks. Play each agency off against the other. Make sure the president knows what the people who're supposed to be working for him aren't telling him. Zen bureaucracy."

"That what you did at Foggy Bottom?"

"That's an interesting question," Michaelson said. "The State Department is very low on the Central Intelligence Agency's routing list. Part of my job in the Foreign Service was to remedy that situation."

"Gotcha," Cunningham said.

Michaelson stepped into his modest Georgetown apartment twenty minutes later. He poured half a tumbler of Johnny Walker Black Label scotch, turned his television to CNN, and flipped his answering machine on to replay any recorded messages. There were several, but only the last one really grabbed his attention.

"This is Ginny McNaghten, Chesapeake News," a clipped, professional no-nonsense voice said. "I'd like to talk with you about the Luttwalk execution story."

THE SECOND DAY AFTER THE EXECUTION

CHAPTER SIX

D ahl pressed himself so hard against the floor that he could feel the clammy, rough-finish concrete right through his fatigues. His pistol gripped tightly in his right hand, he crawled through sluggish, clinging fog toward the doorway. Just short of it, he paused and listened for a telltale scrape of leather on cement. Ears straining, literally sweating from the intensity of his concentration, he heard nothing.

He brought his feet up underneath him. Coiled and tense, he paused again and listened. Then he dove through the opening into the corridor beyond.

He glimpsed a figure scrambling for cover at the end of the hallway. He raised his pistol but didn't fire. Instead he slithered furiously, awkwardly for the doorway ten feet beyond him on the opposite side of the corridor, his elbows biting into the concrete as if he were trying to dig through it. As soon as he reached the doorway he came to his haunches, chanced a hasty look into the room, leaped through, and backed quickly into the nearest corner. He planted his shoulder blades hard against the Sheetrock and swept the room nervously with his eyes.

Nothing. For just a second Dahl started to think about his next move. He thought a moment too long.

Out of the corner of his eye he saw the shoulder and arm and half the head of a man appear in the lower third of a doorway diagonally across the room from him. Dahl whipped his pistol around but the other man was quicker and much steadier. The instant before he would have fired, Dahl felt a heavy, thudding impact in the center of his chest. Something wet spattered over Dahl's throat and face, and he was suddenly looking through vivid red splashes coating both lenses of his goggles.

"You're dead," the man said.

"Shit," Dahl said.

10:35 A.M.

"Like the song used to go," Captain Tim Howard said over the phone to Cunningham, " 'there's a danger when you taste brown sugar.' Kid got in over his head."

"What song was that again?"

"Thought that might get a rise out of you. Just wanted to see if you were paying attention."

"No one ever accused you of sensitivity, did they?"

"I'm unliberated," Howard conceded cheerfully.

"You're unreconstructed. Hell, two days ago I took out the guy that killed the kid. 'Course I'm paying attention."

"You sure it was you took him out?"

"What's that supposed to mean?" Cunningham demanded jovially.

"Either you already know or I can't tell you. This a secure line, by the way?"

"Jesus but CID does strange and powerful things to people. Do you guys really handcuff yourselves to those cute little attaché cases you carry, or is that just infantry jive?"

"Make it to beer call at the Officers' Club some night and I'll tell you about burn-bag drill."

"Reason I called was, I've got to wondering about that very thing," Cunningham said then. "The whole dearly departed Luttwalk thing and what if I didn't know it you couldn't tell me. If Terry Hurst was just a horny kid who got his silly white ass caught in a cross fire while he was walking on the wild side, why were you guys all of a sudden hip deep in the thing practically before his next of kin were notified?"

"Who says we were?"

"Either I already know or you can't tell me," Cunningham said. "Which do you think it is?"

"I'm not saying one way or the other," Howard responded, after a two- or three-beat pause. "I still haven't heard you say this is a secure line. But whatever you know or think you know, remember—the kid was DOD personnel."

"Bullshit. I was in the army twenty years. Paperclip shrinkage in the quartermaster's office gets priority over off-premises murder of a Pentagon civilian."

"What're you tryin' to prove, Alex?"

"I'm the one *raised* the question of who really took out Luttwalk."

"So you have a personal interest in this thing?"

"Call it that if you want to," Cunningham said.

"It's in good hands. That's all I can say."

"You just said plenty," Cunningham muttered as he hung up the phone.

11:14 A.M.

". . . as a result of an overdose of thiopental sodium introduced into his system no more than approximately thirty minutes before the lethal injection began," FBI Special Agent Harvey Estabrook was saying.

Estabrook was sitting directly across from Michaelson at a round, cherrywood table that seemed oddly out of place in the windowless basement office in OEOB where they had gathered. To his left sat Cunningham and a woman in civilian clothes. A man in an army uniform sat to his right.

They were all being very cool about it, but OEOB was special and Michaelson could tell they knew it. No matter how sophisticated you were, no matter what your security clearance was, no matter how long you'd been in Washington and how many presidents you'd seen come and go, there was something about coming to work twenty-five feet from the west wing of the White House, showing your credentials to the first uniformed Executive Protection Service officer at the end of West Executive Avenue, showing them to the second officer, and then walking through the door while that guard saluted that produced a gut-tingle and made you know you were suddenly playing in a different league.

"Wasn't he supposed to get a shot of thiopental sodium prior to the execution?" Michaelson asked.

"Yeah. Only enough to tranquilize him, though, put him under. Not enough to kill him."

"Obviously. But the doctor who gave him that injection could have made a mistake and given him too much."

"That's one possibility," Estabrook conceded.

"What are the other possibilities?"

"I don't know that the bureau's satisfied with any conclusions it's reached on that score yet."

"That's curious. Do you mean we're not certain whether Luttwalk got the overdose in the course of the prescribed thiopental injection or in some other way?"

"No way to be sure," Estabrook shrugged. "It could've been that way. It could also've been a separate injection. Or it could have been given to him in something he ate or drank. Theoretically, he could even have given it to himself."

"A prisoner under a deathwatch could have given himself a hypodermic injection?" Michaelson asked.

"Thiopental sodium can be taken orally, in paste form. If he got his hands on some, he could've put it under his tongue and it would've reached his bloodstream very quickly. But that's all pretty academic. We don't think it was suicide."

"Let's explore the live possibilities, then," Michaelson said.

"Fine," Estabrook continued. "If Luttwalk got the overdose in what you call the prescribed injection, it could've been because the doctor somehow miscalculated the dosage, or it could've been because the doctor deliberately killed him, or it could've been because somebody switched syringes on the doctor. And then there's the last-meal theory."

"That one seems like a reach," Michaelson said. "The steak, salad, potatoes, and cola were picked at random from the officers' mess at Fort Leavenworth and prepared at the base kitchen. The warden made that decision only on the morning of the execution. The killer had no way to anticipate it, and I take it there hasn't been an epidemic of thiopental sodium overdoses among ranking base personnel."

Michaelson paused and glanced around the table. Estabrook had two Styrofoam coffee cups in front of him, nested one inside the other. Captain Arliss Posner, the man in uniform, sipped sparingly from a red cardboard cup with the Coca-Cola script logo written on it repeatedly in white. The woman, Mary Ellen Standish, kept her eyes fastened on a lined, white notepad.

"Thank you for your exposition," Michaelson said then to Estabrook. "I couldn't help noticing, however, that you told me nothing I couldn't have learned by reading the reports that have been filed thus far in the case."

"We try to put everything material in the reports," Estabrook smiled.

"Not everything, I don't think," Michaelson said quietly.

"What do you mean?"

"What I would be particularly interested in knowing, actually," Michaelson said, glancing at Posner, "is what progress has been made toward identifying the person or persons who were waiting in the back of the van when Luttwalk kidnapped Hurst."

"Come again?" Estabrook asked.

"Oh it's quite clear, isn't it?" Michaelson responded. "Luttwalk put Hurst in the back of the van, then went around to the front to drive it. If he'd been planning on both driving the van and keeping Hurst under control all by himself, he'd presumably have forced Hurst into the front seat."

"There's, ah, evidence that the decedent's hands were, ah, restrained," Estabrook said.

"Indeed there is. Tied behind his back tightly enough to abrade his wrists and leave particles of number nine hemp embedded in the lacerations, according to the medical examiner's report."

"What I'm saying," Estabrook said, "is Luttwalk coulda thought that'd be plenty to keep the decedent under control all by itself."

"But there's a timing problem," Michaelson said. "Having just rather loudly killed a woman, Luttwalk was certainly in a major hurry to leave the scene. We can assume that he didn't take the time to bind Hurst— indeed, the young woman who witnessed Hurst's abduction, and saw things clearly enough to spot three digits on the van license plate, mentioned nothing about Luttwalk's tying Hurst up. The fact that Hurst was bound tends if anything to reinforce the conclusion that Luttwalk had at least one accomplice in the back of the van."

"I'm not sure I follow you," Estabrook said.

"I suggest that you understand me perfectly and are playing dumb," Michaelson answered without a trace of irritation. "Hurst had to have been tied up after he was in the van. Luttwalk couldn't have handled both that chore and driving the van. Therefore, he had to have one or more confederates."

"Well—" Estabrook said.

"Now, you know all this as well as I do. I imagine that you and your efficient colleagues started trying to find out who else was in the van within twelve hours after Mr. Hurst launched his bark on the dark seas of eternity. What I'd like to know—and to know sooner rather than later—is what you've accomplished in that direction."

"There wasn't a trace of anyone but Luttwalk in the van when the state trooper stopped it," Estabrook said. "And we haven't picked up anything since. Based on what you say we have a very nice theory. What we don't have is evidence."

"Very well. Then let's reason together, shall we? No physical traces, and so the accomplice or accomplices must have absconded before

Luttwalk was stopped. They could have left at the scene of Hurst's murder."

"Which meant they were in for a long march on a cold night," Standish said. She was a civilian analyst with the Defense Intelligence Agency. It was the first substantive comment she'd made in the course of the meeting.

"A car could've met them there," Estabrook said. "By prearrangement."

"Then why not pick up Luttwalk too and ditch the van?" Cunningham asked.

"They didn't know the van was blown, or half blown anyway," Posner said. "They wouldn't want to leave it at the scene as long as they could have Luttwalk take all the risk of getting rid of it somewhere else."

"All of which suggests, doesn't it," Michaelson asked, "that the person or persons who got away had a rather more important role in whatever it was that led to Hurst's death than Luttwalk did?"

"Luttwalk, as far as we can tell, was just a trigger man, hired muscle," Estabrook said. "He certainly wasn't very important. But it'd be natural to split everyone up once Hurst got dead. What makes you think the accomplices—if there was more than one—weren't just more muscle, just as unimportant as Luttwalk himself was?"

"Because the point of what they did wasn't just to kill Hurst," Michaelson answered. "If the idea had merely been to assassinate Hurst, Luttwalk could've done that at the house in Washington. There had to be some other reason for the long ride."

"Interrogation," Standish volunteered. "They picked a place more than half an hour's drive away from where they kidnapped Hurst because they wanted at least thirty minutes to ask him questions."

"That was the thought that occurred to me," Michaelson said.

"But they had to know there was a *risk* the van'd be hot by then," Estabrook protested. "Why not just take him to a house or apartment or some other safe place, question him to their hearts' content, and meanwhile get the van into a chop shop where it couldn't incriminate anyone?"

"I can think of at least one reason," Posner said. "If they kill him in a house they have the problem of getting rid of the body. They avoided that problem by taking him to where they were going to kill him before they shot him, and questioning him on the way."

"And of course a second possibility," Standish said, "is that what they wanted to ask him was where something was. If he told them, they'd have to drive somewhere to check out what he said before they could risk killing him."

"Another possibility is that they were just stupid, like a lotta crooks are, and that we're giving them too much credit," Estabrook said.

"And giving ourselves too much credit in the process?" Michaelson asked.

"You said it, not me."

"I think that's a possibility worth exploring. What about it, Captain Posner, Ms. Standish? If the interrogation theory's right, then the interrogation had to be about something the killers thought was important. What could it have been?"

"I wish we knew," Posner smiled.

"You certainly do know," Michaelson assured him. "That is, you know what it *could* have been about. I'm satisfied that the CID got involved in Hurst's case the very day his death became known. Hurst must therefore have been working on something important enough that the mere possibility of its being compromised triggered your involvement in a criminal matter you otherwise wouldn't have touched with a ten-foot pole. What was it?"

"You're making us sound a lot more systematic that we are," Posner said disarmingly.

"This evasiveness is getting old, Captain," Michaelson said, suddenly peevish. "I'm working for the White House. I'm on a very short leash. My assignment is to get in, get the job done, and get out. If you wish to lie to your superiors, each other, the media and Congress, that is no concern of mine. But I must insist that you not lie to me. I don't have time for it."

"Those are serious charges, Mr. Michaelson."

"Oh come off it, Captain. No one's taping the meeting. You don't need to make comments for the record."

"That wasn't—"

"Yes, yes, I'm sure. Now let's get down to business, shall we? I propose that we break until tomorrow at nine o'clock. By this afternoon, I would like each of you to get in touch with whoever's in charge of this case in your own shops, and tell him or her that Michaelson is being a self-important asshole, throwing around weight that he may or may not have and insisting on full disclosure. Or if not full disclosure, at least on not being actively misled in response to direct questions."

"As long as we're putting cards on the table," Estabrook said, "do you really think you can make that insisting part stick?"

"I don't know," Michaelson replied. "But I know how we can both find out."

Three seconds of relative quiet followed. Only the scratching of Standish's mechanical pencil on her notepad broke the silence.

"Tomorrow at nine," Posner said then, standing up.

"Meanwhile," Michaelson said immediately, as if he were merely continuing his earlier thought, "I'd like a copy of every piece of paper that's been generated by anyone in the course of this investigation. Please don't explain to me that I can flip a computer terminal on and peruse the documents at my leisure in electronic files. I don't know how to use computers and I'm too old to learn."

11:55 A.M.

"So, your side won, huh Mr. Dahl?" the black-haired young man at the counter said.

"Yeah. Finally. But I got nailed in the first twenty minutes. Gimme a pack of paint pellets, willya? I'm gonna practice a little bit at home."

"Sure. But don't try it in the District. Even that gun's not legal in the District."

Dahl accepted a package of six plastic-nosed cartridges roughly the size and shape of .30-.30 bullets and buried them in the bottom of his duffel bag, underneath his camouflage fatigues and combat boots, next to his pistol. His face and neck glowed from the vigorous scrubbing he'd done to get the red paint off. His chest still hurt a bit where the paint-pellet had hit him earlier that morning.

"Tomorrow," he told the counter attendant. Then he paid for the paint pellets and left.

It took Dahl the better part of twenty-five minutes to drive from the War Games Combat Simulation Center ("Realistic Fun for Dad and Son") in Alexandria to Appomattox Condominium Estates in McLean, where he lived. Before he'd even turned off the engine on his Lincoln he saw Ginny McNaghten clambering out of an eight-year-old Escort and scurrying toward him. He got out and met her halfway to the front door of the eight-unit building where he lived.

"I'd have thought Chesapeake News Service would lease a Lexus for you," he said to her. "Or at least a Celica."

"My father didn't fight in the Pacific for three years so I could drive a Toyota," she answered tartly. "And I notice you don't have a Lexus either. Or even a BMW."

"The station has a lease-American policy," Dahl explained apologetically.

"Why don't you invite me in?"

"You trying to pick me up?"

"At my age I'd be more likely to wash your mouth out with soap and send you to bed without dinner."

"I'm sorry about that crack yesterday about your being older, Ginny, I didn't mean it that—"

"No, I'm not trying to pick you up. I'm working on a story. Feature about the execution yesterday. Life and death at Leavenworth. That kind of thing."

Dahl looked appraisingly at McNaghten. Sunlight made her hair shine, and her eyes gleamed with an eagerness that the prospect of doing twenty-five hundred words on life and death at Leavenworth couldn't account for. It occurred to him that she didn't look all that bad for forty-four.

"Come on in," he said.

12:25 P.M.

"They basically stonewalled us, didn't they?" Cunningham said to Michaelson as he finished a cup of boysenberry yogurt. "Didn't tell you anything you didn't already know."

"Yes." Michaelson dabbed delicately with a napkin at the right corner of his mouth to wipe away a trace of mustard from his roast turkey sandwich.

"You said it'd be an unproductive meeting and it sure was that."

"Short term, at any rate."

"What do you mean by that?"

"A couple of things," Michaelson said. "First, unless I miss my guess, you should be approached sometime this afternoon or this evening by at least one of the agencies represented at this meeting."

"Why do you say that?"

"Call it intuition."

" 'Intuition.' That doesn't sound much like you."

"Best I can do. The important thing is, when this contact does take place we should find whatever the contacting agency says quite illuminating."

"I can't wait. What's the second thing?"

"Just that we should get the computers on. There should be some very intriguing material put into electronic files sometime this afternoon."

CHAPTER SEVEN

I sn't that sort of a strange thing for grown-ups to do?"
This question came from McNaghten. Dahl had just explained the
camouflage fatigues visible through the half-open zipper of his
duffel bag by telling her about the War Games Combat Simulation
Center and playing capture the flag and urban terrorist there with
four-man teams armed with pistols that fired red paint pellets.

"Not really," Dahl shrugged defensively in answer to her question. He
dropped the duffel bag just inside his front door and gestured toward a
white leather armchair in his living room. "Other guys play basketball,
touch football. It's the same thing, really. Every sport simulates battle.
War games are just a little closer to the real thing."

"Okay. If you say so. Did the station repeat your feed from Leavenworth?"

"Yeah they did, actually. They were real pleased with it. So you're
thinking of doing some kind of a feature on it, huh?"

"Something like that," McNaghten said. "Smell-the-dust-feel-the-sun-
see-the-paint-peel kind of thing. Detached and dispassionate with a little
tonal irony in case someone on the *New Yorker* reads it."

"Sure," Dahl nodded. He didn't have the faintest idea of what she was
talking about.

"That's what I was hoping you could help me with."

"Me help you?" Dahl asked with a generous dose of tonal irony. "You
sure I'm up to it?"

"I'm talking about impressions," McNaghten said. "Striking details here and there, one word worth a thousand pictures."

Dahl got up from the arm of the couch where he'd parked himself and moved toward the kitchen.

"You want something to drink?" he asked.

"Diet Coke. Caffeine free."

"I think I might have that, actually."

McNaghten followed Dahl into the kitchen. It seemed underused, as bachelor kitchens often do. The appliances sparkled with a little too much sheen, like equipment in a model kitchen at a home show. The countertops hadn't had much food sliced or grated or chopped on them.

Dahl handed her a can of Diet Coke without caffeine. He opened a cupboard, didn't see any glasses, and gave her a green coffee mug instead. McNaghten poured Coke into the mug. She brought the mug up to her face and let the effervescence tickle her nose. When the foam had dissipated, she poured in a little more Coke, then set the can on the counter near the stove.

"I thought you didn't smoke," she said, nodding at an open pack of Kents lying on the Formica.

"I had a guest earlier in the week who does. She's the kind of guest that I'm willing to overlook things like smoking and eating crackers in bed for."

McNaghten winced inwardly but kept her face impassive. She was just old enough to regard the comment as sophomoric swagger rather than disarming candor.

"So," she said after a brief pause. "Like we were saying. Any little detail that sticks in your mind. The kind of thing that'd make the whole scene more concrete for somebody who wasn't there."

"I really don't know," Dahl said. Holding his own can of La Croix water in his left hand, he shrugged broadly in a parody of frank and complete sincerity. "We were in the same place at the same time with the same people. I can't imagine I saw anything you didn't."

"Sure you did," McNaghten said casually. She turned a three-quarter profile to him and took a couple of steps toward the kitchen window in an effort to make her comment seem offhand. "For example, you told me you got some good stuff from the doctor. That's the kind of thing I'm talking about."

"Well, sure." Dahl retreated until his back was flat against the refrigerator door. He crossed his arms across his chest. "But wouldn't that sort of be like Tom Brokaw telling Bob Woodward?"

"You're flattering at least one of us." McNaghten smiled without showing her teeth. "I'm not trying to pump you. If you're actually going to use what the doctor told you in a story of your own, then it's your personal property and I wouldn't dream of asking you for it. But I'd assumed that as far as you were concerned the Leavenworth story ended when you went off the satellite. Not true?"

It wasn't an unfriendly question. Not even particularly challenging. But it made Dahl feel as if he were right up against it. Either he was working on a further story about the Luttwalk execution, or he had no good reason not to tell McNaghten what he'd learned from the doctor. Which was nothing. The doctor hadn't told him a thing. Which meant that he'd look silly, because he'd told McNaghten that he'd gotten something good.

"The fact is," he stammered—and then, blessedly, inspiration flooded over him. "The fact is I am working on a more in-depth story about the execution. In fact, I think I'm working on the same story you are."

McNaghten couldn't completely hide her reaction to that. Her expression didn't change but her face paled slightly and a sudden caution replaced the playfulness in her eyes.

"What story is that?" she asked evenly.

"I don't think you came here after material for some prose-portrait think piece. I think you know what story I'm talking about."

"I hope one of us does."

"Look, Ginny, let's work on it together." He sensed instantly that he was overplaying his hand, but all at once he couldn't stop talking. "Join forces. Pool our resources. We can agree to a simultaneous release. I can guarantee you more play than—"

"You're bluffing." McNaghten was smiling calmly as she said this, and that made the words cut more deeply than if she'd spoken harshly. "You spend your mornings playing soldier and your afternoons playing reporter. You don't have a story. You don't have the first idea for a story. You show me you've got something before you talk about pooling resources."

"Doesn't that kind of work both ways, actually?"

"I *work* for my leads, Ken. I squeeze 'em right out of the asphalt. I'm in a tough business in a hard city in an evil world. And I know you don't sell something by giving it away for free. Thanks for the drink."

She put her cup on the counter and left the kitchen. Dahl stood quite still until he heard the front door close.

Thirty-five minutes later, when he was back in his car driving to Washington, it occurred to Dahl that without specific effort he couldn't remember anything after McNaghten's exit. He could tell he had showered again and washed his hair and he must have changed into a muted gray three-piece suit because that was what he was wearing now. But he'd done all of that on automatic pilot.

What McNaghten didn't know was that he did have a little something on the Luttwalk story. Over two years before, at a time when he had only three months as a local Washington news anchor under his belt, he'd gotten a message that someone named Terry Hurst wanted to get in touch with him. He hadn't gotten around to returning the call before Luttwalk had blown Hurst's brains out. So that was one story he'd kissed off.

Well, he wasn't going to kiss off another one. In there, somewhere, was a story and he was going to get it.

If he could just figure out what it was.

And how to go after it. Which was going to be a problem, because he didn't even know where to start.

That was when his car phone beeped.

"Dahl," he said after he'd pushed the speaker button.

"Ken," a female voice he recognized from the station said, "a Mr. Matsuyama says he's anxious to get in touch with you. He says he'll be leaving in twenty minutes and won't be available again for the rest of the day. Do you want me to put you through to the number he left?"

"Sure."

"Mr. Ken Dahl?" a masculine voice asked after the promised operation had been completed. Only the suggestion of an accent and an unusual distinctness of pronunciation indicated that English was a second language for the speaker.

"Yes, this is Ken Dahl."

"Mr. Dahl, my name is Ishiro Matsuyama. I would like to make arrangements to speak with you. I have some information in which I think you might be interested."

This struck Dahl as a providential stroke of luck. In his present state of mind, it simply didn't occur to him that this contact needn't be related in any way to the Luttwalk execution story.

CHAPTER EIGHT

O ne of the few things you can really count on in Washington,"
Michaelson said, "is being consistently underestimated."

Cunningham watched Michaelson flip dextrously through
screenfuls of data on the computer monitor. As Michaelson's fingers
flicked over the keyboard, Cunningham noticed for the first time that half
of the pinkie on Michaelson's left hand was missing.

"Is that a general thing or are you just talking about your own
experience?" Cunningham asked.

"I think the observation applies pretty widely. A president we had not
long ago owed a good deal of his success to the fact that lots of very
smart people in this city stubbornly and persistently underestimated him
for almost twenty-five years."

"So you expect a lot of hairy stuff to show up on the computer
because Posner and his buddies believed you when you said you didn't
even know how to turn one on?"

"Probably not. What I expect to show up on the computer is a lot of
electronic mail among the senior case officers at each of the agencies.
'Call so-and-so before seventeen-hundred hours today. Urgent.' That
kind of thing."

"Then where does the underestimating come in?"

"That comes in when Captain Posner, or someone reading a script he
wrote, gives you a call at home tonight."

"And why is that going to happen?" Cunningham asked.

"It may not happen," Michaelson conceded, smiling. "None of this is scientific. If it does happen, it'll be because Posner thinks I'm nothing but a striped-pants pencil pusher from Foggy Bottom and you're just a by-the-book pony soldier, and that neither one of us could possibly have figured out on our own that Luttwalk must've had an accomplice in the back of the van."

"But we did figure it out. Or you did, anyway. And this morning you told Posner and the other two all about it."

"Just so. And Posner will assume that we must have gotten that from one of the other two, instead of puzzling it out for ourselves. The other two will assume the same thing. I expect Posner to call you to try to verify that, and if possible to get you to say which of the others leaked the information to us."

Cunningham spent a few seconds digesting this. Several minutes before, he'd been reflecting silently on the fact that Michaelson really hadn't told him much more than the agencies had told Michaelson—that there was no hard evidence yet that Michaelson actually trusted him. He wasn't sure whether what he was hearing ought to change his mind or not.

"What do you want me to say when this call comes?" he asked.

"I doubt that it makes any difference. If you say we got the information from Estabrook he'll assume we got it from Standish, and vice versa. On the other hand, the more adamantly you insist that we came up with the idea on our own, the more convinced he'll be that we had an inside source."

"What's all this going to accomplish?"

"No guarantees," Michaelson said, "but it will quite possibly cause Posner to put pressure on Estabrook and/or Standish to shut off the leaks to us that Posner will impute to their agencies. This will reinforce the suspicion of both Estabrook and Standish that we have an inside source. Sooner or later, this accumulating suspicion will reach critical mass."

"What happens then?"

"Then we will in fact have at least one and very probably three inside sources."

"Why?"

"Because each agency in self-defense will start providing us with under-the-table information that makes that agency look good, or at least not as bad as the information it's assuming we're getting from the other agencies makes it look. They'll each assume that the other two agencies are doing that, and they'll each react by doing the same thing."

"That sounds more like second-rate English satire than the real world."

"We're talking about Washington, D.C., not the real world," Michaelson said. "Woodward and Bernstein destroyed a presidency using essentially the approach I just described."

Cunningham shook his head briefly and sighed. He pulled an empty, battleship gray file drawer out about two feet and slid it shut again. Fists on his hips, he walked a few steps away from Michaelson, then turned back toward him.

"I thought we were the good guys," he said, as much to himself as to Michaelson.

"A key part of our assignment is to figure out who the good guys are," Michaelson responded. "As you yourself pointed out yesterday, a junior member of the White House staff could pull together reports from three agencies and summarize them once a week. If that's all Lever wanted, he wouldn't need us."

"Well," Cunningham said, "I'm not sure who the good guys are. But I'm pretty sure they're not gonna turn out to be by-the-book pony soldiers who lie to their brother officers. Which is what you're asking me to do."

"I must not have expressed myself clearly. I thought I'd asked you to tell the truth."

"Technicality. You asked me to deceive Posner."

"I asked you to let Posner deceive himself."

"No matter how thin you slice it, it's still baloney."

"And no matter how sentimental you get about it, it's still Washington," Michaelson said. "Captain Arliss Posner may be a brother officer, but he's also a bureaucrat who's deliberately concealed material information from someone whom he knew to be representing his commander-in-chief. So did Estabrook. So did Standish. They may have done it for noble motives or base ones or ordinary human ones, but they did it. We don't know much but we do know this: we aren't going to learn what we have to know by sending everyone a memo saying, 'Tell us the facts and this time we really mean it.' "

"Translation: it's a dirty job but someone has to do it," Cunningham said. His smile as he spoke was biting and bitter. "I've heard that one before."

"It's not so dirty as all that, in my judgment. But whatever kind of job it is, someone does have to do it and I'm rather glad I'm one of those people."

"That's one difference between us."

"Major Cunningham, there are a great many useful and constructive things you can do in connection with the Luttwalk investigation without involving yourself in this oblique and manipulative aspect of it at all. If you don't feel comfortable in an adversary relationship with agencies of the United States government, there's no need to put you in that position."

Cunningham abruptly made full eye contact with Michaelson. Consciously, deliberately, he relaxed his muscles, let the tension flow out of his shoulders and neck. He thrust his hands into the hip pockets of his trousers, leaving the thumbs hooked on the outside.

"Begging the gentleman's pardon, sir," Cunningham said, smiling icily, "but the hell with that. I'm in or I'm out."

"Fair enough," Michaelson said. "Which is it?"

Cunningham paused for a moment before he answered. He closed his eyes during the interval, as if he really were thinking about how he was going to answer that pointed question. He decided that he still didn't have any hard evidence that Michaelson trusted him.

"I'm going to head on home," he said then. "And wait for Posner's call."

CHAPTER NINE

7:40 P.M.

A riane?"

"Hi, Ken. Thanks for calling back. Great show. Did you hear from Matsuyama yet?"

"Yeah. He said you gave him my name."

"Right. He's a client and you're a friend. I think you can do each other some good."

"You're really into leveraging things like that, aren't you?"

"Synergy. That's why they call me Ariane Daniels."

"I'm doing the eleven o'clock as well as the seven o'clock this week," Dahl said. "But I can squeeze in an hour between them to meet him. How about if I stop by around midnight and tell you how it went?"

"Sounds great, tiger. Bring Ted Koppel."

"Huh?"

"Joke, Ken, joke. See you then."

"Sure."

8:05 P.M.

"He's smarter than you think he is," Cunningham said into the receiver. "Far as I know, he figured it out for himself."

" 'Far as you know?' " Posner asked.

"That's what the man told me and I believe him. What else can I say?"

"You can say you trust me as much as you do him."

"I trust you as much as I do him. Happy?"

"I have the feeling I'm not getting through to you, Major," Posner said.

"You think I'm lying to you?" Cunningham demanded, an edge to his voice.

"I think you're not giving me the whole story. I think you're not telling me everything you know."

"Where's it say I'm supposed to tell you everything I know?"

"You ever seen the file on Michaelson?"

"Negative. Should I have seen it?"

"If you had I don't think you'd be holding back on someone from the right bank of the Potomac."

"I'm all ears, Captain. Tell me about Michaelson."

"It's the kind of thing I'd rather not get into over the phone."

"This CID paranoia's wearing a little bit thin."

"What's that supposed to mean?" Posner asked.

"It means I said put up or shut up and I haven't heard anything since."

"You get yourself on a secure line and you'll hear plenty."

"What are you doing tomorrow at oh-six-hundred?"

"You tell me," Posner sighed after a pause.

"C and O towpath at Rock Creek near the Marine Reserve Center. You can talk to your heart's content because I'll be breaking in Nike Air trainers and trying to do three miles in under twenty-five minutes. It'll be all I can do to breathe."

"See you tomorrow, Major."

Cunningham hung up the phone. He took a sip of Schlitz Malt Liquor from the stein that Cynthia Cunningham had set beside him on the den desk when it started to look like the phone call might last a while. He stood up and pulled a thin, olive-covered booklet from the bookshelf above the desk. *The Engagement at Djebel Berda, Tunisia, 31 January 1943.* By Major Alex Cunningham, U.S.A. Without dropping the first pamphlet he picked up a second, slightly thicker. *The 41st Division From Hollandia to Inchon.* By Major Alex Cunningham, U.S.A.

Unit histories and engagement accounts. Twenty years on the right bank of the Potomac, and the main thing he had to show for it was twenty-seven unit histories and engagement accounts with his name on them and his words inside them.

"Is Posner the shavetail we knew at Camp Roberts when you did Ranger training?" Cynthia Cunningham asked.

Alex Cunningham turned around and looked and his wife.

"That's the one," he said.

"Well it can't be him has you shook, then. It must be the other one. Michaelson?"

"I'm not sure I'd say shook, exactly," Alex Cunningham smiled.

Cynthia folded her long legs underneath her as she sank into a corner of the divan across the room from the desk.

"Well he's sure made some kind of impression on you," she said.

"I ever tell you about the Advanced Warrior Program at Fort Bragg, summer after my second year at the Point?"

"Probably. But go ahead and tell me again."

Cunningham took a long drink.

"The highlight is jousting on foot," he said. "You take two soldiers and you put 'em in football helmets and thick gloves and this oversized, external crotch pad that's basically an industrial-strength outside jock-strap. Then you give 'em each a pole that's about five feet long with padded leather nubs on each end, and have 'em go at it."

"That's 'advanced'? What's the Primitive Warrior Program like?"

"We cadets get down there for AWP and the guy in charge is this old red-neck sergeant from Cracker Barrel, Georgia, or someplace. He has a couple of grunts demonstrate and then the first two cadets he picks to joust are me and this buddy of mine. We didn't impress him much. So he puts on the gear himself and squares off with my buddy and cold-cocks him in about five seconds."

"Not exactly a surprise, was it?"

"That was the point. Very important lesson for future lieutenants to learn about sergeants."

"Does this have something to do with Michaelson?" Cynthia asked.

"I'm coming to that. So my buddy's hunched over groaning, and this cracker sergeant turns to me. And he throws away his pole. Then he takes off his football helmet and tosses it aside. He strips off his gloves and his crotch pad. And he stands there in nothing but fatigues and he raises his bare hands and nods at me and says, 'Sir, come and get me, sir.' "

"Get to the part about Michaelson."

"That was it right there."

"You'd better explain it then, 'cause I missed something."

"Watching Michaelson operate reminds me of that sergeant dropping his pads and protective gear, just contemptuously shrugging them aside. You look into Michaelson's eyes and listen to his voice and you realize that's his attitude about Washington: I don't need illusions, I don't need rationalizations, I don't need to kid myself about what I'm doing and everybody else is doing, I don't need the crap ordinary people use to get by here; I can look it right in the face and really know exactly what I'm seeing and live with it."

"That man must have one deep pair of eyes."

"Like you said, he made an impression."

"What happened with the sergeant?"

"He put me flat on my face. But it took him half a minute, and he knew he'd been in a fight."

8:45 P.M.

Across the oversized office Dahl saw Matsuyama silhouetted against the bright, steady beam of a high-intensity desk lamp. With tweezers Matsuyama was holding something very small up to the light. Delicately he dabbed paint on the object with a long, pinpoint-tipped brush.

Dahl hesitated. He turned toward Hiro Tanaka, who had met him at the street-level door of the Connecticut Avenue office building and shown him to the suite occupied by Ohatsu Ltd. Smiling minimally, Tanaka touched the knot of his red-and-white striped tie and gestured toward the interior of the office.

Dahl moved uncertainly forward. He saw that Matsuyama was holding a molded human figure less than half an inch high in the tweezers. The figure depicted a uniformed man holding a musket. Matsuyama had already painted the soldier's coat and pants dark blue and his boots black. With patient, minuscule strokes of the brush, he now daubed dark brown paint on the soldier's specksized backpack and belt.

"Forgive me," Matsuyama said. "But if the paint fails to dry evenly, much of the effect is spoiled."

Matsuyama set the figure down on the metal base of the desk lamp. He dunked the brush in a tiny bottle of clear liquid and then, extending his hand, rose from his chair and turned unhurriedly toward his visitor.

"You are Mr. Kenneth Dahl?" he said.

"Yes, sir."

Dahl automatically added the honorific as he shook hands. Matsuyama looked like he was in his early fifties. He was spare and elegant, with dark, liquid eyes that looked with polite dispassion from behind rimless glasses.

"My name is Ishiro Matsuyama. I am happy to meet you."

"Same here."

"Please sit down."

Dahl glanced around until he found a straight-backed chair. He sank into it.

"Ms. Daniels made it clear that you are a busy man," Matsuyama said, "so I will try not to waste your time on preliminaries. You are a news reporter?"

"Anchor. That is, yes," Dahl said.

"Just so. I am the founder of a company called Ohatsu, Limited, that is based in Yokohama. We specialize in computer applications and miniaturized electronics."

"I see."

Dahl glanced over his left shoulder in response to a gesture from Matsuyama. Tanaka stood silently just behind Dahl, holding an ice-filled glass and a can of lime-flavored La Croix water on a tray.

"Oh, thanks," Dahl stammered as he accepted the beverage.

"It is a very competitive field," Matsutyama said.

"I can imagine."

"But we are developing a product that excites us very much. It is this."

He tapped what looked like a pocket flashlight with a glassy, slightly oversized end lying on the table beside him.

"What is it?" Dahl asked.

"It is easier to show than to tell. Mr. Tanaka?"

Tanaka strode toward the back of the office and disappeared through a door in the corner. In less than a minute he came back holding a videotape cassette. Passing behind Dahl, he opened a chest-level cabinet in the wall to Dahl's right, revealing a television and a VCR. He slipped the tape in and clicked on the TV. In a moment, Dahl saw a ghostly, black-and-white image of himself stroll into the picture; heard himself speak; saw himself shake hands, sit down, assume a vacuous expression, and finally take the soft drink that Tanaka offered him.

"That's incredible," Dahl whispered. "It's simply incredible." Matsuyama beamed. "How in the world do you do it?"

"This device represents a combined application of two well-established concepts: first, electronic transmission and remote reception and recording of sound and light images—television, in other words; and second, miniaturization of the process through use of computer microchips. Once you replace wires with chips, there is in principle nothing that requires a television camera as such to be any larger than the minimum diameter of a lens capable of receiving enough light to define an image."

"Okay," Dahl said, nodding decisively. "Right."

"Just so." Matsuyama glanced away, licked his lips, then continued. "The trick is in recording the image that the camera defines. If the videotape or other recording medium is to be incorporated into the camera, this obviously introduces another constraint limiting the minimum possible size of the camera. The most common alternative is to have the tape separate from the camera, using cables to transmit from the camera to the tape the images to be recorded. Unfortunately, this largely defeats the purpose of making the camera smaller, because the cables then become a limitation at least as confining as the size of a normal camera would be."

"Of course," Dahl said. He repeated his emphatic nod.

"At Ohatsu, however, we asked ourselves this: what if the image were transmitted to the recorder electronically, just as a television station transmits images from wherever it is to television sets in individual homes? Obviously, with a miniaturized transmitter, the image could not be sent very far or to very many receivers—but it does not have to be, does it?"

"I see. I mean, no, it doesn't."

"So," Matsuyama said. "It would seem we have made a very good start on the application of this concept, no?"

"You certainly have."

"Unfortunately, we are far short of commercial practicality. The device you see here is one of four prototypes. A production-line model at this point could not be sold for less than three million dollars."

"That's a lot to pay for an inconspicuous security tool."

"I beg your pardon?" Matsuyama said.

"I assumed that's what it's made for," Dahl said. "To let someone keep an eye on something without anyone knowing it."

"I suppose that is one possible use," Matsuyama said after a small cough. "Mr. Tanaka, please make a note of it."

"Certainly."

"The applications we have in mind are somewhat broader," Matsuyama continued.

"Like what?" Dahl asked.

"Advanced robotics, to take one example. The greatest limitation on industrial uses of robots right now is that they cannot be made to see except in the very crudest sense. Computerization is the obvious solution conceptually. But you can hardly save money by replacing human workers on assembly lines with robots if each robot requires a three-million-dollar computerized television system for vision alone. Even the UAW is cheaper than that."

Matsuyama paused to give Dahl time to laugh at the joke. Dahl looked earnestly straight ahead.

"This is very interesting, Mr. Matsuyama. Ah, I guess, uh, the next question is whether you see some practical solution to this problem."

"Precisely the subject of your visit, Mr. Dahl."

"Oh." Dahl was glad to hear this.

"You see, an American company has developed a computer-controlled device and the necessary software that I am convinced could be used to deposit electronic transmission commands on microchips. If I am right, then this prototype could become a commercial proposition, as our British friends say."

"Well," Dahl said, smiling nervously, "I guess that problem is solved then."

"Not quite, unfortunately."

"Why not?"

"Ohatsu would like to buy the device and license the application software. The American company would like to do business with us. We have agreed on a price—a price that would have a quite positive impact on the United States trade deficit. Curiously, though, the U.S. government has raised difficulties about the sale."

"How could it do that?"

"The items in question are on the strategic technology list. Their sale to a foreign company must be specifically authorized."

"Oh," Dahl said.

"I of course understand this. What I cannot understand is why there is any problem about the sale to Ohatsu."

"Maybe they're afraid you'll give it to the Russians?" Dahl suggested.

"Mr. Dahl, the Russians need soap and toilet paper and forklifts. The one thing they don't need is cheap mechanical labor. They have plenty of the cheap human variety."

"Then what do you think the problem is?"

"I am mystified," Matsuyama shrugged. "I have naturally consulted American legal counsel. And in addition I have engaged Ms. Daniels' consulting firm."

"And they haven't come up with any answers?"

"On the contrary, they have come up with an answer which disturbs me very much. According to Ms. Daniels, it has been made clear to her that Ohatsu's problems could be solved if one hundred thousand dollars were paid to the right person."

"What?" Dahl jerked forward, his eyes wide open, his hands rigidly gripping the arms of the chair. For the first time in twenty minutes he'd heard something he understood. "Are you telling me someone in the United States government is shaking you down?"

"I am afraid that is precisely the implication."

"Good God." Dahl settled back into the chair. He groped for his glass of La Croix water and drained it. He wondered if Bernstein felt this way the first time he talked to Deep Throat.

"In many countries I would not have been alarmed by this information. I would have found it disturbing to be sure—the amount is not trivial, the expense would be unproductive, and the payoff would be technically illegal. But with many governments—in Chicago or the Third World, for example—things like that are simply part of doing business."

"Not in Washington?"

"Not at the national level. I have done business in America for many years. I have spent an average of six months each year in the United States since the mid-seventies. America's federal executive has its share of faults. But this variety of petty corruption is not among them."

"Well," Dahl said. "Yes. This sounds like a story that I'd really like to get to the bottom of. What's the agency involved?"

"Our thought is the same as yours," Matsuyama said. "A thoughtful maxim of American government has it that the best cure for many ills is exposure to light."

"Right. Yeah. What's the agency involved?"

Matsuyama stood up.

"If as you say you do have an interest in this matter, then I think you should discuss it further with Ms. Daniels."

"Ariane Daniels?"

"Yes. As I said, Ohatsu engaged her firm in this connection. She will know what to do and the proper way to say things. For myself, I am a simple manager. I understand finance and electronics. I do not understand politics."

Dahl remained rooted for the moment in his chair. Matsuyama advanced two steps and held out his right hand. Taking the hint at last, Dahl stood up, shook hands with Matsuyama, and let Tanaka escort him to the door.

When Tanaka got back, Matsuyama was critically examining the soldier he had been painting when Dahl arrived.

"What did you think of Mr. Dahl?" Matsuyama asked without taking his eyes from the tiny painted figure that he held three inches from his nose.

"He seemed remarkably obtuse," Tanaka said. "Too much so to have been affecting simplemindedness for our benefit."

"I agree at least with the first part of your assessment." Matsuyama strode toward the room where Tanaka had retrieved the videotape. "Still, Ms. Daniels is quite certain he is the right person for our purposes," he said over his shoulder.

Tanaka followed his superior into the rear room. A green-painted plywood board rested on a rectangular table beneath the room's only window. Gray-and-black-painted plastic simulated a quarter-inch wall running the entire width of the three-by-four-foot board. On one side of the wall crouched dozens of gray-painted figures the same size as the blue soldier Matsuyama now carried toward the table. Scattered across the green expanse on the other side of the wall were scores of other blue figures. Each soldier on both sides had been painted as meticulously as the one Matsuyama put into place.

"Have you had an opportunity to read Mr. Foote's account of the American Civil War?" Matsuyama asked Tanaka.

Tanaka glanced at the three-volume history on the back of the table: *The Civil War, A Narrative*, by Shelby Foote.

"Of course. You suggest that each executive at Ohatsu read it."

"Do you recall the description of the Battle of Fredericksburg and its aftermath?"

"Not specifically."

"It was a terrible defeat for the Union. The Army of the Potomac piled up stunning losses in charge after futile charge against a well-entrenched rebel position."

"Yes. There were many battles like that in that war."

"Indeed there were. After the news of the battle reached President Lincoln, he spent considerable time reviewing the casualty reports. Then he told an aide, as I remember, something like this: 'They say we are beaten. But if the same battle were to be fought over again twenty times, with casualties in the same proportions, the Confederate Army would be destroyed and the Union would still have a hundred and twenty thousand men in the field. If I find a general who can stand the arithmetic, I'll win the war.' "

"Yes, sir," Tanaka said.

Matsuyama pivoted gracefully and gazed for a moment at the younger man. The muted light in the room glinted from his rimless glasses.

"He found his general, and he won the war," Matsuyama said. "We must never underestimate the Americans, Mr. Tanaka. Terrible things happen when we do."

10:05 P.M.

Marjorie Randolph looked through Michaelson's largest window at the late-night activity on Wisconsin Avenue. She was forty-eight years old and would soon be forty-nine. Despite the long hours she spent under the fluorescent lighting of Cavalier Books, the store she owned on Connecticut Avenue, her face showed a healthy glow that her chestnut hair set off.

"Your move," Michaelson called from the couch, where he sat before a chessboard set up on the coffee table.

Half turning, Marjorie craned to look at the board eight feet away. "Knight to queen's bishop seven," she said. "Check."

"That's extremely aggravating, Marjorie," Michaelson said as he completed the move for her. "I spent seven minutes considering my own move."

"Ten," she corrected him. "But it was the only intelligent move you had."

"Perhaps I should just resign now."

"You might as well. It's mate in four."

"My word." Michaelson tipped his king over and stood up. "How did you get to be so expert at this game, Marjorie? It's not a gentry kind of avocation at all. More an East Side coffeehouse type of activity."

"The first month after I opened Cavalier Books we averaged three customers a day. The only books I could stand to read were the chess books, because I could put them down without regret if I had to do some work."

"You learned well."

"Thank you. I have a feeling, though, that the biggest factor tonight wasn't my skill but your preoccupations. You played like someone with something on his mind."

"Your discernment has lost none of its penetration."

"Is this the project you're working on for Nat Lever?"

Michaelson let a suggestion of wonder color his expression as he handed Marjorie a glass of Cabernet Sauvignon.

"Is there anyone in northwest Washington who doesn't know I've taken something on for Nat?" he asked.

"It certainly isn't any particular secret. Something to do with the execution earlier this week, isn't it?"

"Yes." Michaelson sipped from his own glass. He used the interval to review the pros and cons of discussing details of the matter with her and decided on disclosure. "I came across something mildly provocative while I was reviewing files early this evening," he said.

"What was that?"

"The victim of the crime that led to the execution was a young man named Terry Hurst. His father is a veterinarian who lives near Topeka, Kansas."

"That doesn't sound particularly provocative so far," Marjorie said. "But I'm sure there's more."

"Well, you see, the execution took place at Leavenworth Federal Penitentiary."

"Rather near Topeka?"

"Yes. And even nearer Fort Leavenworth."

"What's special about Fort Leavenworth?" Marjorie asked.

"Several things. It's a major U.S. army base. It's the site of a disciplinary barracks which is reputed to be the toughest military prison in the United States. And it's the home of a surprisingly large number of quadrapeds that periodically require the attention of a vet specializing in large animal practice."

"Hurst's father, for example?"

"Correct again. He seems to have been one of the regular vets called in there on a systematic basis over a period of some twenty years."

"At the risk of appearing dense," Marjorie said, "so what?"

"So. Wouldn't you expect this information to have been included in the reports of the Army Criminal Investigation Division's activities in the case?"

"I suppose I would."

"It was. That is, it was included in the computerized file that I retrieved electronically. But it somehow got omitted from the physical paper files that the CID sent over to me after I demanded them this morning."

"You know something?" Marjorie said. "I think you might be up to another game."

THE THIRD DAY AFTER
THE EXECUTION

CHAPTER TEN

When we get to the Khyber Pass
When we get to the Khyber Pass

We'll load our rifles and kick some ass!
We'll load our rifles and kick some ass!

The antiphonal chant—the clear, piercing shout of the squad leader followed by the fuzzier but louder repetition of the men running with him—reached Posner and Cunningham long before they could see the group that produced it. Posner, jogging beside Cunningham through the gently falling drizzle, his training shoes smacking loudly against the rain-glistened asphalt surface of the towpath, had finally hit his stride just as the muscular couplets became audible.

"Marines?" he asked.

"Yeah. We've got a good quarter mile on them though. We won't hear them again for a while now that they're around the curve too."

"Good."

Cunningham puffed with the effort of talking and running at the same time. Dark perspiration stains discolored the upper chest and armpits of his unadorned gray sweatshirt.

"So what do you have to tell me about Michaelson?"

"He wants to be in the next cabinet so bad he can taste it."

"I was raised to believe that ambition is a healthy thing," Cunningham panted.

"He's been doing favors for up-and-comers for years. Including before he retired from State. His specialty was digging stuff out of the spooks and shopping it around to people he liked."

"Was it the spooks who clipped him for half a finger?"

"No, that was the other side. He caught a ricocheting bullet during a riot at a Near Eastern embassy where he was deputy chief of mission a few years back."

"How about the people he shopped information to?" Cunningham asked. "Which side were they on?"

"Sometimes it's hard to tell. Most of them were politicians. He's really not much better than a politician himself."

"So"—pant—"what?"

"So you're in this thing to find out what really happened to Luttwalk. We're in this thing for the same reason. But Michaelson's in it for Michaelson. Strictly self-promotion."

"Seems to me the best way to promote himself is to accomplish what the guy who signed him up asked him to accomplish."

"If he can," Posner said. "But what if he can't?"

"I give up."

"His best bet then is to find a convenient scapegoat to pin the failure on."

"Like CID?" Cunningham asked.

"Like CID. Or like retired Major Cunningham."

"I'll take my chances. What's the worst they can do? Yank my ticket to the Army-Navy game?"

"You must have a lot of friends from the service."

"After twenty years? I hope so."

"You really want them to blame you if the army gets dumped on to cover some screw-up by a bunch of bureaucrats?"

"What makes you think he's got such a hard-on about the army?" Cunningham demanded.

"I don't. I just think he's the type who always knows which side his bread is buttered on. Someone's leaking to him. It's not us, and whoever it is sure as hell isn't gonna bend over backwards to make us look good."

They ran twenty-five strides without talking while Cunningham gathered more breath. Most of their quarter-mile lead over the marines had evaporated. The leathernecks in their gold T-shirts and olive-drab shorts were now less than a hundred yards back and the rhythmic pounding of their in-step running rattled over that short distance.

If I die in a combat zone,
If I die in a combat zone,—

Wrap me up and ship me home!
Wrap me up and ship me home!

Pin my medals upon my chest!
Pin my medals upon my chest!

Tell my momma I done my best!
Tell my momma I done my best!

The marines came even with Posner and Cunningham, who unconsciously quickened their pace a bit. The marine squad leader shifted his eyes right and grinned.

Look to my right and what do I see?
Look to my right and what do I see?

Has-been grunts from the infantry!
Has-been grunts from the infantry!

Cunningham involuntarily shook his head. Smiling at himself, he sucked breath into his lungs until his right side nearly split with the pain.

"Look to my left and what do I see?" he bawled then.

"Look to my left and what do I see?" Posner took up after a moment's puzzled hesitation.

Buncha jarheads yellin' at me!
Buncha jarheads yellin' at me!

The marines guffawed and pulled steadily beyond Posner and Cunningham.

"Know what I'd do if I were you and believed what you believe, Captain?" Cunningham asked as the marines' backsides faded into middle distance.

"What's that?"

"I'd butter some bread myself."

CHAPTER ELEVEN

8:45 A.M.

Ariane Daniels gripped her Kent far back between the first two fingers of her left hand, manipulating it and her BMW's steering wheel simultaneously with the reflexive and joyless skill of someone who smokes about a pack a day. In her right hand she clutched the receiver of a car phone. She wore her blond hair swept stiffly back and off her neck on either side of a part over her left ear. Her skin, cream-colored with just the hint of a tan, was luminous and unblemished. Her violet eyes sparkled.

Cars often hung just behind or beyond hers so that the men driving them could examine her at leisure. Daniels was used to this. She was twenty-nine and she'd been used to it since she was fourteen.

"Ken?" she said into the phone.

"Yeah, love."

Daniels's face showed no pleasure at the tender form of address, but her voice remained dulcet and coaxing.

"I've got it set up."

"Great. Thanks. I really—"

"The lawyer's name is Cadwallader. Reed Cadwallader. He's at Harlan, Ellis and Wilhelm. That's a boutique firm with offices in that bank building at the intersection of Connecticut and Penn."

"Right." Dahl wondered what a boutique firm was.

Daniels knew what "right" meant when Dahl said it in that tone.

"You know," she said. "A small firm that specializes in a single, narrowly focused practice area. Put all their eggs in one basket and take good care of the basket."

"Right," Dahl said.

"Anyway," Daniels sighed, "I just got off the phone with him. He's expecting you at 10:30 but call him to confirm the time."

"Will do."

"Call him right away, Ken."

"I will."

"It's on the deepest possible background. Make sure he knows right up front that you understand that."

"Sure," Dahl said. He heard a long exhalation over the line. In his mind he saw a ribbon of smoke streaming out of Daniels' pursed lips toward the windshield.

"He'll give you names and dates," Daniels said. "It should be enough to get a producer interested."

"I'll get it done. See you tonight maybe. Bye for now."

"Right," Daniels said to herself as she recradled the phone. "Ciao-time."

9:12 A.M.

"There was no contact between Luttwalk and nonprison personnel between the time his lawyer shook hands with him following the last interview with reporters and the time the outside physician injected him with thiopental sodium," Estabrook said. "He was escorted back to his cell, where he stayed until they brought the gurney for him."

"Am I correct that he'd already had his last meal?" Michaelson asked, glancing around the table at Posner and Standish.

"Yeah."

Silence hung over the conference table for a second or two. Estabrook's exposition was routine, almost a time killer. Everyone was waiting for Michaelson to raise the question that Posner had ducked at the end of the previous day's meeting: What could Terry Hurst, Luttwalk's victim, have been working on that excited the interest of the Army's Criminal Investigation Division in a routine civilian murder?

"Anything else you'd like to know?" Estabrook asked.

"Yes. How much contact was there between Terry Hurst's father and the physician who administered the soporific to Luttwalk?"

"Not a great deal that we know of," Estabrook shrugged after a puzzled hesitation. "They lived in different cities."

"Topeka and Leavenworth aren't that far apart by midwestern driving standards," Michaelson said mildly. "In fact, I understand that Hurst's father frequently provided veterinary services at Fort Leavenworth."

"Is that a fact?" Posner asked, glancing at Estabrook.

"Yes," Michaelson said. "It is a fact. I wouldn't have thought that the modern army would have much demand for those skills, but apparently there's more livestock at Fort Leavenworth than I'd imagined."

"Tradition," Standish interjected.

"Leavenworth's not a small town," Estabrook said at the same time, impatience coloring his voice. "Even if Hurst was out to the fort every week, it's not like he and the execution doctor'd necessarily have tripped over each other crossing Main Street. We don't have any reason to believe that they spent much time together or even that they were acquainted."

Michaelson nodded, affecting the complacent satisfaction of a committee chairman who's successfully completed an agenda item.

"Next topic," he said. "I was going over the prison's visitor log for the day of Luttwalk's execution. There were two FBI agents from the bureau's Kansas City field office present. Why?"

"Standard procedure," Estabrook said.

"Standard procedure?" Michaelson demanded, arching his eyebrows. "Before Luttwalk the United States government hadn't executed anyone since the early 'sixties. How could there be a standard procedure for something that's rarer than Democrats winning presidential elections?"

"If it's a bureau investigation and a bureau arrest," Estabrook insisted stolidly, "we're there when they close the file, too."

"And what is bureau procedure on discussing pending investigations with the press?"

"What's that again?" Estabrook snapped. "What're you referring to?"

"The prison's visitor log," Michaelson answered mildly. "One of the press people attending the execution was a reporter for Chesapeake News Service named Regina McNaghten."

"And—?" Estabrook prompted.

"And," Michaelson said, his voice even, "Ms. McNaghten has gotten in touch with me. She's made it clear that she's chasing a rumor or a hunch about some kind of problem with Luttwalk's execution. Some of the questions she's asked suggest access to information that could only have come from one of the agencies represented at this meeting."

"Which one are you accusing?" Standish asked, amused.

"I'm not accusing anyone—yet," Michaelson said. "I bring the matter up merely to emphasize the importance of discretion."

"Meaning what?" Posner asked. "Don't leak? Or leak only to the right people?"

"I mean don't leak," Michaelson said, smiling pleasantly. "And if you do, don't get caught."

Glancing around the table, Michaelson thought of asking again about Hurst's last Pentagon assignment. He sensed that the time wasn't quite ripe. If someone was about to break, that wasn't going to happen in front of the others. With Cunningham now about thirty thousand feet over West Virginia, Michaelson decided that the best thing for him to do was keep his mouth shut and bring the meeting to an anticlimactic conclusion.

CHAPTER TWELVE

A source familiar with the background.' How about that?" Dahl asked.

Reed Cadwallader frowned. He was tall and slender with wispy, sandy-colored hair. His once well-conditioned, patrician body was going slowly but inexorably to seed, as muscles that had pulled oars for four years at Georgetown and swung squash rackets all the way through the University of Virginia Law School had gradually been limited to lifting aluminum-shaft golf clubs every other weekend at Burning Tree.

"Perhaps a little too close for comfort," he said after considering Dahl's suggestion. "I'd prefer just 'a knowledgeable source.' "

"Fine."

"Is that on?" Cadwallader asked, glancing at the palm-sized tape recorder on Dahl's lap.

Hesitating for a moment, Dahl clicked the machine off, glanced up at Cadwallader, then punched the cover open and removed the cassette. Cadwallader beamed and Dahl basked for a moment in his approval as he laboriously wrote 'a knowledgeable source' on the legal pad resting on his lap.

"Now," he said. "Who's trying to shake down your client?"

"It's not quite that simple," Cadwallader said. "Let me give you a little background, if I might."

"Okay," Dahl shrugged.

"The first thing you have to understand is that the United States Department of Commerce likes exports. I mean really *likes* them. If you're asking for an export license the only way you don't get one is for some other agency to come in and muscle Commerce around."

Dahl nodded and scribbled on his pad.

"Now, the thing is, it's not even clear that the seller *needs* an export license for the Ohatsu transaction. We thought we'd get a don't-bother letter, as it's known in the trade. That way, no one at Treasury or Defense would even have a chance to throw their weight around."

"Why would they care about a sale to a Japanese company anyway?" Dahl asked, drawing on Matsuyama's comments in an effort to sound knowledgeable. "It's not the kind of thing the Communists would be interested in, is it?"

Cadwallader hadn't gotten where he was by being clumsy, and only for an instant did his expression betray his astonishment at Dahl's question.

"The, ah, problem goes beyond that," he said gently.

"What do you mean?"

"Ten years ago you'd see bumper stickers on Mustangs or Chevys that said, 'Hungry? Out of Work? Eat your Toyota!' Four or five years ago you started finding Lee Iacocca on TV saying, basically, 'Remember Pearl Harbor—buy Chrysler.' Now if you look at the paperback racks when you go to the airport you can't help noticing that the Japanese have replaced the Russians as America's all-purpose bad guys."

"I'm not sure I get the point," Dahl admitted gingerly.

"The point is that America really is a democracy in at least a broad sense," Cadwallader said. "The bumper stickers gradually get noticed, and then those attitudes start getting pandered to, and then taken seriously, and finally accepted within the power structure."

Dahl didn't say anything, because he was afraid of sounding stupid. His expression, though, asked plainly what the punchline was. Cadwallader decided that he'd better supply it.

"I guarantee you," Cadwallader continued evenly, "that slapping Japan around will be a *leitmotif* of the upcoming presidential election campaign. And if you were a fly on the wall in the Pentagon's Strategic Planning Department, you'd see at least as many brass hats noodling about the next war against Japan as you'd see figuring out how to stop the Red Army."

A chilly little thrill of excitement ran through Dahl. He looked at Cadwallader sitting at his mahogony desk in front of bookshelves that groaned under the weight of thick, squat black binders with titles like *CCH Common Market Antitrust Regulations* and *Trading With China*, and he felt as if he were finally being admitted into some inner circle, made privy to really inside information known only to mysterious and quietly powerful people who carried their saddle-leather briefcases to the seventh floor of the Department of State and the Office of the Secretary at Treasury and other precincts of power. Cadwallader was good at making people feel this way.

"Okay," Dahl said. "So you thought you could do sort of an end run around these people by getting what you called a don't-bother letter. What happened?"

"Well," Cadwallader said with a self-deprecating smile, "I thought things were going along swimmingly enough. Problem was, it kept getting bumped farther and farther up the staff level until it finally reached the political level. It landed on the desk of one Arnold Hapner."

"Who's he?"

"He's a loyal member of the party in power. Election before last he made a kamikaze run against an entrenched incumbent congressman in Ohio or Idaho or someplace, and his reward was that he got a Commerce appointment after the incumbent creamed him."

"And what did this Hapner guy do?" Dahl asked.

"Mr. Hapner kept finding all sorts of new hoops for us to jump through. It got to be rather annoying. Finally five, no"—Cadwallader swivelled around and looked for several seconds at the calendar open flat on the credenza behind his desk—"six days ago I saw him and asked what in blazes the problem was. He hemmed and hawed and then after he got tired of beating around the bush he said, 'You know, what you guys need is a consultant who really knows his stuff in this area.'"

"I thought Ariane Daniels was Ohatsu's consultant on this deal."

"She is. That's what I told Hapner. We already have a consultant and we're very happy with her. Guess what Hapner said."

"You tell me," Dahl prompted.

"He said, 'You know who's really good at this kind of thing is the MacDonald Clover firm. They know it inside and out, and on something like this I'm sure you could get them for a hundred thousand.'"

Dahl scribbled with furious intensity on the legal pad, covering two pages with a large, looping hand.

"MacDonald Clover?" he asked as he wrote.

"Right. They're in the phone book. I'm sure I don't need to add that that firm was founded by recent alumni of the present administration."

"Aren't there laws about that?" Dahl asked.

"Several. There are also several ways around them."

"Is there any possibility that MacDonald Clover really is better at this kind of project than Ms. Daniels's firm is?"

Cadwallader smiled with patronizing tolerance.

"If they were better than Ms. Daniels we'd have hired them in the first place. 'Consultant' in Washington is just a fancy word for someone who knows the right fannies to pat and can call real decision makers without getting put on hold. Ariane Daniels is as good at that as anyone."

Dahl felt the backs of his ears burning. He wondered in embarrassed amazement if he could possibly be blushing. He wouldn't have said he was in love with Ariane Daniels, exactly. At first he'd simply thought it natural and right that he should have someone like her, just as he had a luxury car to drive. But he felt now that their relationship had grown beyond that, actually. He was sure she needed him, and he felt protective toward her, solicitous of her vulnerability.

"So you think Hapner would be getting a kickback on the fee if you hired the firm he recommended?" he asked Cadwallader quickly.

"I don't know if it's that gross, or if he's just making sure that there'll be a cushy spot for him at MacDonald Clover when he gets tired of the civil service pay scale. He's gotten a dose of Potomac fever and you can bet he doesn't want to find out how many people remember his name back in Idaho or Ohio."

"Okay," Dahl said earnestly then, looking at his notes and unconsciously gesturing with his pen, "so—"

"Excuse me, Mr. Cadwallader."

Dahl and Cadwallader both glanced up at the interruption. Cadwallader's secretary had pushed his door open and stuck her head in.

"I know you asked me to hold your calls, but Mr. Merriweather is calling from London."

"Thank you very much, Delores," Cadwallader said. He picked his phone up from the cradle. "Hullo, Peregrine. Hold on a moment, can you?" He covered the mouthpiece and looked apologetically at Dahl. "I wasn't expecting this. Terribly sorry. It's nearly five in London and this is rather a time-sensitive matter. Could I ask you to wait outside for a few minutes?"

"Sure."

Dahl stood up and exited under Delores's watchful eye. As she swung the door smoothly shut behind him, he wondered if Peregrine Merriweather's call had something to do with Cadwallader's accent and diction going from East Coast street-smart to Alistair Cooke.

He spent an uncomfortable minute or two between the two secretarial work stations that crowded the area immediately outside Cadwallader's office. There wasn't anything for him to do or even any place for him to sit.

"Can I get you some coffee, Mr. Dahl?" Cadwallader's secretary asked.

"No, thanks. I'm interested in reversing the operation, actually." He gave her the postcard smile. He figured she deserved a break.

"I beg your pardon, Mr. Dahl?"

"Which way to the men's room?"

"Oh." Now she understood what reversing the operation meant. "Go to your right down the corridor, past the library double doors and on down to where the corridor sort of jogs to the left a little bit. Then just before the corner after the jog there's a kind of a side hallway leading to a lounge and coffee maker and soda machine, and right beside that is the men's room."

"Thanks."

He made it past the library before he got lost. The jog turned out to be about twenty feet long. This confused Dahl, but he wasn't absolutely sure he was lost until he'd gone around another corner and found himself at the head of a completely different corridor. It was when he turned around to retrace his steps that he saw it.

MR. BALDWIN.

All caps in raised gold letters on a dark wood panel mounted on the wall of a suite just before the corner-office suite.

Of course, it didn't say *Corky* Baldwin. On the other hand, what were the chances that there were two powerful Washington lawyers both named Baldwin? Well, they were pretty good, actually. Maybe he should ask one of the secretaries in the work-station part of the suite. Just step past the divider and ask: Is this the Baldwin who defended that big murder case where the guy just got executed?

Dahl was still pondering this possibility when he heard two voices coming down the corridor to his right. One was female and sounded young. The other was male and sounded southern. Not a southern drawl. More like a southern twang, like a flat midwestern accent turns into after a stay in the mid-South followed by twenty years' exposure to the bastardized pseudo-southspeak that's been in style in Washington since Jefferson's inauguration.

"We told you this was an international-slash-intellectual property practice," the southern voice was saying. "But we didn't tell you it was all negotiations in Brussels and arguments before the Court of Customs and Patent Appeals. If you want to replevy a patented German mold being held by some outfit that's technically a co-citizen of a plaintiff-in-interest, you've got to go into the local trial court—just the same as a used car dealer who hasn't been paid. I know it's grubby, but that's the way it works."

"It's not the court, it's the judge. Gordonstan is the most racist, sexist judge on the D.C. Superior Court."

"Nothin' I can do about that. I can't be there and you're the only other one who knows the file. You're just gonna have to grease it up, bend over, and enjoy it."

The conversation stopped abruptly at this point, because the two speakers turned the corner and found themselves face to face with Dahl. The male was Corky Baldwin. Dahl didn't recognize the female.

"Good morning," Baldwin said after a pregnant pause. "Can I help you find someone?" Law firms don't approve of people with unfamiliar faces wandering around their hallways.

"Ken Dahl," Dahl said, stepping forward and extending his hand. "We met at the Luttwalk execution. I'm with WRKO here in Washington. I'm here seeing Reed Cadwallader."

"Absolutely," Baldwin said, his voice all sunny warmth. He gripped Dahl's hand tightly and shook it firmly. "Good to see you again."

"I just wanted to stop by your office and say how much I admired what you did in that case. Taking it without a fee, I mean, and fighting it all the way through like that. I know you must get emotionally involved with a death penalty case, and most lawyers wouldn't have done it for nothing."

Baldwin nodded slightly, in frank appreciation of the flattery.

"Law's not just a way to get rich, it's a profession," he said. His voice had become solemn and unctuous. "You know, the professor I had for commercial transactions my third year told the class on the last day, he said, 'You've all learned a lot of law and if you work hard you'll make plenty of money. But you'd better make sure that when you're through practicing law you've got more than the money. Because if you don't, no matter how much it is, the money won't be enough.' I've always remembered that."

"Well, good seeing you again," Dahl said. "I think I'd better see if I can find my way back to Reed Cadwallader's office now."

Dahl nodded at the young woman next to Baldwin and strode away, much impressed.

"Ah, there you are," Cadwallader said when Dahl had made his way back to the area of Cadwallader's office. "We were about to send out a search party. I know it can seem like a maze when you're not used to it."

"Right." Dahl thought it best not to mention that he never had found the men's room.

"I think we've pretty much covered the high points, don't you?" Cadwallader asked as he led Dahl back into his office. "Were there any more questions you wanted to bring up?"

"Let's see," Dahl said tentatively, paging back through his notes.

"I'd be the last one to tell you how to do your job, of course," Cadwallader said. "But there is one observation I might make."

"Sure."

"The less idea they have of what you're looking for, the more chance there is that you'll find it."

"Uh, yeah," Dahl acknowledged.

"If you go in full bore asking about the Ohatsu deal, you can be sure they'll have their ducks in a row and their stories straight before you get anyone on tape. You might want to start by just asking about any license deals where MacDonald Clover was involved and Hapner's fingerprints showed up. Even just an FOIA request for that might shake some interesting things loose."

Dahl wrote "Freedom of Information Act" on his pad.

"Okay," he said. "Good idea."

"I want you to feel free to call me if you come up with any more questions," Cadwallader said, standing up abruptly from behind his desk and holding a business card out to Dahl. "Good luck on this."

Dahl took the card. He surmised that the interview was over and that he wasn't going to be asking any more questions for the moment. He didn't really mind. He couldn't wait to get to a producer with the stuff he already had. He allowed the lawyer to usher him smoothly to the reception area. Cadwallader had padded back toward his office and Dahl was about to get on the elevator when he noticed the young woman he'd seen with Baldwin approaching him.

"I hope you enjoyed your stay, Mr. Dahl," she said. Her voice was smooth and professional. Her eyes smoldered with resentment. "I thought you might want to take one of our firm brochures along."

Dahl accepted a glossy, four-color, eight-page booklet from the young woman. She held his gaze for just a moment as she handed the brochure to him, made sure he saw the eyes. Dahl started to turn on the postcard smile but then the elevator came so he just thanked her, nodded, and stepped onto it.

He paged idly through the brochure on the way down. Smiling middle-aged male lawyers sitting in leather swivel chairs. Smiling young male and female lawyers handing documents to each other, playing tennis, jogging with the Washington Monument in the background. Pretty standard stuff, he thought.

Just as the elevator door opened, he found the page of bond stuck in the middle of the brochure. After a moment's surprise, he stepped into the building lobby and examined the document with puzzled attention:

Ohatsu, Ltd.
c/o 1020 K Street, NW
Suite 1313
Washington, DC
To Services Rendered, May 1–May 31

May 1:	WWB/		Draft license app.; attn. to corresp.
	SSK	15.2	re: same
May 2:	WWB/		Rev. & revs. license app.; teleconf.
	SSK	16.5	w/agency, client re same.
May 3:	WWB/		Rev. & revs. license app.; research primary
	SSK	16.8	juris. issue; draft memo re: same.
May 4:	WWB/		Rev. & revs. license app.; rev. & revs.
	SSK	15.9	primary juris. memo; attn. to corresp.
May 5:	WWB/		Finalize & submit license app.; draft,
	SSK	17.0	rev. & revs. project chronology.

PAGE TOTAL: 91.9 Hours at $375 (blended rate): $30,025.00

That's where the page ended. He shook the brochure, but nothing else fell out. He wondered what conceivable significance the cryptic array of initials and numbers on what was obviously a bill could have.

Then, from the depths of the Luttwalk preparation his producer had crammed into him, a couple of dates struggled valiantly to the surface of his memory. Suddenly he knew who W.W.B. was and he knew why the young woman whom Baldwin had told to grease it up, bend over, and enjoy it had given him this piece of paper.

CHAPTER THIRTEEN

Cunningham could already hear the dogs baying when his GSA motor pool sedan was still fifty yards up County Highway G from the packed-rock driveway. The driveway led to the side of a rambling, single-level frame house painted sunshine yellow. A neat black-on-white sign mounted on the front porch roof read "Randall Hurst D.V.M."

Cunningham recognized the man with dull red hair who was standing on the front porch as Hurst. He wore a faded plaid shirt, Levis, and brownish yellow leather boots that laced up to the middle of his shins.

"You didn't waste any time getting out here, I'll give you that," Hurst called as Cunningham pulled the car to a stop behind a pre-Taurus Ford station wagon and climbed out of it. "You call me from Washington early this morning and here you are in the flesh in Topeka, Kansas, early this afternoon."

"Guy I'm workin' for can make things move fast when he wants to," Cunningham said. Cunningham's first inkling that he'd be traveling to Topeka today to meet with Hurst had come around 7:20 that morning, when he'd called Michaelson to report on his chat with Posner.

"That racket you hear's the noisiest part of the practice," Hurst said. "Spaniels, collies, and retrievers. Nearly a dozen of them on hand right now."

"I thought you were a large-animal vet."

"Every farmer's a hunter," Hurst said. "Every hunter has dogs. If you can't take care of a man's dogs, he's not gonna trust you with his cows and horses. C'mon inside."

Hurst led Cunningham through a screen door into a sparsely furnished room with a concrete floor. A counter not quite chest high ran along the back part of the room, about five feet in front of the rear wall. Mounted on the wall behind the counter were Remington reproductions—"Ridden Down" and "Coming Into Town" were the ones Cunningham remembered—and Audubon prints that presented a relentlessly uplifting view of the animal kingdom. In the midst of these works, not doing anything to call attention to itself, just hanging there waiting for the double take, Cunningham noticed a framed epigraph, calligraphy on eggshell parchment. The text read, "It'll be a happy day for America when the last ecologist is drowned in the blood of the last bureaucrat." A tag line attributed this ferocious sentiment to the American Farmer.

"Reception room," Hurst said. He waved his arm at a swinging metal door in the far corner behind the counter. "That leads to the treatment area."

Hurst turned toward the opposite corner. Cunningham followed him through a firmly latched wooden door that gave onto a hallway demarcating the veterinary clinic from the Hursts' living quarters. The soothing rumble of a room air conditioner drew Cunningham inexorably toward a paneled den on the other side of the hallway. He glided thankfully into the room behind Hurst.

"Have a seat," Hurst said, nodding toward an overstuffed leather armchair near the door. He crossed to the chair's twin and sank into its ample cushion after glancing irritably through the window behind it. "Soon's Francie's through lolling in the pool I'll have her get us some iced tea," he said.

"Sounds great."

Something that looked like a nineteenth-century oil portrait hung in the V formed by crossed sabers near the center of the wall opposite Cunningham. It depicted a man with longish, dark hair and a flowing mustache. He was wearing some type of uniform. His eyes were cold and a bit wild at the same time. Below the portrait was a glass-front gun cabinet holding three rifles and a shotgun.

"I recognize the thirty-thirty lever action, the Remington ADL bolt-action thirty-ought-six, and the twelve-gauge automatic shotgun with the ventilated rib. What's the other one?"

"Winchester two-forty. Varmint gun. Prairie dogs, coyotes. Not enough muzzle velocity for them on a thirty-thirty."

"Why do you have two deer rifles?"

"One for Missouri and one for Kansas. The thirty-thirty's fine for open country, but if you're gonna nail whitetails in woods and forests you need a shell that can go through brush and leaves without getting deflected."

"It sounds like farmers aren't the only ones who're hunters," Cunningham said.

"You grow up in rural Kansas, you come of age with a rifle or a shotgun in your hand. Besides, it's good marketing. Farmers can't afford to be sentimental about animals, and they can't afford vets who're sentimental about them either. One good place to prove you're not is a duck blind."

Hurst craned his neck and glanced again through the window behind him.

"Isn't this about where you take out that little wallet doohickey with your badge on top and your picture ID on the bottom and tell me about how you're with the FBI and you're here to ask me some questions?" he asked as he completed his survey and raised his feet to a hassock in front of his chair. "That's the way they did it with Dr. Dennison."

"You lost me somewhere," Cunningham said. "I'm not with the FBI. I can show you a Maryland driver's license, if that'll make you happy."

"Pretty lame," Hurst said.

"Tell you what you can do if you want to," Cunningham said. "Call information for area code two-oh-two. Get the number for the White House. When you reach the White House switchboard, ask for Richard Michaelson at extension three-five-one-seven. Describe me to him and he'll tell you who I am."

"Skip it," Hurst said. He shook his head. "If you're pulling something, it's too slick for me to outfox. Whoever you're with, what do you want to know?"

"The first thing I wanted to know was how well you know Dennison, the official doctor at Luttwalk's execution. But I guess you've already told me that."

"I'd've told anyone who asked," Hurst said. He shrugged. "Not like it's any big mystery. We've known each other for nearly fifteen years. I take care of his horses."

"That why he called you to talk things over after the FBI came out to see him?"

"That's the reason, I expect," Hurst nodded. "Happened the afternoon of the execution. He said he'd barely got back to his office before they were all over him like a coat of paint. I figured right then something pretty damn serious must've gone wrong."

"What do you suppose it was?"

"Got me. If Dr. Dennison turns out to've had anything to do with it, though, you could win a year's groceries having me bet the other way."

"Why?" Cunningham asked.

"He's a first-rate internist and I've seen him work a fishhook out of an eyeball without flinching. But he gets sweaty palms and jelly legs if he's stopped for driving forty-two in a thirty-five zone. He's not the fella who'd pull something funny in the middle of a federal penitentiary."

"He wouldn't necessarily have to know he was doing it."

Hurst shook his head.

"You mean maybe someone switched syringes on him without his knowing it? I can't see it. I don't think anyone could pull a switch like that on me without my at least having a feeling about it. I can't believe Dennison or anyone else who's given more than ten injections in his life wouldn't know."

"When was the last time you saw Dennison before the execution?" Cunningham demanded quietly.

"Day before." Hurst offered Cunningham a thin, tight smile that said, Make something of it. "He has a show jumper that he's really pinned his hopes on for the American Royal in Kansas City next week. He was worried that it might have a hoof infection and I drove in to look at it."

"Okay," Cunningham said.

"Looks like Francie's taken up permanent residence in that pool," Hurst said. "Not that I can blame her when it's over ninety in September. I'll be right back."

Cunningham relaxed in his chair as Hurst rose and left the room. He glanced again around the dimly lit den. No pictures of family or friends. No degrees or certificates mounted. A handful of textbooks on the scanty shelves, and some trade journals and *Reader's Digest*s lying on top of the television. Nothing that Hurst had taken much trouble to display—except for the long guns and that nineteenth-century portrait above the crossed sabers.

Hurst strode back into the room. In one hand he cradled two bottle-green glasses half filled with ice. In the other he held a water-beaded metal pitcher. Cunningham accepted one of the glasses from Hurst, picking up a strong odor of medicinally scented soap from Hurst's hands.

"I'll tell you something," Hurst said after he had made his way back over to his own chair. "Long as you're wondering whether I tried something funny on Luttwalk, I mean."

"I didn't know I'd suggested anything like that."

"It came through loud and clear, my friend." Hurst chuckled mordantly. "Anyway, lemme let you in on something. Nobody asked me how that sniveling bastard Luttwalk should die. If they had, I'd've suggested, maybe, nail his testicles to the floor of a dirty tool shed, give him a rusty razor blade, and set fire to the shed. If he makes it out of the shed his reward is we kill him quick. If there was any damn way in the world I could've hurt him, I would've done it. But I'm not such a damn fool that I'd risk a tax audit, much less a jail sentence, for anything short of a chance to put that sorry piece of shit through some pretty considerable agony."

"You sound like you have a lot better idea of what you think I'm here about than you could've gotten from anything I've told you so far. Nobody said anything about switching syringes or hurting Luttwalk. You've been jumping to some conclusions, haven't you?"

"You got here fast, but you were late," Hurst said. "Day of the execution, even before Doc Dennison's call, some woman reporter gave me a buzz. She was fishing but she sure wasn't coy."

"What'd she say?"

"She just wanted to know about reports that something'd gone wrong with the Luttwalk execution. I asked her what she was talking about, and it came down to her thinking the guy who put the needle in acted like he was surprised by the way Luttwalk felt and reacted when he did it. Then some guys with badges paid a visit on Dr. Dennison and had lots of questions for him."

"I see," Cunningham said.

"Then," Hurst continued, "out of a clear blue sky a couple of days later I get a call from Washington, D.C., from someone who says he'd like to fly out and see me today. And when he does, he turns out to be the executioner that this reporter thinks was surprised."

Cunningham stopped himself from taking another sip of iced tea. He lowered his glass and met Hurst's level gaze.

"I was wondering if you'd recognize me," he said.

"It didn't come to me right away. But I've seen people in surgical masks before and a few minutes ago the memory finally clicked. I didn't really need that anyway to come up with the conclusions you said I've jumped to. I didn't have much trouble figuring out that someone thinks something pretty bad must've happened to Luttwalk before Uncle Sam managed to kill him."

"Any ideas?" Cunningham asked.

"Nope. Seems like a strange thing to do. Take a huge risk just to mess with a man's about to die anyway."

"Seems strange at that."

"Anything else you'd like to know?" Hurst asked as he stood up.

"There is, to tell you the truth," Cunningham said. "But I don't know how to get into it. I'm not trained for this kind of thing. I'm just an old cavalry officer who went out to do his job one morning and found himself up to his ass in alligators before lunch."

Hurst had strolled over to the window at the front of the house. He'd been staring up County Highway G, die-straight eight miles to I-35. When Cunningham mentioned "cavalry" Hurst looked quickly back over his shoulder, a spark of interest flickering in his eyes as he focused for the first time on the medallion around Cunningham's neck.

"First Air Cavalry Division?" he asked.

"Right."

"Nam?"

"Full tour."

"Ever stationed at Leavenworth?"

"About nine months," Cunningham said. "They promised to find a Ranger-training slot for me if I'd get my ticket punched out here, so I did. Turned out the most important thing I did was organize the detachment for the American Royal parade that year. I was the only cavalry officer they could find in the Pentagon that week who knew which side of the horse you mount on. That was my first American Royal."

"There've been others?"

"Since I got out, yeah. I've made a lot of the shows. Turned out there're people who'll pay me a lot more than the army did to sit on top of a horse."

Hurst nodded.

"That other thing you wanna talk to me about is Terry, isn't it?" he asked quietly.

"Yeah," Cunningham admitted.

"All right," Hurst said decisively. "I've had enough air conditioning for a while. Let's step out on the deck."

Hurst strode from the room, leading Cunningham down the hallway, through a small kitchen, onto a redwood deck built onto the back of the house. At the far end of the deck and slightly above it, protected by an enclosure of vertical redwood planks, was a round swimming pool perhaps twelve feet in diameter. A plump young woman in a purple, one-piece swimsuit floated lazily in it.

"Francie," Hurst said, " 'bout two minutes from now we're gonna have some visitors. Get something on and when they get here tell them I'll be tied up for ten more minutes or so and if they wait I'll be with them then."

" 'Kay, Dad," Francie said as she pulled herself effortlessly from the pool. Hurst waited until she'd gotten inside before he spoke again.

"I said vets aren't sentimental about animals," he said then. "But it takes about six years of dissecting them and a few years of treating them when half the time the 'treatment' is to shoot them or put them to sleep to squeeze that sentimentality out of you."

"If you ever do," Cunningham remarked.

"When I went back to K-State after semester break my freshman year, I didn't say good-bye to my dog. I knew if I did I'd cry, after the way I'd missed him during that first term."

"Nothing to be ashamed of."

"I didn't say it was. When Terry turned twelve, I got him a solid black Labrador puppie. Named it Loki, after the Scandanavian god of mischief. Terry thanked me and cared for the dog and took him along when he went plinking with his .410. He was a good boy, considerate, cared about my feelings. But when it came time for Terry to go off to college, he went to KU instead of K-State. He said good-bye to that dog and there wasn't a tear in his eye. The closest he came to crying was when he saw the computer I'd bought for him to take with him. That was what he loved."

Cunningham thought of four different banalities to mouth, decided against all of them and kept his mouth shut.

"I knew then that I'd lost him," Hurst continued. "Knew it as soon as I saw him walk through the door of that dormitory. I knew he'd never be a vet, never come back to Topeka, never really be comfortable with the way he'd grown up. I knew KU was gonna take my boy and send me back a stranger. That's what happened."

"You're telling me you didn't have any idea of what Terry was doing in Washington, that he never talked to you about what he was working on."

Hurst had thrust his hands in the hip pockets of his Levis, thumbs hooked over the seams as he leaned against the railing around the deck and looked at what seemed like an acre full of barking, romping dogs. He jerked his head around and stared at Cunningham, his eyes as cold and clear as a night sky over the Great Plains in January.

"Yeah," he said. "That's what I'm telling you."

"Listen," Cunningham said, groping for words that could retrieve the opportunity he felt sure he'd just blown, "I'm not—"

"Have a good drive back," Hurst said. He swiveled around and marched into the kitchen with Cunningham in his wake.

The two men who were waiting in the reception area when Hurst and Cunningham got there didn't match Cunningham's stereotype. They were wearing light-hued, summer-weight suits instead of blue wool ones, and neither of them had hats. Even so, Cunningham was certain that he knew who they were. He was right.

"Dr. Hurst?" the nearer one said as Hurst came through the door ahead of Cunningham.

"Yes."

The man opened a wallet-sized leather folder. On the top was a badge. On the bottom was a credential with a color picture on it.

"My name is Vince Halperin," the man said. "This is my partner, Steve Romero. We're with the FBI. We'd like to ask you some questions."

CHAPTER FOURTEEN

As that morning's meeting was winding down, Estabrook had asked Michaelson casually where he could get a good, cheap lunch in the neighborhood, and Michaelson had responded casually that he generally took an apple or a sandwich and ate it while strolling around the Tidal Basin. Michaelson figured this was a good sign.

It was. Estabrook met Michaelson about an hour later on the path leading to the Jefferson Memorial.

"I'm not sure how much Posner's telling you," Estabrook said as soon as the preliminaries were out of the way. "But I know he's holding out on the main thing you want to know. If he'd already told you what Hurst was working on before he was killed, you would've asked about that at this morning's meeting so he could duck the question again on the record."

"I see," Michaelson said. "And are you now going to let me in on what Captain Posner and Ms. Standish have thus far been holding back?"

Estabrook nodded.

"Security measures for psephometric computer programs," he said.

"I see. Most illuminating. What might psephometric computer programs be?"

"Vote counting," Estabrook said. "Computerized ballot tabulation."

Dropping his apple core into the paper sack he'd brought for the purpose, Michaelson gazed past Estabrook at the elegantly domed monument to America's most enigmatic president: the slaveholder who wrote that all men are created equal, the strict constructionist who bought half a continent without a by-your-leave from Congress or a nod at the Constitution, the peace lover who'd waged undeclared war on the Barbary pirates.

"Why was the United States Army concerning itself with computerized vote counting?" Michaelson asked very quietly, no suggestion of banter left in his voice.

"I don't know," Estabrook said. "But if it was because somebody told it to, you wouldn't think Posner would've been so shy about saying so, would you?"

"What explanation has he offered?"

"None."

"You mean you haven't asked?"

"We've asked," Estabrook affirmed. "He just hasn't felt like giving us an answer. He uses the phrase 'need-to-know' a lot. Need-to-know is something he thinks we don't have."

"I see," Michaelson said. "Thank you. Most helpful. I wonder if you could enlighten me on one further point."

"What's that?"

"The real reason that FBI agents were present at Luttwalk's execution."

"I told you: procedure."

"That's nonsense and you know it as well as I do," Michaelson said without rancor. "They were there in the hope that Luttwalk would try to save himself by offering to talk. Weren't they?"

Estabrook started to answer, then stopped and considered the question more carefully.

"If you already know," he said finally, "why are you asking?"

"Because if you were a bit more forthcoming concerning your own agency's activities, the tales you're telling about Posner and the army would be that much more credible."

"It's obvious," Estabrook shrugged, not even slightly offended by the insinuation. "If Luttwalk decided at the last minute that he wanted to make a deal, sure, we wanted to have personnel on hand to take care of the situation."

"Surely he'd been approached about that long before the execution date."

"We told his lawyer from day one he could save his hide if he'd sing. He never took the bait."

"That's simply incredible," Michaelson said. "You said he was just hired muscle. I can understand his holding out as long as he had a chance in court. But once his last appeal was denied and he knew there wasn't any more hope, why in the world would a simple thug go to his death rather than betray the people who hired him?"

"You got me," Estabrook conceded. "That's what we were counting on. That's why we had people there. We figured when he got word he was out of court on the habeas petition and the president had turned down any reprieve, he'd finally spill his guts. But his lawyer came in that morning and must've given him the news and still, nothing."

"That morning? I thought the appeal had been decided long before the execution."

"The basic appeal had," Estabrook explained. "The direct appeal from the trial. But in criminal cases you get more than one kick at the cat. His lawyer started a habeas corpus action, claiming some constitutional rights had been violated that hadn't been decided on the first appeal. He brought it real late in the game and asked for an emergency stay of execution. The Supreme Court denied both the morning of the execution. And unless Luttwalk decided to talk there was never any hope for an executive reprieve."

"Suppose Luttwalk *had* decided to talk. Suppose when the doctor came to give him the soporific he'd started yelling that he was ready to make a deal. What would've happened?"

"Our guys talked to his lawyer just before the doctor came in. The lawyer said no dice. Then they went in with the doctor and talked to Luttwalk. They told Luttwalk that if he was ready to cave they had a direct line to the White House counsel, who had a stay of execution sitting on his desk. They reported that Luttwalk just lay there on the gurney, smirking, like he was half out already."

Michaelson shook his head slowly.

"Well," he said, "it's most unfortunate."

"That's the way it goes." Estabrook shrugged. "But we'll catch the guys who did it. We'll ask them the same questions and sooner or later we'll get some answers."

"I'm not at all sure of that," Michaelson said.

"What do you mean?"

"Based on what you've told me this afternoon, I'm coming reluctantly to the conclusion that the odds are against finding whoever's responsible for murdering Luttwalk. Efficient police work won't be enough, I'm afraid. It's going to take either a piece of good luck for our side or an incredible mistake by the perpetrator. Barring that, I don't think the murderer will be caught."

"We'll see," Estabrook said.

"Fortunately," Michaelson added cheerfully, "finding the murderer isn't my job. Have a pleasant afternoon."

CHAPTER FIFTEEN

Ken, that's great news," Daniels said. "Cadwallader came through, huh?"

"Yeah he did, actually," Dahl said. "I'm going to talk to my producer as soon as I get in for the seven o'clock 'cast tonight and I figure I'll get a green light no problem."

He meant to stop right there. He really did. But when he heard Daniels' voice and imagined her standing at her desk with midafternoon sunlight shimmering in the window behind her, he couldn't stop himself from going on.

"Plus," he said, "I dug something out on my own, actually."

"Oh?" Daniels responded after a half-beat pause. "What was that?"

"Little sidelight on the Luttwalk execution that I covered earlier this week. It looks like Luttwalk's lawyer didn't handle that case for free after all."

"What do you mean?"

"He charged Ohatsu for at least a week of the time he spent in Luttwalk's trial."

"That sounds pretty serious, Ken. Is that just gossip or do you have some documentation for it?"

"It's documented, all right," Dahl said. "I'm holding the document in my hand. I'm looking at it. I can't wait 'till my producer sees it."

"You might hold off on that part of it," Daniels said.

"Why?"

"Ohatsu is my client, Ken. Phantom billing a foreign account isn't going to make the front page of the *Post* but it's damn important to the company that pays the bill."

"I can see that," Dahl admitted, "but—"

"I'll have to look into this, and if it checks out I'll need to report it to Mr. Matsuyama. I can't make a charge like that until I'm sure it's true, but at the same time I'd hate for him to hear it from somebody else."

"Well, sure," Dahl said. "Still—"

"Besides," Daniels continued, "you're going to need Cadwallader's help to follow up on the Ohatsu-shakedown lead. That's the story, not some bullshit sidebar on some stiff who's already yesterday's news. You start threatening Ohatsu's relationship with Cadwallader's firm and you're going to chill him real fast."

"Well, Ariane, I know you're right about that, but—"

"I'm not saying forget about it. I'm saying just keep this to yourself until I've had a chance to look at it. Tell you what. Why don't you come over after the eleven o'clock and we can talk about it?"

"Better idea," said Dahl, who felt like he was drowning in the torrent of Daniels's words. "Why don't you come over to my place about half past the witching hour tonight. We can look at it together, and then comes the dawn I'll get some croissants in for breakfast."

"*Fabulous* idea, Ken. You're the best. See you then."

Dahl hung up. He started whistling. Daniels's last words made him feel sunny, and the tough talk preceding them excited him. Standing naked in the living room of his apartment, a limp towel slung casually over his left shoulder, he tingled with heady excitement at the thought of spending another night with her.

"Come see me and in the morning I'll get breakfast." He glowed with satisfaction at controlling someone like Ariane Daniels with words as simple as these. He felt magical. He felt omnipotent.

Magically, omnipotently, he punched McNaghten's number into his phone.

"You said to call when I had something to show you," he said after he'd reached the recording telling him to leave a message. "Well, I have something to show you."

CHAPTER SIXTEEN

Thank you for calling me about your talk with Dr. Hurst before you left Kansas City, by the way," Michaelson said to Cunningham. "After Estabrook's revelation this afternoon, I prepared a rather snippy directive calling for a complete report on the army's psephometric computer program by noon tomorrow. Thanks to your call, I was able to add a demand for a complete rundown on Fort Leavenworth's relations with what has to be the most interesting veterinarian in the Midwest. Punched the directive up a little bit."

"I don't expect it needed very much punching. I'll bet all hell broke loose when that thing hit Posner's terminal screen."

"Not to mention Nat Lever's. Soda?"

"No, thanks," Cunningham said. "I like scotch by itself."

"A traditionalist," Michaelson said approvingly. He settled further into the tall-backed, navy blue leather club chair across from the sofa in his apartment. "You know I never had a drink of scotch in my life until I joined the Foreign Service?"

"Really?"

"I knew I was *supposed* to like it, but it never fit into my budget at Harvard or the Fletcher School, so I didn't acquire a taste for it. Then, when they were giving us our orientation before our first overseas postings, the briefing officer said, 'Gentlemen,'—it was all men back then—'you will leave with beer tastes, and you will come back with scotch tastes.' And that's the way it happened."

"I got acquainted with scotch a bit earlier than that," Cunningham said. "Where I grew up, bourbon was the good ole boy drink, so you didn't dare bring that into my mother's house. But scotch was what they drank at the country club, so that was all right. She never touched a drop of it herself the longest day she lived, but she'd let it in the house."

"I know you had misgivings about going out to see Hurst in a rush," Michaelson said crisply, after a contemplative pause. He set his glass down on top of a copy of *Foreign Policy* and leaned forward to emphasize the change of subject.

"I had the feeling it was more that you wanted to stir something up than that you really expected me to find out anything. When you told me to have someone meet me at the airport with a sedan from the GSA motor pool instead of just renting a car, I thought, cripes, everyone west of the Mississippi who gets a green cardboard paycheck's going to know who I am, what I'm up to, and why I'm doing it. Then I figured, that's exactly what he wants. He's trying to light a fire under someone."

"That was part of it," Michaelson admitted. "But I also thought there was a good chance you'd learn something. And it looks like I may have been right. If I'm reading you correctly, you think Hurst might very well have murdered Luttwalk."

"He's tough enough to do it and he's mean enough to do it. He certainly had the chance to do it, especially if a syringe switch actually could've worked."

"His argument that it couldn't have worked struck me as unconvincing."

"Me too," Cunningham said. "Syringes are mass-produced and I'd be willing to bet that doctors give wrong injections somewhere every week. But where Hurst really rings the bell with me is that portrait."

"Yes. You said over the phone it was a portrait of William Quantrill. I didn't have the faintest idea who he was. I meant to look him up before you got back, but I didn't get the chance."

"He was a Confederate guerrilla leader during the Civil War," Cunningham explained. "Frank and Jesse James rode with him. I don't think Hurst realized that I recognized the portrait. Without the sabers up there to give me a hint, I'm not sure I would have."

"It certainly suggests an offbeat taste in portraiture," Michaelson said. "But I'm not sure I understand why you attach so much significance to it."

"Soldier for soldier and gun for gun," Cunningham said, "guerrilla fighting in Missouri and Kansas was as bloody and brutal as anything in the Civil War. When I called Cynthia from the airport I had her pull the encyclopedia down and fill in some details on Quantrill. In the summer of 1863, he and his men raided Lawrence, Kansas. They burned it to the ground. They killed a hundred and fifty people. Most of the casualties were civilians, lots of them women and children shot down in cold blood."

Michaelson sipped scotch, closed his eyes for a moment, and nodded.

"Lawrence is where the University of Kansas is, if I'm not mistaken," he said then.

"Right."

"And Hurst told you he blamed KU for taking his son and sending back a stranger."

"Exactly," Cunningham said. "I'll bet a month's pay that that's what got Quantrill's picture up on Hurst's wall. I saw that and I said to myself, here's a guy who knows how to hate."

"Agreed. But doesn't that strengthen the argument Hurst offered in his own defense: that if he'd done anything to Luttwalk, it would've caused Luttwalk a lot more pain than a tranquilizer overdose did?"

"It's a smart argument," Cunningham acknowledged. "But I'm not sure I buy it. Hurst has his own ideas about how a man's supposed to act. I could see him saying to himself, 'I mean for it to be *me* that puts that son of a bitch away—not some bureaucrat in a surgical mask.'"

"You may be right. In any event, with this little nudge in the right direction we can be sure that the FBI will be pursuing that possibility very aggressively. Congratulations. It was an extremely productive interview. I don't see how it could have gone better."

"I do," Cunningham said.

"Oh? How?"

"I had the feeling right there at the end that he was ready to tell me something. I felt like I'd finally gotten on his wavelength when I talked about being in the cavalry. We were cruising along then, and I thought he was opening up and was just about to let go of something important. Then I asked the wrong question and he brushed me off from there on out."

"That's an intriguing notion," Michaelson said. "If it really was a missed opportunity, we'll just have to see if we can think of some way to go after it from a different direction."

"That may take some doing. I have a feeling that Hurst is the kind of guy who says, One strike and you're out."

After taking his most generous sip of scotch so far, Michaelson glanced at his watch.

"I don't think we'll resolve the issue tonight," he said. "You've put in over twelve hours today, starting with your dawn run beside Captain Posner. I think I'd better let you get back to your wife."

"Sure." Cunningham drained his own glass and stood up. "By the way. I assume you know what Posner told me about you. Am I right?"

"I can pretty well guess. Looking for a top job. Weakness for self-promotion. Not quite as fanatical about stonewalling Congress as most people on both banks of the Potomac are. Used to play cat and mouse with the gents at Langley. Does that basically summarize it?"

"Basically."

"It's quite true, incidentally. You can package it to make me look like a self-interested careerist or you can package it to make me look like a slightly less scrupulous, slightly more ambitious version of George Kennan. Or anything in between. But the essential data are perfectly accurate."

"I assumed as much. He also told me that you'd called my personnel file up."

"I most certainly did," Michaelson said. "That doesn't surprise you, does it?"

"Not particularly. I was just wondering what you think you found out."

"The main thing I accomplished was to surprise myself. I'd assumed that you'd left the army for the same reason most career officers do: because it's up or out and you'd been passed over twice for promotion. But I found out I was wrong."

Cunningham smiled. "I wasn't sure how clear it'd be to someone from the left bank of the Potomac," he said.

"I didn't have any trouble with that part. I know how to read efficiency ratings. I know why you didn't leave. What I didn't figure out was why you did."

"It's not an easy question," Cunningham said. "What it comes down to is that after Nam I couldn't get back to being part of what the army's about."

"I certainly wouldn't have guessed that. First Air Cavalry Division. Paratroop qualified. Ranger training. Special Forces. In my untutored way I would've said that that's the kind of thing the army's about."

"That was just it. I did all those things, and the army let me do them to keep me happy. But what the army really wanted me to do was sit at a desk in the Pentagon and write military histories. I put in for Jump School and they said, fine, go to Jump School. I got my ticket punched, then found myself back at a desk writing unit histories and engagement accounts. Same thing with Ranger training and Special Forces. I'd get my beret and my braid and then, pow! I'm back reading about Fort Hood in the archives instead of serving there."

"I understand what you're saying," Michaelson said.

"I know you do. You were a foreign service officer and you did what foreign service officers do. I was an army officer and I wasn't doing what army officers do. Unit histories and engagement accounts are important. Tradition's a significant weapon for a military outfit. But what the army's about is men taking rifles and going in harm's way. If I couldn't do that, I wasn't going to be in the army."

"It's really the same thing you told me yesterday afternoon. You're either in or you're out. I either trust you or I don't, and it's time for me to fish or cut bait."

"I guess that's what it comes down to."

"You don't accomplish the really tough jobs in Washington without luck," Michaelson said. "I got lucky when I sent you to talk to Hurst. You also don't accomplish anything in Washington without enough brains to keep doing the things that were lucky the first time you did them. I intend to keep on being lucky."

After Cunningham left, it took Michaelson several minutes of searching to come up with the telephone number of former United States Senator Desmond Gardner, now out of prison and back home in the Midwest, thanks in part to Michaelson.

"Hello?" a young, rather impatient female voice answered after he placed the call.

"Hello. This is Richard Michaelson. Is that you, Wendy?"

"Sure is." Her voice brightened. "How's D.C.?"

"D.C. never changes. Are you still serious about running for your state's legislature when the seat in your district comes up next?"

"Absolutely. I quit smoking last year and I'm reviewing the state budget right now."

"You no doubt know a great deal more about the subject than I. I wonder if I might speak with your father for a moment."

"Dad's not home right now. Want me to have him call you?"

"I'd appreciate that very much. I have a rather unusual request. I'd like to find out if he happens to know anyone who owns a show horse."

Silence intervened for a long moment.

"As a matter of fact," Wendy said thoughtfully then, "he does know someone like that."

CHAPTER SEVENTEEN

T
he station really doesn't like me to leave between the seven and eleven o'clock programs," Dahl said to McNaghten as he maneuvered his Lincoln through McLean, Virginia's nighttime traffic, over pavement still slick from a downpour that had stopped only an hour before. "And this is the second night in a row I've done it."

"You're a regular rebel, Ken. There's something existentially thrilling about your reckless contempt for establishment rules."

"It just would've been a lot simpler if you could've come by tomorrow morning, that's all."

McNaghten gazed at the windshield's faint reflection of her thin-lipped smile.

"I have a real job," she said. "You know, mail to open, bills to pay, subscribers who expect me to keep regular office hours—that kind of thing. I can't start the workday by traipsing off to the suburbs."

By now they were driving alongside the ash gray, fieldstone-faced wall defining the northern boundary of Appomattox Condominium Estates.

"Shit, look at that," Dahl said absently. "Some kid's cut through the wire on top again. Security at this place's a joke."

"The problems of the wealthy," McNaghten sighed.

Dahl turned his car into the Estates' driveway. His headlights shown on a wrought-iron gate that swung open after he inserted a stiff card into a discreet box mounted beside the driveway. She doesn't think I have anything worth looking at, he thought. She thinks I'm bullshitting her. He drove through the opening and nosed the Lincoln into his assigned parking space.

"If you're really worried about security," McNaghten said, gesturing briefly toward the second-floor quarters that Dahl occupied, "you shouldn't leave a light on when you go out before dark. It's a signal that nobody's home."

"Right," Dahl muttered. He started to open his door. "What did you just say?" he demanded. "I didn't leave any light on."

"Well there's one on now, shining behind the shade on that middle window."

Dahl, with mounting understanding, looked anxiously at the second story of the building where he lived. He hadn't left any shades drawn either.

"NO!" he yelled suddenly, smacking the steering wheel with the heel point of his balled right fist. Then he pushed the car door violently open. "Call the police!" he ordered McNaghten over his shoulder as he hustled out of the car.

"What are *you* doing?" McNaghten asked. But then she saw that Dahl was already opening the Lincoln's trunk and she knew exactly what he was doing.

"No, Ken!" she shouted uselessly at the car's cavernous back seat. "Jesus, what a child," she said then to herself.

She clambered out of the car and scurried around to its rear. Dahl had dug his paint-pellet gun out of his duffel bag and was frantically loading it.

"Call the police," he directed her again. He did it this time without looking at her as he concentrated on feeding cartridges into the weapon.

"You come with me and we'll call the police together," she said in the exaggeratedly placatory tones that might be used with a lunatic or a toddler throwing a temper tantrum.

"Bullshit," he said grimly.

He turned toward the building about thirty feet away. With both hands McNaghten grabbed his right arm near the shoulder.

"They might very well still be in there," she said.

"That's exactly what I'm counting on." He jerked his shoulder free.

"Ken, they'll be using real bullets, not paint pellets." She seized two fistfuls of the back of his coat. "Now, come with me and we'll call the police together."

He spun around, his face savage with frustrated determination.

"Stop treating me like an infant," he barked.

Putting his left hand not ungently on McNaghten's right shoulder, he gave her a stiff, decisive shove. McNaghten gasped as she stumbled backward and her bottom smacked the pavement. She lifted her head in time to see Dahl sprinting toward the narrow lawn that led to his building. Simultaneously, in the white glow of a mesh-protected light-bulb above the service door on the side of the building, she saw that door start to open.

"Ken!" she yelled.

Dahl saw the door swinging open at the same time. A dark-clothed, heavily encumbered figure was pushing through the door, and it looked like there was another one behind him.

"Freeze!" Dahl yelled.

Gripping the pistol with both hands, arms extended and slightly bent at the elbows, hips back, knees flexed, he leveled his gun at the first exiting figure.

A crash of splintering glass split the air as the man dropped a portable television and a VCR wedged under his left arm. He swept his left hand inside the suede jacket he was wearing. He didn't drop the maroon leather attaché case in his right hand.

Dahl squeezed the trigger. His pistol cracked. The first man jumped back against the service door, smacking his head on it. He reached with his still-empty left hand for the apex of his collarbone just to the right of his throat, now the center of a red spatter that covered most of his throat and part of his upper chest.

"Christ, I'm hit!" he screamed.

The second man shouldered through an opening that his disoriented colleague partially blocked. With both hands he pointed something at Dahl.

Dahl belly-flopped instantly onto the rain-sodden lawn. Dredging sloppy mud and black water up with his churning elbows, he crawled forward and to his right.

A long burst of rapid automatic fire rattled from the second man's gun. Dahl reflexively buried his face in the mud, then raised it and re-aimed his pistol.

McNaghten had come to a crouch behind the Lincoln. Now she flattened herself behind it as whistling bullets shattered its windows and perforated the still-open trunk lid.

"Uzi," she muttered. "Every two-bit punk in Washington has to have an Uzi. Doesn't anyone just use thirty-eights anymore?"

Steeling himself beneath the hail of bullets, Dahl squeezed off a second shot. A piercing scream ripped from the first man as the pellet exploded in the center of his face. He dropped the attaché case.

McNaghten crawled awkwardly to the safe side of the Lincoln, opened the front passenger door, and groped for Dahl's car phone.

"Gunfire at Appomattox Estates," she said after she'd punched 911.

The second man fired another inexpert volley, this one as high as the first one had been. Then he grabbed his companion's right arm and began pulling him at a run toward the back of the building. They disappeared around the corner. Dahl missed with a last shot that he fired in sheer combat exhilaration.

Coming to his feet, he ran toward the attaché case still lying on the asphalt outside the service door. His fingers clumsy with tension and excitement, he fumbled it open and pawed through the contents.

He didn't see it the first time through. Black, panicky despair gripped him. Oblivious to the wailing squad-car sirens and the lights snapping on above him, he went methodically through the papers again.

There it was. The bill. He took the precious piece of paper out and stood up, gazing lovingly at it.

McNaghten edged gingerly toward him. Sensing her presence, he turned to face her. Sweat glistened on his mud-spattered face. Filthy water dripped from his saturated clothing. Grass stains and more mud streaked his once-elegant Ralph Lauren suit, his cotton-broadcloth Arrow shirt, and his YSL silk tie.

"That was pretty goddamned impressive," she said quietly, gazing up at him.

"I was highly motivated."

CHAPTER EIGHTEEN

I thought you didn't smoke."

"I don't," McNaghten said. "Anymore."

She held a cigarette with delicate elegance in the first two fingers of her left hand, about two inches from her left cheekbone. Smoke from its tip curled lazily toward the opening at the top of the window in front of her. Her right forearm nestled under her breasts, her left elbow resting on top of her right hand, she presented for once a picture of serene contentment. She glanced over her shoulder at Dahl and the surrounding wreckage of his living room. A playfully sly smile nudged the corners of her lips.

"There's a time and a place for everything," she explained. "And an hour after you've come through a shoot-out okay is a pretty good time for a cigarette."

"I guess so," Dahl said, returning her smile. "You finished with the phone?"

"Yep. Story's with the service and the service's putting it on the wire. Thanks for letting me tie your line up."

"No problem. Professional courtesy."

"You earned that shot," McNaghten conceded as Dahl picked up the phone and started punching in a number. "Why haven't you showered and changed? Don't you have a remote crew on the way?"

"Sure have," Dahl said. "That's why I haven't changed. My producer thinks the story'll be more visual if I still look just the way I did after the fight."

McNaghten opened her mouth but Dahl started talking into the phone before she could say anything. She turned silently back toward the window.

"Hi, Ariane, Ken. . . . No, I'm at home. I've been burgled. . . . I'm okay, thanks. . . . Yeah, unbelievable. Place looks like a cyclone struck it. You'll be able to see it on the news tonight. . . . No, they didn't get it. . . . I don't know if they were after it or not. They were taking a lot of other stuff too, but that could've been a blind. Anyway, I've gotten a couple of copies of it off in the mail, one to you and one to, uh, someplace else safe, so it's okay now. . . . No, no sense coming over tonight. The station's doing a remote from here and the place's a mess, like I said, and I'm not even sure it's that safe to be here. . . . No, uh, I think I, uh, better stay here tonight. . . . Look, I'll give you a call tomorrow and we'll see if we can make sense of it then. . . . Yeah, me too, babe. Later. Right."

McNaghten turned around as Dahl hung up the phone.

"The friend who likes Kents. Am I right?"

"Yeah," Dahl said.

"Are they just going to tape three minutes on the Second Battle of Appomattox, or are they going to try to have you remote-anchor the eleven o'clock news from here?"

"Story only. Live remote, then a tease and tape for eleven. They'll bring in a sub for the late news."

"I guess that makes you a reporter."

"At least for tonight."

McNaghten drew briefly on the cigarette and put it out.

"Listen," Dahl said, shrugging nervously again. "I'm not sure how to say this. I brought you out here and after the remote I'll drive you home. Or get a cab for you, if you want. But, uh, if you want to, you know, spend the night, that'd be okay too."

McNaghten turned and looked searchingly at Dahl.

"That's kind of sweet, the way you said that," she said.

"Well I, you know, meant it, actually."

"I don't think I've had a really sweet proposition since the day Agnew resigned."

Dahl smiled sheepishly. His achingly vulnerable expression made him seem incredibly young—more like nineteen than twenty-six.

"So," he said. "Whattaya say?"

"I know it's the best offer I'm likely to get for a long time," McNaghten said. "And someday soon the answer might be yes." She strolled over toward Dahl and looked up at him. The D.C. insider hipness dropped from her eyes, making her face seem frank and sensitive. "When I was growing up, girls were taught not to drop their panties too casually in mixed company. That was then and this is now, but some things stay with you. So maybe we could"—suddenly tongue-tied, she rolled her eyes, searching awkwardly for words—"revisit this topic later. Okay?"

"Sure," he said.

Almost desperately, she searched his face, trying to find out whether it really was all right or she'd blown it.

"Really?" she asked anxiously.

"Really." Dahl held out his hand to shake McNaghten's. "But I think maybe I liked it better when you were treating me like an infant."

McNaghten shook hands with him. Her smile was relieved, delighted, just short of girlish.

"Would you feel better if I made you stand in the corner?" she asked.

They laughed together.

THE FOURTH DAY AFTER THE EXECUTION

CHAPTER NINETEEN

8:05 A.M.

T hat's odd," Marjorie Randolph said. She put the front section of *The New York Times* in her lap and leaned over to retrieve the Metro section of *The Washington Post* from the pile of discarded newspapers on the floor beside her.

"What's odd?"

Michaelson waved away the waitress approaching with a steaming silver coffee pot. The Carlton Hotel Coffee Shop on Massachusetts just beyond Du Pont Circle offers one of the most enjoyable light breakfasts in northwest Washington. By budgeting carefully, Michaelson could afford to eat there once a week.

"What's odd," Marjorie said, "is that *The New York Times*'s account of that shooting incident in McLean last night is a lot more complete than the *Post*'s. The *Post* has a run-of-the-mill police blotter story in eight paragraphs. The *Times* reads like someone actually developed enough energy to have a reporter on the scene."

"That does seem strange," Michaelson agreed, his interest piqued. "It should be the other way around."

Marjorie pulled the *Times* from her lap and glanced back at it.

"It looks like Ginny McNaghten may have stolen one from the big kids. Good for her."

"Ginny McNaghten?" Michaelson asked sharply.

"She's Chesapeake News Service," Marjorie explained. "I mean that literally. She and Chesapeake News Service are the same thing. The *Times* is a subscriber and the *Post* isn't, and from the credit line it looks like the *Times* ate the *Post*'s lunch on the McLean story as a result."

"May I see the *Times* account, Marjorie?" Michaelson asked.

"Sure. Do you know Ginny?"

"Not yet," Michaelson said.

9:35 A. M.

"Good news and bad news, Ken. The good news is I've saved your ass." Ariane Daniels's telephone voice was as usual aggressively self-assured.

"Saved my ass how?"

"I scoped out that bill business. And I got the story without your name coming up."

"Okay. What's the story on the bill? And what's the bad news?"

"Same answer to both questions. Basically, it didn't mean what you thought it did."

"Then what does it mean? That Baldwin could be in two places at once?"

"Did you notice when they gave the hourly charge on the time sheet they said 'blended rate'?" Daniels asked.

"Yeah."

"Well, that's a standard law firm smoke screen. It means they have two or more lawyers working on a matter during a certain period, so they charge a single hourly rate that's supposedly an average of both lawyers' hourly rates. You with me so far?"

"Sure. There were initials for two different lawyers on the bill, and one of those lawyers was Baldwin."

"And the other one wasn't. See, that's the point."

"No, Ariane, I don't see."

"The other lawyer's like this very junior associate. Low billing rate. So maybe he works on something for Ohatsu from eight-thirty in the morning until ten at night with six minutes off to piss. And sometime that night, after Baldwin's through in court for the day, maybe this associate calls Baldwin and talks about Ohatsu for sixteen minutes. That means Baldwin and the junior associate both worked on Ohatsu stuff that day, so they put down both initials and they charge a blended rate

106

for the associate's thirteen-point-five hours plus Baldwin's point-three hours."

"Bottom line being what?" Dahl asked a trifle impatiently.

"Bottom line being, there's nothing inconsistent with Baldwin being in court all day defending Luttwalk and having his initials appear on an Ohatsu billing item for that same day, even though the total billing item amounts to a lot more than an ordinary day's work. An item like that doesn't mean Baldwin worked twelve hours on Ohatsu, it just means someone at the firm did, and Baldwin contributed some fraction of the time."

"It still sounds to me like Ohatsu's being gouged."

"Of course they are," Daniels said with exaggerated patience. "But padded bills are one thing and phantom bills are something else. In Washington, a law firm's *overcharging* its clients is in the dog-bites-man category."

"Maybe," Dahl said dubiously.

"How are you coming with the shakedown story?"

"The producer likes it. She wants me to get more before we do anything with it. I'm working on a Freedom of Information Act request to file today."

"Okay. Sounds good. How about you, Ken? Are you all right after last night? That was crazy."

"I'm just fine."

"Ken? I've been wondering about something."

"What's that?"

"How you mentioned that bill to me in a telephone call yesterday, and then burglars suddenly hit your place last night. It seems like a very strange coincidence."

"You could say that, yeah." His expression blank, animation faded from Dahl's face. He'd been trying to ignore uncomfortably suspicious thoughts. Except for the generic message he'd left on McNaghten's answering machine and a couple of cryptic hints to his producer, he hadn't mentioned the bill to anyone except Daniels.

"So," Daniels continued, "I know this sounds, like, paranoid, Ken, but do you think there's any chance your phone was tapped?"

"Who'd wanna tap my phone?"

"Who'd want to send people with machine guns over to pay you a visit when you weren't home?"

"I could have it checked, I guess."

"It's probably too late now. If there was a tap on your phone and the burglars were connected with whoever tapped it, they probably took any eavesdropping stuff away with them."

"Maybe so."

"Just a thought."

"Yeah. Thanks. I'll keep in touch on the Ohatsu shakedown story."

" 'Kay, Ken. 'Bye."

10:15 A.M.

"This is a usually reliable source at DOJ," the male voice on the phone said.

"I'm listening," McNaghten said, although she didn't stop typing the invoice she was working on.

"I'm calling about that FOIA request you filed for the Luttwalk autopsy."

"What about it?"

"You should get an answer in about twenty-three more days."

"SOP," McNaghten said.

"When you get the answer, here's what it's going to say: 'The medical procedure in question was performed under the auspices of the Veterans' Administration Hospital in Kansas City, Missouri. Please check below if you wish to have your request forwarded to the appropriate agency for further action.' "

"Son of a bitch," McNaghten said. She stopped typing.

"Just thought you'd like to know."

"Thank you *very* much, Department of Justice," McNaghten said. "Let me know if there's ever anyone you'd like me to kill."

McNaghten hung up, finished the invoice that was already in her typewriter, then dug out a Freedom of Information Act request form and typed "Department of Veterans' Affairs" on the first line.

10:55 A.M.

TO: Nathaniel Lever/PERSONAL AND CONFIDENTIAL
FROM: Michaelson

Push has come to shove. Posner is stonewalling.

"No," Michaelson said, removing his fingers from the keyboard as he read the text on the monitor's blue screen. "That allusion's too heavy-handed."

He deleted the last three words and typed, "No response from Posner.

Please call as soon as convenient." He added his initials at the bottom.

Cunningham read the change expressionlessly over Michaelson's shoulder.

"It'd be nice to talk to the man face to face," he said.

"There are three people in the world who can plausibly ask to see Lever personally without getting an appointment two weeks in advance," Michaelson answered. "I'm not one of them."

"Think we'll get a response to this?"

"Of course. As long as we remember that failing to answer is an answer."

Michaelson moved the cursor back to the end of the top line. After "Personal and confidential" he typed a slash and then added, "eyes only."

"Just to make absolutely sure it gets read by every senior member of the White House staff," he explained. "We'll send it at five minutes after noon."

11:50 A.M.

They all think they're the ones who'll be able to bring it off, Maureen Lowry thought to herself as she watched Arnold Hapner pace around the modest office provided to a staff attorney with the Commerce Department. She relaxed a bit behind her desk while she pretended to study the document Hapner had put in front of her. They come in here from the hinterlands, from Georgia or Massachusetts or California or Kansas, and they all think they'll be the exception—they'll be the outsider who can out-hustle Washington, play the capital game better than the permanent government.

They all find out the hard way how wrong they are. This is going to be a personal pleasure, she thought.

"What is this?" Hapner demanded.

"It appears to be a Freedom of Information Act request from a local television station," she said innocently.

"I know that. I can read. I mean what's he driving at? What in the world is he after?"

"If I had to speculate," Lowry said gravely, "I'd say he's fishing for evidence that this consulting firm mentioned here"—she paused, wanting to find exactly the right lawyerly term, the phrase that would tell Hapner that he'd be lucky to get off with probation and community service—"that this consulting firm corruptly procured favors from the department," she concluded.

"What in the world could make them think anything like that happened? Or had anything to do with me?"

"I have no idea."

"Well, we'll object to this, won't we? I mean, a lot of this stuff's very confidential."

"I'll review the request carefully with that in mind," Lowry said. Right. Like tonight while I'm watching "L.A. Law." "In general, however, the confidentiality exceptions to the Freedom of Information Act are rather narrow, and receive a very strict construction from the courts." Hapner looked unhappy. "Especially the D.C. Circuit." Hapner looked stricken. "Of course," she added casually, "if you feel that your personal interests are implicated, you would be entitled to engage private counsel of your own choosing to review the matter."

Hapner looked panicked.

"Okay," he said in a low, distracted voice. "Okay. I'd appreciate it if you'd get me your report as soon as possible."

"I'll have a memo to circulate by early next week."

Hapner mumbled his thanks and left Lowry's office.

Welcome to Washington, asshole, she thought.

12:43 P.M.

"Michaelson," the retired FSO said after picking the phone up before the end of the first ring.

"Mr. Michaelson? I'm sorry, I was trying to reach your secretary."

"She's still at lunch. Can I help you?"

"Yes. This is Mr. Jacobs's secretary." Michaelson's eyebrows went up. He mouthed "White House chief of staff" at Cunningham, sitting a few feet away. "Mr. Jacobs was wondering whether you and Major Cunningham could attend a meeting in Mr. Jacobs's office at 1:30 this afternoon with Mr. Lever."

"Certainly."

"Good. See you then."

Michaelson pushed the disconnect button without putting down the receiver. With unusual quickness and intensity, he punched a new number into the phone.

"Marjorie?" he said after a few seconds' impatient waiting. "This is Richard. Is your computer on?"

"Of course it isn't, Richard. I thought I might spend a few minutes this afternoon selling books."

"I'd like to impose on you. I'd very much appreciate it if you'd put your machine on, connect the phone modem, load the store-and-file program and a formatted blank disk, and let me tie it up for about forty-five minutes."

"I'd be more than happy to, Richard. That's exactly why bookstores have computers—to accommodate requests like that."

"Thank you, Marjorie."

Michaelson again pushed the disconnect button. Then he put the receiver on the modem for his own computer, dialed the number that would connect it with the computer at Cavalier Books, and retrieved from his computer's memory the FBI summary of the Luttwalk autopsy report. When he saw green lights blink on both the modem and his own terminal, he typed in a Transmit command.

"Can I ask what you're doing?" Cunningham wondered in a bemused voice.

"I'm making an unauthorized disclosure of government documents."

"Any particular reason?"

"Yes," Michaelson said, his eyes still fixed on the screen. "There's a very good chance that in less than an hour you and I will be fired. And if we are, we won't see the inside of this room again."

CHAPTER TWENTY

J acobs slouched behind his desk, his right arm draped over the back of his chair. His unbuttoned suit coat revealed a nondescript tie slightly askew on a white, button-down shirt. One of the collar buttons was undone, and the point of the collar curled insubordinately upward. A shock of Jacobs's brown hair hung down to within an inch or two of his brown-framed glasses, giving him a boyish appearance that belied his fifty-two years. The presidential seal on his tie clip matched the one on his left cuff link.

Eight feet directly behind him stood an oak door leading to the Oval Office, where the president of the United States was working.

French cuffs, Michaelson thought. The first thing they do after they join the president's staff is buy five shirts with French cuffs, so that they can wear the cuff links that go with the power clip.

Michaelson had chosen an armless, straight-back chair near the right front corner of Jacobs's desk. He had shifted the chair so that he could look directly either at Jacobs or at Lever and Cunningham, sharing a chesterfield couch across the room from him.

"You've done an excellent job, Dick," Lever was saying. "Really first rate. Major Cunningham also. I feel that you're exactly the right people for this project."

"Excellent, as you're kind enough to say so, but incomplete," Michaelson said. "I haven't been able to get Captain Posner to answer the question that the next phase of our effort turns on. He hasn't been seduced by my charm, and he seems unimpressed by my authority."

Michaelson glanced at Jacobs, who looked like a poker player about to toss one card and anxious not to tip whether he was drawing to a flush or a full house.

"Why don't you let me work on the Posner angle from my end?" Lever proposed. His quietly confident, gently patronizing smile suggested a Mercedes dealer about to close a sale.

"Precisely my object in asking you to call," Michaelson said.

"They do things differently across the river. An oblique approach sometimes works where a frontal assault wouldn't."

"You don't say."

"You can continue pursuing the other aspects of the project. I'll think of some way or other to shake some information loose from Captain Posner. Between the two of us, we should be able to keep the president pretty well up to speed about what's really going on here."

"Let's hope so," Michaelson said. "So then, when your effort to outflank Captain Posner succeeds, would you expect him to provide the report directly to me, or will it be channeled to me through you?"

"We can cross that bridge when we come to it, can't we, Dick?"

"If you prefer."

"Good. Then—"

"As long as we're clear that one way or another I'll get the information," Michaelson interrupted.

"What are you saying?" Jacobs snapped. "Is coordinating data flow somewhere on your job description? I thought the president gave me that job."

Michaelson turned his body slightly and gazed into the green-flecked brown eyes that glinted behind the plastic lenses in Jacobs's glasses.

"I'm saying that I was asked to undertake a particular assignment and I accepted. Should it become clear that I no longer enjoy the confidence of those upon whom my effectiveness depends, then any possibility of a constructive contribution on my part will be over and my course will be obvious."

"Confidence isn't an issue, Dick," Lever said soothingly. "You know that. We're talking—"

"Let's cut the Mickey Mouse, okay?" Jacobs directed. "The pillars of the republic aren't gonna crumble if the door hits your ass on the way out. You're helpful but you're not necessary."

"No one knows that better than I."

"If you're bent outta shape because some paper stops before it reaches you, I'm sorry. I can find fourteen different ways to stroke you if that's what it takes to make you feel better about the whole thing. But the bottom line is, no one elected you—and the guy that people did elect didn't pick you to be chief of staff, he picked me."

"I entertain no illusions on that score. Those people you refer to also elected some other ladies and gentlemen who do their work down the street. They—"

"Look," Jacobs said. For the first time he smiled. He raised the arm that had been dangling over the back of his chair and held his right hand palm out toward Michaelson. "One thing, okay? Don't threaten me. I don't react well to that kind of thing."

"I'm not threatening you. I'm trying to explain why my insistence on access to information I was promised from day one is important for reasons transcending my own self-importance."

"What's Congress have to do with that?" Jacobs demanded.

"There are three things I won't do if I'm summoned before a congressional committee. I won't lie. I won't evade questions. And I won't take the Fifth."

"That leaves spilling your guts," Jacobs said. "That sounds like a threat."

"Not at all. If the president directs me in writing to refuse to answer questions, I'll refuse to answer them—but on grounds of executive privilege, not the Fifth Amendment."

"Until a court lets you off the hook by overruling the privilege, you mean."

"Until nothing," Michaelson said. "The courts are entitled to their opinion, and the president is entitled to his. In a constitutional crisis I'll continue to take my orders from the president—as long as he's personally and publicly accountable for those orders."

"Hell of a choice," Jacobs snorted. "We court impeachment or you sell us out."

"It is in order to avoid precisely that dilemma that I'll resign if I can't get the information I need to do my job. If there are pertinent facts that I can't be trusted with, then I'd better get out before I learn anything that you wouldn't want to hear Peter Jennings talk about on ABC."

Jacobs looked steadily at Michaelson without saying anything. Lever glanced for a long moment at Jacobs, then turned his own gaze back to Michaelson.

"Do me one favor, Dick," he said. "Sleep on it. Okay? Just take tonight to think it over. On something like this, it's more important to do it right than to do it fast."

"I quite agree. I won't make any irrevocable decision until tomorrow."
He glanced at his watch. "Tomorrow at, say, eleven A.M."

Lever went back to his Mercedes dealer smile.

"You'll be hearing from us before then," he said.

THE FIFTH DAY AFTER
THE EXECUTION

CHAPTER TWENTY-ONE

S orry to come by so early, especially on a Saturday," Cunningham said, "but it was something I thought you ought to see."

Michaelson turned the audio cassette over in his hand, as if visual inspection could reveal something about it.

" 'Is it live or is it Memorex?' " he murmured. Then he glanced back up at Cunningham. "How did you get it?"

"It was in a tightly sealed zip-lock baggie inside my front door when I went out to get the paper this morning."

"Have you tried to play it?"

"Negative. Thought I'd get it over here as soon as I could and we'd hear it together."

"Fair enough."

Brushing dry corn flakes from the front of his trousers, Michaelson left the kitchen of his apartment, where he and Cunningham were sharing coffee, and took the cassette to the stereo cabinet in his living room. After he'd inserted the cassette and pushed Play, two seconds of hissing tape was succeeded by a guttural male voice.

"So. Any word?"

"Not yet." The second voice was also male. "Probably a good sign. Like I told you—"

At that point, a piercing hum intervened, obliterating all other sound on the tape. Michaelson endured it for fifteen seconds, then pushed Fast Forward to spin a quarter of the way through the tape. At that point he stopped it and hit Play again. The hum continued. Seven minutes of repeating this process on both sides of the tape convinced him that the hum had wiped out everything except the initial, brief exchange.

Michaelson wound the tape back to the beginning of the first side and played through the aborted dialogue again. When the hum started, he turned his volume up almost as high as it would go and put his ear as close to the nearer speaker as he could stand to. He couldn't make out a particle of intelligible sound underneath the hum.

He wound the tape again back to its starting point and ejected the cassette from his tape player.

"Do you recognize either of the voices?" he asked Cunningham.

"Hard to say for sure. The first one could be Luttwalk. I only heard him talk a couple of times, but it sounds quite a bit like him."

"Well, I hate to sound pessimistic," Michaelson said, "but I don't think we're going to extract much more from this, at least with our own resources."

"Someone who knew what he was doing and had the right equipment might be able to pick something up underneath that noise, even if we can't," Cunningham said.

"If there's anything underneath it to pick up," Michaelson said, nodding. "I rather doubt that there is. But if we can talk Estabrook into it, it's certainly worth a try."

"Doesn't there almost have to be something else on the tape?" Cunningham asked. "I mean, it might've been erased so far that it can't be recovered, but if there was never anything on there, why bother to cover it up with that ungodly noise?"

"Suppose the noise was used to drown out whatever was on another tape—call it the original tape, for the sake of hypothesis. Then suppose this tape was made by recording what was still audible on the original. If that's what happened, then you could do acoustic enhancement tricks on this copy all day long and you wouldn't turn up a thing."

"What would the point of all that be?"

"Bureaucratic hardball," Michaelson said.

"You're over my head."

"I think someone's telling us that all we've accomplished by pressing as hard as we have is to make people destroy evidence—with the implication that if we keep pressing, they'll destroy some more."

Cunningham accepted the cassette from Michaelson and flipped it a couple of times in his hand.

"Then maybe getting this to Estabrook right away isn't such a hot idea after all."

"We should have a better reading on that before noon today," Michaelson said. "One way or the other."

120

CHAPTER TWENTY-TWO

Posner looked different. He was standing, for one thing. He was wearing an everyday uniform, but it looked like the best one he owned, with spit and polish noticeable from the toes of his gleaming shoes to the shiny silver parallel bars pinned to the stiff collar tabs on his pale green shirt.

He was standing in the bay of a horseshoe-shaped table that dominated a windowless office in the White House basement. At the apex of the table's bend sat Jacobs, with an aide beside him busily taking notes. Next came Lever, and Lever's note-taking aide sat between Lever and Michaelson. Michaelson and Cunningham, sitting to his right, took their own notes.

The balding man immediately to Jacobs's left was in mufti but his military bearing was as unmistakable as Posner's. The ashtray accumulating Winstons in front of him testified to his contempt for Washington's current official hostility to cigarettes. His face, calm but alert, always awoke memories of the picture *Time* had run when he was appointed deputy director for national security affairs—the picture showing Vice Admiral Stanley Jennings, then a lieutenant junior grade, standing in the prow of a river patrol craft in Vietnam, .45 in one hand and microphone in the other, dispassionately calling artillery fire down on his own position.

Jennings's note taker sat to his left. Then came Standish, Estabrook, and a uniformed aide to Posner. The aide also had a pen and pad ready.

If you want to know the number of factions involved in a White House fight, just count the aides taking notes at the meeting where the issue comes to head.

It was 11:15 on the morning after Michaelson's meeting with Lever and Jacobs.

"All right," Jacobs said to Michaelson, "the ball's in your court."

"Thank you," Michaelson said. "Captain Posner, do you have the report I requested two days ago?"

"Affirmative."

"May I see it?" Michaelson extended his hand toward a black binder lying on the table in front of Posner's aide.

"It's not—" Posner began.

"A few last-minute revisions?" Michaelson asked mildly. "Some finishing touches? Correcting a bit of stray syntax and a typo here and there? That's quite unnecessary. I'll accept it as it is."

Posner stiffened.

"Pursuant to directive from General Vernon Jeffries to A. Posner oh-nine-hundred this date, the report is to be delivered orally."

Michaelson settled back in his chair, a resigned smile playing at his lips.

"By all means proceed," he said.

"Project Sapphire initiated two years, seven months, eleven days ago this date. Task force directed by General Jeffries. Total personnel assigned: seven. Objectives: one, determine feasibility of software security measures sufficient to eliminate or minimize risk of interference with or manipulation of computerized ballot tabulation; two, prepare action plan for design of same in anticipation of near-term implementation; three, prepare report describing same."

"I see," Michaelson said. "Project Sapphire. And where did General Jeffries get the idea to embark on such an ambitious undertaking?"

"Begging the gentleman's pardon—"

"He wasn't off on a random frolic, was he, Captain? Who told him to do this?"

"The captain does not have first hand knowledge responsive to that question," Posner said.

"He didn't ask you whether you had first hand knowledge," Jacobs barked. "He doesn't care whether it's firsthand, fourthhand, or gossip around the water cooler. He wants to know who told Jeffries to do this."

"Begging the gentleman's pardon," Posner said, "that information is available only on a need-to-know basis."

"I have a need to know it," Jacobs said. "And you have a need to tell me."

"Begging the gentleman's pardon, the captain will require written instructions to that effect. From a superior officer."

"What the hell do you think this is?" Jacobs exploded. "Some two-bit skirmish between the Corps of Engineers and the Interior Department over an environmental impact statement? I'm the chief of staff of your commander in chief, and if I tell you I have a need to know then I by God have a need to know."

Posner stood stiff and stone-faced. And silent. Jacobs threw his pencil on the desk in front of him and hurled himself violently back in his chair, rolling his eyes in disgust at the ceiling.

"Captain," Jennings said then in a voice that was quiet but all business, "do you know who I am?"

"Affirmative," Posner said.

"When you address a superior officer, Captain," Jennings said, a clipped, intense edge sharpening his tone, "you will call him 'sir.' Is that clear, Captain?"

"Yes sir. Begging the admiral's pardon, sir."

"Good. Now: be advised that the people at this table have a need to know the information requested. And now hear this, Captain: you *will* provide that information to the fullest extent of your knowledge forthwith. Is *that* clear, Captain?"

"Quite clear, sir." Posner almost relaxed, as if an immense burden had been lifted from his shoulders. "It is the captain's understanding that the directive to General Jeffries came from Mr. Jacobs."

"What?" Jacobs demanded, surprise rather than anger coloring his yelp.

Posner's aide flipped open the binder in front of him and unsnapped the rings. He handed a sheaf of photocopied pages to Posner. Instead of handing them on to Estabrook so that he could take one and pass the sheaf around, Posner walked around the inside of the table himself, laboriously putting a stapled three-page packet in front of each principal and skipping the aides. When Michaelson got his three pages, he saw his name neatly typed on a plastic-cased tab attached to the right edge of the top page. Somebody had stamped the pages in red with a Bates consecutive numerator. The stamp on the top page of Michaelson's packet read "0001M." The top page of Cunningham's was stamped "0001C." Anyone who wanted to leak this memo would at least have to take a couple of deliberate precautions to avoid leaving tracks.

Jacobs flipped with irritated impatience through the pages, unconsciously running his thumb and index finger down the center of each page as he absorbed the text at a thousand words a minute.

"Jesus H. Christ," he said after he'd flipped to the third page with the scrawled "OK—J" at the bottom. "No wonder we have a deficit big enough to fill the Marianas Trench. No wonder you people can't buy a goddamn toilet seat without spending eight thousand dollars." He picked the pages up and waved them at Posner. "This didn't tell anybody to set up a seven-man task force and launch a multiyear project. It asked one, simple question: Is it possible to infiltrate a vote-counting computer program and produce a false but plausible report of the results? All Jeffries had to do was find a propeller-head who could tell him yes or no."

"Definition of the project parameters was refined in the course of interactive liaison with the ultimate intended recipient of the information," Posner said.

The room ventilator labored through several quiet moments while those present translated this khaki-speak into their own particular dialects of bureaucratese. Jacobs got it first.

He picked up a phone mounted underneath the table directly in front of him.

"Put me through to Sellinger at the national committee," he said after a moment. "Jacobs," he said a few seconds later. "Who the hell are you? This is supposed to be a direct line to Sellinger. . . . Well where is he? . . . . Well you find him. And you tell him to get his ass over here right now."

CHAPTER TWENTY-THREE

Michael Francis Sellinger, assistant to the chair of the national committee of the party in power at the moment, was in his early forties. His dark hair lay flat against his scalp. He sat at the end of Michaelson's side of the table, leaning forward with his forearms flat on the surface, attentive but relaxed as Jacobs approached the conclusion of his tirade.

". . . tell you you can ask the brass hats one simple question, and the next goddamn thing I know some brigadier general across the river's set up his own little empire that's probably spending the gross national product of half the countries in sub-Saharan Africa every eight hours. Goddammit!"

Sellinger didn't blink or break eye contact with Jacobs. He waited two full seconds, as if to be absolutely sure that Jacobs had finished speaking. When he finally replied, his even tones suggested polite but rather detached interest.

"What's the question?" he asked.

"The question is how the hell it happened," Jacobs snapped.

"When I asked brass hats about computerized vote fraud, I got roughly this answer: Every known method of injecting a gross data-manipulating virus into a sophisticated computer program runs an extremely high risk of discovery before it operates; if it evades discovery and actually does impact data, it leaves tracks so clear that discovery of the distortion is inevitable after the fact; however, the theoretical possibility of developing a virus that could impact data without being discoverable either before or after the fact cannot be totally excluded."

"In other words," Michaelson said, "the answer to your question was, probably no but possibly yes. Is that right?"

"I wasn't sure, so I pressed the issue," Sellinger answered. "I asked if this theoretical possibility was science fiction, like the theoretical possibility of time travel derived from particle physics, or is it something that's unlikely but that could conceivably happen in the real world. The answer was the latter."

"Is there any example of a virus like that actually getting to the point of operating without detection in a computer system with halfway decent security?" Jennings asked.

"No known example," Standish interjected when Sellinger hesitated. "The Israeli Defense Ministry computer system is one of the most sophisticated in the world, and it was successfully infiltrated with a delayed-action virus several years ago. But the virus was discovered before it could have any impact."

"Unfortunately," Sellinger said, "we aren't necessarily talking about computer systems with sophisticated protection when we get into ballot tabulation. We're talking about systems run by individual states, with access given to lots of people without security clearances."

"At the same time," Michaelson said, "you're talking about an exercise that would be self-defeating unless the distortion of the ballot count were undetectable after it happened as well as before. Even if the virus—is that the right word?—weren't discovered before the election and produced a bad count, as long as the fact that the count had been fiddled were clear, the computer tabulation would be thrown out and they'd find some way to recount the ballots. You might delay the results of the election by a week or two, but you wouldn't change the legitimate outcome."

"Exactly the point of my initial follow-up," Sellinger said. "If there really were no way—understand, literally *no way*—to change the count without making it obvious that that was what you'd done, then there wasn't any problem. Unfortunately, as you'll recall, the answer was that it might be conceptually possible to do precisely that."

"Star wars," Jacobs sighed, shaking his head. "Fucking star wars."

"In my judgment," Sellinger continued, "for which I of course take responsibility, even a slight risk that such a thing could happen mandated that we take the analysis further. I determined that we had to find out just how theoretical this theoretical possibility was."

"So you asked General Jefferies to initiate Project Sapphire?" Jennings wondered.

"Correct."

"Meaning that we had members of the United States Army trying to develop software defenses to a hypothetical undetectable computer virus with effective but theoretically undiscoverable impacts."

"Right."

"And of course the first step in doing that would be to come up with the best possible virus for that purpose in the first place," Jennings continued.

"That's my understanding," Sellinger said.

"Are you telling me that the army's been working on a computer program that could rig a national election?" Jacobs demanded.

"It has."

"And that it started with a memo that I initialed?"

"Correct," Sellinger said. No hint of defensiveness distorted Sellinger's tone as he delivered precise, unhurried answers to the rapid-fire cross-examination.

"I see," Jacobs said. "And do you folks over at the national committee have some answers we can give when a special prosecutor asks why this administration set up a secret project to subvert the Constitution?"

"As explained," Sellinger said, "the intent of the project is on the contrary to thwart such subversion."

"Bullshit," Jacobs said, his low, almost jovial tone contrasting sharply with the vehemence of his rhetoric. "You just woke up one morning and said, 'Hey, computer viruses. Big problem. Action plan today.' My ass. You expect me to believe that? Well, let me tell you something: I don't. And the House Judiciary Committee isn't going to either."

"The threat was quite real," Sellinger responded coolly. "The grounds for recognizing that threat were substantial. The potential national security impact is obvious, as you have just pointed out."

"Perhaps we're getting somewhere," Michaelson said. "You just mentioned grounds for recognizing the threat. What were they? What provoked your interest in this whole area?"

Sellinger paused before answering. Quite deliberately, he looked at Jacobs, then at Lever, then at Jennings. Only after getting impassive stares in return did he answer Michaelson.

"About six weeks before the authorizing memo," he said, "a consultant who has a reputation for being able to deliver came to see me. She said she was representing a client whose identity she couldn't at the moment reveal. She told me that this client could provide a service which would guarantee—flat-out, no-ifs-ands-or-buts guarantee—that our party's candidate, whoever he or she was, would win the next presidential election."

"What service was she offering?" Jacobs asked.

"She was deliberately vague on that point. She came very close to saying that I didn't really want to know. She just said that the money—the serious money, five million a year for four years—wouldn't have to be paid until after they'd delivered."

"That is to say," Michaelson asked, "after the next election?"

"Right. All her client asked initially was twenty-five thousand dollars a year until the next presidential election."

"I know that a hundred thousand bucks is just pocket change to you guys over there," Jacobs said, irony and disgust mingled equally in his voice. "But what exactly was this twenty-five thousand a year for four years supposed to pay for?"

"Computer security services. Measures to prevent infiltration and manipulation of data on our own computers."

"Christ, it was a protection scam," Jacobs said. "Just like those guys in Newark who make the shop owners fork over fifty bucks a week to keep from getting their windows broken and their stores trashed."

"That's the way I read it," Sellinger said. "She was saying her client had a capability that could be used for us. It could just as easily be used against us. If we didn't want to buy it, the clear implication was that she could walk down the street and sell it to the other party's national committee."

"And so you surmised that when she proposed to guarantee the outcome of the next election, combined with the news that her undisclosed client was in the business of preventing computer viruses, she was really telling you that her client could manipulate the computerized presidential vote count and make it come out any way the client chose."

This summary came from Michaelson.

"I thought the inference was obvious," Sellinger nodded. "We won the last election forty states to ten. If the right seven states had gone the other way, we would've lost, even though we'd have carried thirty-three states and the other guy only seventeen. All of those seven states either use computerized vote counting in statewide elections already or will be using it by the next election." He paused and waited for a moment. He had the undivided attention of everyone in the room. "That's why I thought the risk was quite real. I still do."

"What's the consultant's name?" Michaelson asked.

"Ariane Daniels. She's the head of Ar-Dan Associates."

"Is she really that good?" Jacobs asked. "Good enough to make a threat like that credible?"

"She's extremely effective. She's only twenty-nine or thirty but she's been in Washington a long time and she knows her way around. She's been a Senate page, a congressional aide and a campaign staffer. Before she opened her own shop she learned lobbying and consulting by working for a year or so with some real pros."

"When did she go off on her own?"

"Just over four years ago," Sellinger said.

"At twenty-*five?*" Jacobs asked. "That's incredible."

"She made her consulting reputation representing the Snack Institute," Sellinger explained. "Every six months some bunch of do-gooders tries to get Congress to say that food stamps can't be used for junk food. She had Hostess and Frito-Lay and the other heavies in the Snack Institute start a nonprofit group dedicated, as Ariane liked to say, to bringing the benefits of fine desserts to the underprivileged. People inside the beltway nicknamed the outfit Let Them Eat Cake. Bottom line is you can still buy Twinkies with food stamps. When she brought that off people really noticed her. She found some money somewhere and put her name on her own door."

"You know," Jacobs said, "I'm beginning to think you might actually have believed that she could rig a national election."

"Who are her clients now?" Michaelson asked.

"The main one I know about is an outfit called CAPE-G." Sellinger looked toward the ceiling as he tried to remember what the acronym stood for. "California Alternative Public Employees' Group," he said then. "It's for state employees who're so far out that the regular state union's too right-wing for them."

"Why would they need a Washington consultant?" Jennings asked innocently.

"Save the whales, save the dolphins, save the cannabis plants, you name it. Also, a lot of the membership dues seem to evaporate sort of mysteriously, and the staff needs someone here to explain things to the Labor Department periodically."

"Did you think that this group might be able to do some kind of computer magic that's apparently eluded everyone else who's tried so far?" Michaelson asked.

"They weren't really the client I was worried about, to tell you the truth," Sellinger answered. "After my first conference with her on this, I dug around a little bit and found out she's also representing a Japanese company called Ohatsu, Limited."

"Is that a computer company?"

"Electronics, mainly," Sellinger said, shaking his head. "But they're very big on computer applications."

"And you thought it conceivable that a foreign, private corporation would be involved in election rigging?" Michaelson asked.

"Conceivable," Sellinger shrugged. "Also conceivable that such a company would front for a foreign government."

"Damn nation," Jacobs whispered. "Damn fucking nation."

Nathaniel Lever looked up from his notes. He glanced politely around the room, as if to make sure that he wouldn't be preempting anyone else who wanted the floor. Then he made his first comment since Sellinger had joined the meeting.

"All of this suggests two separate and unequal levels of concern," he said to Sellinger. "The point of Project Sapphire was to find out whether someone really could rig an election through a computer virus without revealing that they'd done that. If the answer is no, then this whole affair is at most a partisan political problem. It's a matter of damage-control for party professionals. If the answer is yes, on the other hand, then it's a national security problem."

"That's exactly right," Jennings said. "Which is it, Mr. Sellinger?"

"The people working on Project Sapphire are represented to me to be extremely talented and to have almost unlimited hardware and software backup," Sellinger said. "And so far, in over two years of trying, they haven't been able to come up with a virus that'll change a vote count without that manipulation's being readily detectable after the fact. They are ninety-nine-point-nine-nine percent confident that, at the present state of the art, it can't be done."

"What a relief," Michaelson said, the irony in his voice considerably less than subtle.

"All right," Jacobs said. "In that case, we got what we came for. Directives: one, no further work on Project Sapphire without specific authorization in writing from me; two, Sellinger will see me at seven-thirty tomorrow morning for further discussion; three, investigation of the Luttwalk murder will proceed under the auspices of the Federal Bureau of Investigation alone, repeat alone, which will direct its efforts through normal channels but will send progress reports at least weekly to my office; and four, the Luttwalk investigation coordinating committee will submit a final report to Mr. Lever, with a copy to me, by the close of business Monday, and all members of that committee hereby have the thanks of a grateful nation for a job well done. Meeting adjourned."

"One final suggestion, if I might," Lever said. "I believe we should all return our copies of Captain Posner's handout to the captain for retention by him."

"Quite right," Michaelson said.

"Concur," Jennings said.

"You bet your ass," Jacobs said.

Posner's aide rose stiffly and began circulating to collect the packets.

"Wait a minute," Cunningham whispered to Michaelson as he turned his over to the uniformed man. "What just happened?"

"Our resignations were just accepted with deep regret," Michaelson said.

CHAPTER TWENTY-FOUR

Estabrook picked the cassette up by its edges, handling it with his handkerchief, and eased it into a bright yellow envelope with "evidence" stamped on it in red block letters.

"Very conscientious," Michaelson said. "But I'll be surprised if you find any fingerprints on that except for mine and Major Cunningham's."

"Nothing that you're ever called on to do in law enforcement is as tedious as explaining later why you didn't do it when it turns out you should've."

"Well, good luck with it."

"I keep waiting for the second shoe to drop," Estabrook said as he sealed the envelope and scrawled his initials across the flap. "I figure that any moment now you're going to let me in on what you want in exchange for this."

"I want a great deal, but I don't feel I'm entitled to ask for anything at all. You're now in sole charge of the investigation, and you can therefore reasonably insist on receiving potentially material evidence as a matter of right, without having to surrender anything for it."

"I'm sorry to hear you say that," Estabrook said. "I was looking forward to telling it to you."

"There is one thing I'd be obliged for a look at, if you're inclined to get it for me."

"What's that?"

"A list of the soldiers sent to the army's disciplinary barracks at Fort

Leavenworth over, say, the last three months, and a roster of the inmates of that institution who were assigned to work details at Leavenworth Federal Penitentiary over the same time period."

"Inmates at the military prison are sent to the civilian penitentiary to work? I didn't know that."

"A not uncommon practice, according to Major Cunningham."

"I don't see any reason why I couldn't get that," Estabrook said. Grinning, he slipped the bright yellow envelope into his inside coat pocket and stood up. "But you're too smart to expect something for nothing from me. What do I get in exchange?"

Michaelson looked up at the stocky, powerfully built man and smiled without showing his teeth.

"If you get those lists for me," he said, "then I'll tell you why I think they're important."

CHAPTER TWENTY-FIVE

Though unable to agree with your conclusion that the coordinating committee has fully served its purpose, I of course defer to your judgment on that issue.' I particularly like that part," Marjorie Randolph said to Michaelson. "Perfect touch for a resignation letter. Ruckleshaus and Elliot Richardson would be proud."

"My model was Acheson, to tell the truth," Michaelson said as he tore the last pages from the printer beside Marjorie's computer in the stockroom at Cavalier Books. "I've been around Washington long enough to know that history didn't start with Watergate."

" '... resignation effective with the submission of the committee's final report.' You sent this in earlier today?"

"Yes. Around four-forty-five."

"You come out of this rather well," Marjorie said appraisingly. "You've demonstrated both your competence and your integrity to a select audience. You've managed to get yourself fired before everything hit the fan. And when this thing does blow up that letter's going to make you look very good."

"You speak as if I'd planned it that way." Michaelson fit the bundle of printed pages into a very old envelope-style calfskin briefcase.

"May I be forced to devote an entire section of this store to books by lawyers if such a vile thought even crossed my mind," Marjorie said piously. "But if you *had* planned it that way, it couldn't have worked out any more perfectly."

"Thank you for the use of your computer," Michaelson said. "Can I buy you a cup of tea?"

Marjorie glanced at her watch.

"A half hour till closing time," she murmured. "Yes, thank you, I should be able to steal another ten minutes."

They passed into the public part of the store and crossed to the small platform against the left wall where book lovers could sit at minuscule tables and discuss Proust and sexual inclinations over coffee, tea, and croissants. Marjorie seated herself at one of them while Michaelson fetched Constant Comment for her and black coffee for himself.

"What are you thinking about?" Marjorie asked Michaelson as he sat down and proceeded to ignore her.

"Aaron Burr. Jefferson Davis. Alger Hiss. Treason."

"My word."

"English treason always seems simple. As far as I can see, it's mostly about sex."

"Well after all," Marjorie said, "they have a thriving tabloid newspaper industry to support."

"American treason isn't as straightforward. Nor as entertaining. A president inherits an administrative bureaucracy. He has the power to incinerate the Soviet Union, but he doesn't have the power to rewrite a Department of Education grant regulation. The bureaucrats spend all their time explaining why anything he wants to do is impossible. So for his own staff he picks people who say, 'Can do, Mr. President,' and get it done. That's the distilled essence of the White House ethic. Any White House."

"What Ollie North had in common with Kenneth O'Donnell."

"You're exactly right," Michaelson said. "That's how it happens. American treason doesn't start with traitors. It starts with patriots."

"Do you think that's what happened here?"

"I don't know. But it *could* be what happened. To paraphrase the Pentagon propeller-heads that Sellinger talked to, the theoretical possibility can't be excluded."

"Richard," Marjorie said skeptically, "all you have to do to look like a twenty-four karat hero within six months is keep your head down. Right now you sound suspiciously like someone who's going to keep his hand in whether he's been fired or not."

"You're speculating, Marjorie."

"Oh, is that what I'm doing?"

"Excuse me," a voice said from six feet away. The voice belonged to a brown-haired woman striding rapidly toward the platform. "You're Richard Michaelson, aren't you?"

"I am," Michaelson said, rising. "And you must be Ms. McNaghten. I see you got my message."

CHAPTER TWENTY-SIX

I've heard a great deal about you, Ms. McNaghten, and I know how
highly regarded you are in your field," Michaelson said as he held
out the chair Marjorie had just abandoned. "But I don't believe I've
had the pleasure of meeting you before now."

"Jesus," McNaghten said. "Where did you pick up a line of bullshit like
that?"

"The United States Foreign Service," Michaelson replied equably.

"You've must've been in it a long time."

"Thirty-five years. What can I do for you?"

"Excuse me?"

"I was returning your call," Michaelson reminded her. "You said you
wanted to talk about the Luttwalk execution. What can I tell you about
it?"

"What went wrong with it? That's for starters."

"From the result-oriented point of view to which we're so partial in
this country, I suppose nothing went wrong with it. The idea was for the
chap to end up dead, and that's what happened."

"You're going to make me work for it, aren't you?" McNaghten
sighed.

"There seems to be a subtext to your remarks that I'm not quite
grasping. You presumably know what you're talking about and I don't
have the faintest idea."

"Something didn't happen the way it was supposed to at that

execution. Within ten minutes of Luttwalk being pronounced dead, I was getting stonewalled by everyone in the Justice Department with a telephone. A little over twenty-four hours after that, a senior presidential adviser was pulling you out of retirement to keep tabs on whatever the hell was going on. I filed a routine request for a copy of the autopsy report, and yesterday I found out I'm scheduled for a runaround on that. If you don't want to answer my questions, that's up to you. But don't tell me nothing went wrong. I'm not an idiot."

"Oh, the autopsy report, that's what you're interested in," Michaelson said dismissively. "Let me see if I can remember. How deep is the background we're talking about here?"

"Knowledgeable source?"

"Fine. I believe the autopsy report noted a large concentration of procuronium bromide in Luttwalk's vein just past the injection point. Cause of death, if my memory isn't playing tricks on me, was an overdose of something or other—thiopental sodium, I think."

McNaghten gaped at Michaelson for three full seconds. He saw surprise, amazement, anger, and irresolution pass in turn across her face.

"Do you have any idea what you just said?" she demanded at last.

"What do you think?" he responded. He dropped the absent-minded professor routine and looked sharply at her.

"I think you do. And I'll bet you could get me a copy of that report if you wanted to."

"I suppose I could. Anything's possible."

"How fast could you do it?"

"It'll have to be pretty fast if it's going to do you any good," Michaelson told her. He took a sheaf of papers from his briefcase and laid it on the table in front of him. "There's a damage-control meeting tomorrow morning at seven-thirty. The preemptive containment effort should be in full swing by noon at the latest. If you want credit for the story before it's old news you'd better have it on the wire tonight."

"Who's meeting tomorrow morning? Where?"

"One thing at a time. We were talking about the autopsy report. I gather you want a copy of it?"

"Of course I want a copy of it. I put a story like this out with nothing to back it up but an oral account from a knowledgeable source and they'll file it somewhere under Elvis sightings."

"You know," Michaelson said, "when you ran through that litany of odd things about Luttwalk, I couldn't help noticing that you omitted the most dramatic episode."

"What're you talking about?"

"I'm talking about a gunfight in McLean involving the same local TV reporter who covered the Luttwalk execution live—a gunfight at which, by striking coincidence, you seem to have had a ringside seat."

"What's that got to do with the autopsy report?"

"You tell me."

"You've been living in this town too long to think you can get away with that," McNaghten snorted indignantly. "Reporters don't do the government's work for it."

Michaelson shrugged.

"I see," McNaghten nodded. "You're saying that's the price for the report."

"You did say you weren't an idiot, didn't you?"

"I'm also not a whore. There're lots of things I'd do for a story. Selling out isn't one of them."

"You reporters have such a charming penchant for self-dramatization. 'Whore.' 'Selling out.' Really now. Mother Teresa is pure good. Stalin and Hitler were pure evil. The rest of us settle for something in between. It's just a question of where."

"Let me try to explain this," McNaghten said. "You're not just asking me to do something I'd rather not do. It's not like letting some Rayburn Building clerk pat my bottom while I rifle a file. You're asking me to compromise my professional integrity. You do realize that, don't you?"

"Yes."

"It's something no self-respecting reporter would do."

"Perhaps not." Michaelson started putting the papers back in his briefcase. "Fortunately, there are plenty of the other variety."

McNaghten settled back in her chair, the beginnings of admiration lighting her eyes.

"I may never have a bigger story than this and you know it. But you want me to sell my soul to get it."

"At least I'm offering the going rate."

"What kind of a bastard are you?" she asked softly.

"First class."

McNaghten smiled gamely. She told him about Baldwin's bill and how Dahl had gotten it. He gave her the sheaf of papers.

"Any sense asking about the damage control meeting now?" she asked as she tucked the pages into her ample purse.

"You have a story to write."

"So I do. I take it there's more where this came from?"

"There is indeed. Give me a call the next time you'd like to do business. I give value for value. And I always pay the going rate."

CHAPTER TWENTY-SEVEN

Latex over Sheetrock, bare linoleum, naked fluorescent tubes: the spartan decor that started the moment the perky young woman led him out of the reception area surprised Cunningham. He'd always thought of television stations as comfortable, affluent places—rather like the suburban-den set of the station's morning program, which he glimpsed through an open studio door as he wound his way down the corridor. Except for the few dozen square feet within the cameras' fields of vision, though, everything he saw was bare bones, low rent, and severely functional.

The news set surprised him too. He'd assumed there'd be a big metal door with a red light over it and a guard in front of it. But there wasn't. He and his escort turned a corner and there, through an open doorway, he saw side-on the curving, walnut veneer desk that Ken Dahl and his co-anchor sat behind while they took turns reading punched-up wire-service copy.

Dahl sat coatless at the anchor desk, scribbling with a gold-and-black fountain pen on a yellow legal pad. Cunningham had some idea of how people worked with words, and to him this looked about as real as stock-shot from a fifties sitcom.

"Hi," Dahl said as he rose to greet Cunningham. "You got something on Hapner?"

"Come again?"

"You told my producer when you called that you had some information you thought I might be interested in. Hapner's the story I'm working on right now."

"I have something on another story I think you're working on," Cunningham said.

"Namely?"

"Do you recognize me?" Cunningham asked. This drew a blank look from Dahl. Cunningham turned his head about eighty-eight degrees to the left. "Maybe if I put a surgical mask on," he prompted.

"The Luttwalk execution?" Dahl said in a burst of illumination. His thin lips lost a little color as he realized that he was within touching distance of the guy who'd actually, uh, done it. "That's old news. I covered that almost a week ago. What makes you think I'd be interested in rehashing it?"

"Article I saw in the paper this morning," Cunningham said. "I caught your story on the news last night about how you found yourself in the middle of a firefight on the way home. Sort of an unusual adventure for a local TV news anchor. Then I saw a piece over breakfast today that made me think a reporter named Ginny McNaghten was right there with you. So happens I know McNaghten's working real hard on something about Luttwalk. I put it together."

Dahl sat down. He cradled his forehead with his thumb and middle finger.

"Why are you interested in all this?" Dahl asked.

"Why do you think?"

Dahl stood up abruptly, almost jerky in his decisiveness. He grabbed his legal pad as if he were afraid someone was about to steal it.

"I hate to do this on the run," he said, moving toward the side doorway, "but I have to be in makeup for the eleven o'clock show in twenty minutes."

Cunningham took this as an invitation to go along. He fell into step beside Dahl.

"There may be a leak somewhere around here," Dahl whispered harshly as they strode down the hall together. "What've you got?"

"Possibly not that much," Cunningham said. "But I had a talk with Randall Hurst. He's the father of the kid that Luttwalk killed."

"Right," Dahl said, less than confidently.

Cunningham followed Dahl through a door with Dahl's name on it. Couch, coffee table, straight-back chair, table, mirror: maybe Dahl really *did* do paperwork at the anchor desk. Dahl closed the door firmly.

"The old man and I had quite a conversation," Cunningham continued. "I really felt like we were, you know, on the same wavelength."

"Sure," Dahl said. Cunningham wondered if minimalism was a new rage in interview techniques. Don't even ask the source his name. Just make comforting noises until the story falls in your lap.

"Anyway," Cunningham said, "toward the end of it, I had the feeling he was right on the verge of talking about something his kid had told him or sent to him."

"What happened?"

"I blew it. I don't know how, but something I said or did turned him off."

"Okay," Dahl said. He paused, the blank expression on his smooth, sculpted face broken only by the slightest tincture of mild curiosity. "Why are you telling me this?" he asked then.

"If he didn't give it to me," Cunningham shrugged, "maybe he'd give it to you. You know, this is your field, you'd know the right way to approach him."

"Well," Dahl said in a drawn-out way as this near total stranger patiently explained how he should do his own job, "it may be worth a try at that. But tell me something: Why do you care? Why is it so important to you that this thing come to light?"

Cunningham gave Dahl a some-things-men-don't-need-to-tell-each-other smile. "I figure you know that as well as I do by now," he said. "It'll be somewhere on the front page tomorrow anyway, I expect."

Dahl nodded knowingly, showing his own perfect teeth, just as if he had some idea of what Cunningham was talking about. "Okay," he said then. "Uh, maybe you should give me your name and a phone number where I can reach you, in case I have to get back to you."

Cunningham did this. Dahl had to scratch his fountain pen three times on the legal pad before he could make the ink flow.

"Did he bite?" Michaelson asked when Cunningham reached him by phone half an hour later.

"He bit all right," Cunningham said. "But I'll be the most surprised ex-major in Washington, D.C., if he comes up with anything. When that boy meets up with Randy Hurst he's going to be a mite overmatched."

"I'm sure you're right about that."

"Then how do you think we're going to extract anything from Hurst by using Dahl as a cat's-paw?"

"I don't," Michaelson said. "What I have in mind is a little more complicated than that. It has to do with an acquaintance of mine who owns a horse."

THE SIXTH DAY AFTER
THE EXECUTION

CHAPTER TWENTY-EIGHT

The movies would've made it a screaming banner headline, black letters two inches high sprawling across all eight columns. In Washington reality it was more modest: four inches by three columns in the lower right-hand corner on the front page of the Sunday *New York Times*'s first section. The *Times*'s modest and dignified headline didn't scream. It offered above Ginny McNaghten's byline a well-modulated observation, after politely clearing its throat for attention.

"Autopsy Raises Questions About Luttwalk Death" was all it said.

That was plenty.

Before the paper had been on the street half an hour, phones were ringing all over northwest Washington and—since it was Sunday and a lot of people had to be called at home—in the more affluent surrounding suburbs. Two national political affairs reporters for *The Washington Post*, their burning ears still echoing their editor's observation that they'd just been aced in their own backyard by a free-lancer whose annual income wouldn't cover the monthly maintenance fee on either of their condos, attacked the story with particular assiduity.

Their enterprise collided headlong with the damage-control strategy that Sellinger and Jacobs had begun hammering out at 7:30 that morning. As Sellinger put it later on in a confidential memo, it made that strategy appear "reactive rather than preemptive." Those familiar with Sellinger's distinctive prose style knew that this was very bad.

"I'm getting the blame for this, you know," Lever told Michaelson when he called him.

"Not on my account, I hope."

"On who else's account? I hired you."

"*Hiring* me didn't cause that leak," Michaelson said. "You know that as well as I do."

"Why are you doing this loose-cannon number?"

Michaelson started to shrug the question off. Then he reconsidered. He closed his eyes and tried to visualize exactly where Lever was sitting in his White House office.

"If you swivel forty-five degrees to your left and look out your window," Michaelson said, "what do you see?"

"A marine in dress blues," Lever answered after a pause, "holding a rifle with a very shiny bayonette."

"How old would you say he was?"

"Nineteen or twenty."

"If the president fifteen minutes from now orders that marine and fifteen thousand others to climb on ships, sail to someplace they've never heard of, and hit a beach under fire, they'll do it, won't they?"

"What's your point, Richard?"

"That is my point. We're talking about the most critical thread in the delicate fabric of this complex society. The president of the United States isn't just another politician. There's got to be something magic about him—something that will make young men and women with their whole lives before them jump out of planes and dodge bullets just because he tells them to."

"This mysticism is something new for you, isn't it?"

"There's nothing mystical about it. Being deputy chief of mission at an embassy that has nothing but a handful of marines standing between it and an angry mob is a very down-to-earth experience. I've been there."

"I know you have," Lever said.

"A leader's magic comes from election," Michaelson said. "Elected by God, elected by fate, elected by destiny, elected by the people. It's all the same idea. If you monkey around with that kind of thing you spoil it. You take away the magic. Once you've done that you're finished."

"For God's sake, Richard, can't you trust me a little? Do you seriously believe that the United States Army is collaborating with a political party to rig a presidential election?"

"Not without more facts than I have now. Nor, until I have more evidence, will I believe that a Japanese company or a group of Japanese companies or the Japanese government have undertaken such an effort. But having reluctantly embraced a responsibility that turned out to involve much higher stakes than I thought it did, I'm not going to shirk

146

it just because Mr. Jacobs has ordered you to assure me that I have nothing to worry about."

"I see," Lever said. The tone of his voice made Michaelson think that he must be smiling gently. "You and Major Cunningham, on nothing but your own resources, are going to take on the Federal Bureau of Investigation, the Defense Intelligence Agency, the Army's Criminal Investigation Division and, if you're right, the centerpiece of the Pacific Rim. You and Cunningham against the world."

"If you like," Michaelson said testily. "That puts the odds slightly in our favor."

THE SEVENTH DAY
AFTER
THE EXECUTION

CHAPTER TWENTY-NINE

"I 'll always think of Vanderbilt as a 'yo daddy' school. The whole time I went there, whenever I met someone, seemed like the first thing he'd ask was, 'What does yo daddy do?' "

Corky Baldwin smiled at Ginny McNaghten across the expanse of Moroccan leather inlaid on the mahogany table he used as a desk. He leaned back in his well-cushioned swivel chair, fingering the brass studs at the ends of its arms. He turned the chair slightly to be sure that its top wouldn't keep McNaghten from seeing the newspaper artist's drawing of Baldwin addressing the jury in a highly publicized white-collar crime case from four years before.

"I was at Vanderbilt on a debate scholarship," Baldwin continued. "Fresh out of Springfield, Missouri, and I thought Nashville was a big city. I told people my daddy pumped gas, and I didn't mean he owned a service station. He was a pump jockey and on busy days he was a grease monkey. I was the only debater at Vanderbilt who knew how to change oil or clear a flooded carburetor."

"How did you get from a place like Vanderbilt to Washington?" McNaghten asked.

"Beginning of my senior year I sent my law boards, my transcript, and my parents' Confidential Financial Statement to every law school I could think of with a letter saying, 'What am I bid?' NYU and George Washington were neck and neck. I figured D.C.'d be cheaper to live in than New York, so I picked G.W. That's why I litigate administrative orders and international trade disputes instead of mergers and acquisitions."

"Administrative orders, international trade disputes, and at least an occasional felony prosecution."

"That's right," Baldwin nodded. "Funny thing. Silk-stocking litigators in New York wouldn't touch a criminal case with a ten-foot pole. In Washington it's different. I don't know a first-rate trial lawyer in this city who doesn't take a criminal case now and then."

"It must pay well," McNaghten said. "But then, it would, wouldn't it?"

"In Washington it does. Highest class of criminal defendant in the country."

"And yet you took Luttwalk for free."

"Professional obligation. Plus, it was a high-profile case. First federal death penalty case in a long time and all that. Trial lawyers have healthy egos and I'm no exception."

"Nice work," McNaghten said. "You took it for free and still got paid for it."

Baldwin's abundant eyebrows bunched slightly. He offered no other evidence of any reaction to the comment.

"What do you mean by that?" he asked, his mild tone suggesting genuine puzzlement.

"I saw a partial bill that showed you charging a corporate client called Ohatsu for time you spent in court defending Luttwalk."

"I remember someone else mentioning that," Baldwin said. He nodded, showing that he was tolerant of the nonlawyer's ignorance. "You just don't understand the way law firms work. This firm, anyway. I may be in trial eight or nine hours, but that doesn't mean my work day stops when the court recesses for the day. The phone doesn't stop ringing and the mail doesn't stop coming and the clients don't stop needing help just because I'm in court all day. Even on a full trial day I might spend two or three hours working on other client matters that night."

"This bill was for a lot more than three hours a day."

"Sure, but it wasn't just my time, was it?"

"No. Your time and someone identified as SSW."

"Well, there you are."

"I don't think so," McNaghten said. "I checked the trial transcript. Steven Smith Wilson second-chaired the Luttwalk case with you. He was in court with you every day. Unless neither one of you was sleeping, you didn't have enough hours left to book the kind of time you billed Ohatsu for after trial."

" 'SSW,' " Baldwin mused. He began paging through a firm directory. "Could be an initial mistake of course. Happens every now and then. These damned computers. I wonder who—"

"Don't bother. I checked Martindale-Hubbel. Wilson's the only lawyer at this firm with initials anywhere close to SSW."

Baldwin dropped the firm directory and smiled appreciatively at McNaghten.

"I guess you had something more than a profile of Corky Baldwin in mind when you came in here to see me," he said.

McNaghten shrugged.

"Okay," Baldwin said then. "I'll share my dirty little secret with you. The firm's fiscal year ends June thirtieth, and the year of the Luttwalk trial I was short some hours. Pure pro bono is fine for Covington and Burling and Hogan and Hartson, but this is a boutique firm. I can't just bury a hundred hours in overhead. Everything goes right to the bottom line. I couldn't in effect take two weeks off and have an associate take two weeks off that close to the end of a short fiscal year."

"So you defrauded a client?" McNaghten asked, her voice rising. She wasn't amazed that he'd done it. She was only surprised that he was admitting it.

"Absolutely not." Baldwin shook his head to emphasize the categorical negative. "I reallocated some time. I knew I had a very big Ohatsu project coming up during the summer and I anticipated the billing a little bit to shift some hours to the gap in the closing fiscal year. I treated it exactly like a retainer. Ohatsu got every hour of work that it paid for."

"Isn't that the kind of thing that'd be illegal if anybody but a lawyer did it?"

"A mischievous question," Baldwin said, grinning. "Ohatsu's not complaining. Neither are my partners. Remember, time is just a unit of measurement, something to keep the bean counters happy. Clients don't pay for time. They pay for results."

McNaghten gazed appraisingly at Corky Baldwin's smooth, self-assured exterior. She had one more question to ask, one more anomaly to throw in his face. She wondered if she should ask it.

Boutique firm. That much was right. Not one of those big, institutional outfits that could smooth out the peaks and the valleys, carry a valued partner through three or four lean years while he reestablished his client base. If Corky Baldwin lost one or two big clients he could go from prince to journeyman overnight, find himself right back in the middle of the pack, scrambling for government contract work and FERC hearings like five thousand other Washington lawyers. She wondered how the poor kid from Springfield would handle that.

She decided to save the last question for later.

CHAPTER THIRTY

Thirty seconds after he sauntered into the Campus Queen, Michaelson spotted H. Seymore Bullitt. Bullitt sat in a booth against the wall across from the door. All Michaelson could see of him was the left cuff of his dark brown Harris tweed suit coat, three-eighths of an inch of cream-colored cotton broadcloth shirt cuff, a pinkish white hand sprinkled randomly with blond hairs, and a half-moon sliver of the left side of his face.

That was enough.

Michaelson strolled through the bar's miniature Munich beer hall decor toward Bullitt's table. On a stage to his right, a young woman wearing a straight blond wig, a black leather motorcycle jacket, and black velvet munchkin boots crooned lyrics that evoked sixties nostalgia spiced with nineties decadence:

> I told you that we were through,
> Just to see what you would do.
> You looked sad,
> And hung your head—
> Made me wish that I was dead.
> Oh, Johnny get an-ga-ry,
> Johnny get mad!
> Give me the hardest spanking
> I ever had!

I want a brave man.

I want a cave man.

Johnny, show me that you care really care for me-e."

Michaelson glanced at his watch as he reached Bullitt's table. It was just after 12:15.

"Hello, Bullitt," he said. "How are things in Rice Paddies?"

Bullitt glanced up, surprise and displeasure combining to perfect a scowl on his face. His hair was thinning but still golden.

"Oh," he said. "It's you."

"Mind if I join you?"

"Suit yourself, I suppose. But buzz off the minute someone interesting shows up, can you?"

Michaelson sat down. He asked the waiter who instantly appeared for Johnny Walker Black Label.

"How did you track me down here?" Bullitt asked. "Times have changed, but I still make it a point not to flaunt anything."

"No great feat of induction. Your tastes always ran to campus neighborhoods. There are three bars like this near Georgetown University. This is the third one."

"Here's to your retirement," Bullitt said. "I can't speak for the rest of the Fudge Factory, but from the perspective of East Asian Affairs I can tell you that the old place has been exactly the same without you."

"Why shouldn't it be? After all, it was exactly the same with me."

"Does this visit by any wild chance relate in some way to the abrupt end of your coordinating committee sinecure that I couldn't help reading about in the papers this morning?"

"Yes."

"What could that possibly have to do with me? I thought it revolved around some thug that we finally managed to execute or tried to execute or something a while back."

"Quite right. Tried to execute, as it happens. One question is whether the Japanese government or a Japanese corporation is involved in the mess."

"Whose silly idea is that?" Bullitt demanded.

"Tell me why the idea is so silly."

"Why would the Japanese government get involved in criminal activity to the prejudice of its favorite customer?"

"Hypothetically," Michaelson said, "because that government concluded that it needed to influence the outcome of an approaching U.S. presidential election in order to retain the customer's business."

"Oh, what perfect rot," Bullitt spat, disgustedly slapping his tumbler back on the table. "Surely even you don't believe that."

"I very much want not to believe it. That's why I sought you out."

"Yes, I'm sure, and all that."

"You are the most talented advocate Japan has in the United States Foreign Service. I want you to explain to me why it is frivolous to imagine that a country whose prosperity depends on exporting expensive consumer goods to the United States might take steps to prevent the election of a president committed to a protectionist trade policy."

"Oh for—" Bullitt sputtered.

"And while you're explaining, please keep in mind that I was in Near East and South Asian Affairs, not East Asia. Speak slowly and use short words."

Bullitt hesitated a moment before responding. His struggle with the tantalizing temptation to display his considerable substantive knowledge and analytic skill played across his face. With a minimal shrug, he succumbed.

"All right," he said. "Who makes the Talon model minivan?"

Eyes closed, Michaelson searched his memory for this obscure datum.

"Chrysler, I think," he said finally.

"Wrong. Chrysler *sells* it. It's manufactured by a Japanese-American joint venture called Diamond Star Motors Corporation. Diamond Star puts the name 'Talon' on half the vans it makes and sells them to Chrysler. It puts the name 'Eclipse' on the rest and sells them to Mitsubishi. Same engineers, same factory, same workers, same components."

"And so?"

"That's only one example. Mazda doesn't just make cars in Yokohama. It makes them in Flat Rock, Michigan. Honda doesn't just make cars in Hiroshima. It makes them in Ohio and Tennessee. Every major Japanese car company has a whole network of manufacturing and marketing interrelationships with major U.S. car companies."

"Your point being that—"

"My point being that *that's* how Japan influences American elections. *That's* how Japan guards against American protectionism. Squeeze Japan Incorporated and you throw millions of *Americans* out of work. They might not belong to the UAW, but they vote. Just ask President Mondale, President Gephardt, and President Dukakis."

"In other words," Michaelson said, "no motive for the Japanese to act illegally, because they play the legitimate electoral game well enough to win."

"As they damn well ought to. We taught it to them. Just like baseball."

"The fact remains that there is evidence of planning for a highly illicit form of interference in a U.S. presidential election. Carrying out the plan would require enormous resources. The only potential actors possessing such resources whose fingerprints have shown up so far are the United States Army, the party holding the White House at the moment, and a Japanese company called Ohatsu, Limited."

Bullitt didn't answer immediately. Deliberately, in time-honored State Department style, he paused, considered the comment, digested it, factored it into his analysis. This took three seconds.

"It won't wash," he said then. "Assuming there's some machination that would give Japan a one hundred percent lock on dictating the identity of the next American president, Japan would still only be improving its position marginally if at all on the protectionism issue. On the other hand, if the machination were discovered, the perfectly predictable backlash is one of the few things that really could guarantee an effective anti-Japanese tidal wave in American politics. The game simply isn't worth the candle. You don't risk everything you have on the chance of a two-percent improvement in your position."

"For the Japanese government, perhaps. How about for a single Japanese company?"

"It's as big a mistake to generalize about Japanese as about Americans," Bullitt said. "But Japanese capitalists tend to be conservative, collaborative, and interested in the long term. The company you're talking about would be pursuing short-term, unilateral advantage at the risk of enormous long-lasting damage to its peers and its country. Anything's possible, but it doesn't sound like a betting proposition to me."

"If your analysis is correct, of course, then the Japanese government ought to be rather anxious to contribute what it can to clearing these troublesome questions up."

"Why don't you ask them? The number for their embassy's in the book."

"It might be more effective if they're approached by someone who speaks the language, so to say."

"Whom do you have in mind?"

"You."

"I'll think it over," Bullitt said sourly.

"Your class was the first group of East Asia hands to come on board after the Dulles-McCarthy purge, wasn't it?"

"Nineteen fifty-five," Bullitt grunted. "Didn't quite make it to the auto-da-fé—a piece of good luck I've never lived down."

"Well, I don't hold it against you, if it makes any difference."

"It doesn't," Bullitt said. He looked up and glanced jerkily around the room. "Harold," he called out, "come over here."

A man in a white turtleneck and royal blue sport coat who looked like he'd just finished a bikini-briefs photo layout session gazed for a moment in the direction of Bullitt's voice. He rambled toward the booth, sipping a beer as he came.

"Hullo, Seymore," he drawled. "Who's your friend?"

"No one interesting," Bullitt said. "He was just taking off."

Michaelson pulled himself from the booth and moved toward the door as the singer warbled,

> Every girl wants someone who
> She can really look up to.
> You know I love you, of course.
> Make me know that you're the boss!
> Oh, Johnny get an-ga-ry,
> Johnny get mad . . .

CHAPTER THIRTY-ONE

"All right, does that take care of all the messages?" Hurst said into the receiver wedged between his shoulder and his left ear.

"Yes," his daughter's voice answered. "Except for the one from Washington. Dahl."

The Ford's engine, bawling in its effort to jerk the station wagon and its two occupants and the horse trailer behind it along I-35, was the only sound for a second or so.

"Go ahead and put me through to him," Hurst directed after the interval.

From the passenger seat, Dr. Frank Dennison glanced edgily at the Ford's speedometer. The needle hovered a click past ninety. Unconsciously, Dennison touched his seat belt.

"Nervous?" Hurst asked, grinning.

"It's not so much dying myself that'd bother me," the physician answered. "But that horse behind us represents a lot of flu shots, abdominal palpations, and physical exams."

"I've been driving ninety miles an hour on the Kansas turnpike since I was fourteen," Hurst said. "Haven't had an accident yet."

"I expect you wouldn't get more than one at that speed," Dennison said.

"Hello?" Hurst said into the phone. "Randall Hurst, returning a call from Kenneth Dahl. . . . No, I wouldn't care to hold for a minute. I'll hold for twenty seconds."

"Mr. Hurst," Dahl said twelve seconds later, "thanks for calling back and, uh, so forth."

"*Doctor* Hurst."

"Excuse me?"

"It's Dr. Hurst. I'm a D.V.M."

"Oh. Right. Well, anyway. Listen, I'm one of the TV newspeople who covered the Luttwalk execution last week."

"I know. I remember you. I asked your station for a videotape of your broadcast. They wouldn't give me one."

"Oh. Uh, well, I'll see that you get one right away."

"Skip it. I got a copy through the network affiliate in Topeka."

"Oh. Well, uh, I guess that's okay, then."

"What's on your mind?" Hurst asked impatiently at that point. "This call's costing me money."

"Well, I'm doing a follow-up on the Luttwalk story, actually, and I was wondering if I could ask you a few questions about it."

"Seems like I've been doing nothing for a week but answering questions from people in Washington. I've already told them everything I know."

"Not quite everything, actually."

"What's that supposed to mean?"

"Mis—uh, Dr. Hurst, I haven't ever told anyone this, actually, but not long before he was murdered, your son tried to get in touch with me."

"Why would he try to contact you?"

"I don't know. Maybe he just liked to watch the *Cheers* reruns that came on after our newscast, so he knew my name. Anyway, it's just a hunch, but I think he had something to show me—and I have reason to believe that whatever it was may have found its way to you."

"Make up your mind," Hurst grunted.

"Excuse me?"

"Either you have a hunch or you have reason to believe. Which is it?"

"Well, actually—"

"Skip it. You don't impress me, Mr. Dahl. Don't call me. I'll call you."

Hurst hung up the receiver and glanced at Dennison.

"It's only about five more miles to the exit for the Clancy place," Dennison said. "You might want to start putting the brakes on now."

"You call this well done?" the man in the khaki ten-gallon hat demanded jovially, flourishing a dark brown rib steak over a blazing barbecue grill. "Why I've seen cows burned worse'n that get up and walk off." A rangy, mop-headed young man behind the grill laughed as

Tyrone Clancy dropped the meat on a paper plate and strode toward Dennison and Hurst.

Gunmetal skies insulated the muddy pasture at the Clancy place, halfway between Leavenworth and Kansas City, from any sense of passing time. You couldn't see where the sun was, couldn't tell how far it had moved, and unless you really thought about it, you couldn't be sure whether you'd been there forty-five minutes or a hundred twenty-five.

Dennison's dark brown gelding stood placidly next to the trailer. Sheila Clancy, sixteen years old and brunette, her English riding costume incongruously emphasizing her youth, stroked the saddled horse's neck with her left hand while she held the bridle firmly with her right. She made soothing sounds that seemed to relax the animal, despite the milling crowd and the other horses and the men in Levis and T-shirts stacking long bales of hay on top of each other at intervals around the pasture.

"Seems to be handling the uproar pretty well," Hurst commented to Dennison.

"Maybe if he can handle it here he can handle something a thousand times more intense at the Royal this weekend," Dennison said. "Anyway, that's one of the things we're here to find out."

The bale stackers had finished. Along with most of the rest of the crowd, Hurst and Dennison moved toward the plank fence that ran along the near side of the pasture.

Three horses galloped in turn around the course before Dennison's gelding. Young people in outfits out of a fifties western rode two of them. A man wearing hunting pinks rode the third. American horsemanship is split between the Pecos and the Thames, and in the lower Midwest partisans show up in almost equal numbers.

Hurst and Dennison then watched with mingled anxiety and pleasure as Sheila Clancy took the gelding satisfactorily through its paces. No refusals, only a hint of a balk at the second barrier, just the right amount of space on the jumps between the saddle and the white cotton breeches stretched over Sheila Clancy's bottom.

"Ribbon material, no doubt about it," Tyrone Clancy said from Dennison's left as the gelding trotted away from the steeplechase course to take a couple of cool-down laps through the overgrown grass next to it.

"Maybe," Dennison said noncommitally to Sheila's father. "Offer material for sure."

"You'll break Sheila's heart if you sell that horse out from under her at the Royal."

"Better bring your checkbook to Kansas City then," Hurst said dryly. All three men laughed.

"Anybody else worth watching coming by today?" Dennison asked.

"Young out-of-state woman named Wendy Gardner called me a couple days ago and asked if she could bring a mount named Fielder's Choice down here. It's up after this cowboy who's on now."

"Never heard of her," Dennison said. "Or her horse."

"It's not the horse that's worth watching, it's the rider," Clancy said. "Someone from out East with a pretty fair reputation supposedly. Said the guy just fell into her lap."

Hurst stiffened. "Someone from out East with a reputation" could in this context mean any of two hundred different people. But the back of Hurst's spine tingled, and he didn't believe in coincidence.

He looked sharply at the lip of the pasture in time to see Alex Cunningham coax a dove gray, white-maned stallion toward it.

As soon as he'd gotten back to his home, three hours and forty-five minutes later, Hurst went to his den and unlocked the gun cabinet. Unfastening the restraining bar, he pulled his .30-.30 from the rack. From a taxicab yellow Winchester box in a drawer at the cabinet's base he took six stubby cartridges and shoved them through the push slot in the breech plate, into the tubular magazine that ran underneath the barrel.

Setting the .30-.30 aside, he pulled the .30/06 from the bracket. The cartridges for that were long and tapering. They came from a red-and-white Remington box. He slipped three of them into the magazine underneath the stock. Just as quickly and expertly, he loaded the .240 and the twelve-gauge shotgun.

He left the shotgun in his den. He put the .30/06 in his bedroom. He stashed the .240 behind the counter in the reception area. And he clamped the .30-.30 to a twin bracket attached to the rear of the Ford's front seat.

CHAPTER THIRTY-TWO

S o," Ariane Daniels said to McNaghten, "media heavies are knocking on tombstones all over town following up on a story you broke. Congratulations."

"Thanks."

Daniels deftly speared the lime wheel in her Tanqueray with a swizzle stick and laid it on a cocktail napkin. She sipped from the drink, using the moment to see whether anyone more important to her than McNaghten had joined the noon crush at the Adams-Mark Lafayette Square's Walnut Room Grill.

"Now that you have some real competition on the story," Daniels said then, "you're looking for an offbeat angle that the others won't bother with."

"I'd rather not get too offbeat. Page one is gratifying."

"Let's face it, you can't go head-to-head with the *Post* and the *Times*. Or even the *Sun*. You started it but they'll finish it."

"We shall see."

"You need the oblique viewpoint stuff. That's why you've come to me."

"I knew there must be a reason," McNaghten said.

"My guess is that Ken told you about the Ohatsu time sheet and you think you can promote something out of that. You figure since I'm one of Ohatsu's consultants, you can get a little background and a couple of quotes from me."

"There is that possibility," McNaghten agreed.

"But don't you think Ken would've done something with that time sheet stuff already if there were anything there?"

"No, I don't."

"You see, that whole thing turns out to be a big yawn. I checked it out for Ken, to keep him from stepping on my toes. There's a very dry and unexciting explanation. You can ask Ken if you want to. He's meeting me here for lunch in a few minutes."

"I've heard the explanation for the time sheet already," McNaghten said. "In fact, I've heard two. From the same source. They were both unmitigated bullshit."

Daniels shook her head.

"I haven't been in Washington as long as you have," she said. "But I've been here since I was sixteen and one of our more heterosexual senators got hot enough for me to make me a page. You're barking up the wrong tree. That dog won't hunt, as the good old boys on the Armed Services Committee like to say."

"I'll just have to do my best," McNaghten sighed.

"I *can* give you a lead, understand," Daniels said. "It's a good lead. It'll get you another front-page byline. But there's a string attached."

"Why am I not surprised? The string is that I have to lay off you and Ohatsu and Baldwin, right?"

"Of course. I mean, cards on the table. No bullshit from A. D. She delivers. Ask anyone from Langley to the Hill. I get paid to protect my clients' interests. What do you expect me to do?"

"Don't ask that question unless you want me to answer it, as I told Ken once."

"Let's hear it," Daniels shrugged.

"Okay. I expect you to sell your client out. I expect you to hand me Ohatsu on a silver platter."

"Why should I do that?"

"To save your skin, A. D., that's why."

"You're talking like you think you know something I don't know," Daniels said.

"I know something you do know. I know that the bill Baldwin's firm sent out was directed to Ohatsu but addressed to your office, not Ohatsu's."

"That's easy," Daniels said, not quite yawning. "But we'll have to continue this some other time. I see Ken coming."

"I also know something else. I know that a lot of the time you bill CAPE-G for isn't spent with the Oceans and Environmental Affairs

Subcommittees in Congress. It's spent with the internal union audits people at the Department of Labor."

"Am I interrupting?" Dahl asked as he reached the table.

"We're just finishing up," Daniels said. She held a folded five-dollar bill out to him. "Would you be a peach and get me a pack of Kent Golden Light One Hundreds?"

For an uncomfortably long moment, Dahl stared mutely at the tendered currency. Bogie would've laughed. Gable would've told her to wipe the smirk off her face before he wiped it off for her. Even Alan Alda would've given her a lecture about how smoking and bad manners seemed to go together.

"Sure," Dahl said evenly after the pause. He walked toward the bar without taking the money.

"Does it surprise you that an association of public employees occasionally has business with the Labor Department?" Daniels asked McNaghten. "You can't hurt me with CAPE-G. They love me."

"The staff loves you, not the membership. CAPE-G's staff collects dues to save the planet and promote social responsibility and then invests a lot of the money in Atlantic City and the Cayman Islands."

"Page eight stuff," Daniels said, shaking her head. "I'm not going to sell out Ohatsu just to keep from taking a few hits like that."

"No. You're going to sell out Ohatsu to keep from doing time. There's some kind of connection between Ohatsu and Luttwalk that stinks out loud, and you're right in the middle of it. I have a source and I'll break the story. The only way to keep your name out of it is to spill your guts."

"Bullshit," Daniels said genially. "I'm twenty-nine years old, I drive a European luxury car, I've met a three-person payroll every month for two-and-a-half years, and I clear six figures annually for myself. I'm doing just fine without brushing up against the Criminal Code. I don't need to take the kinds of risks that you think I've taken."

"That's for the record and you know it," McNaghten said. She stood up and laid her card on the table. "You're doing fine but fine's not enough. The BMW's not enough when people no smarter than you are chauffeured around in Mercedes limos. A hundred ten thousand isn't enough when you see guys that think five times that is an off year."

"You call it greed and I call it ambition," Daniels said. "Whichever it is, everyone that matters in Washington has it. There aren't any altruists here."

"That's not the point. The point is that you were in a hurry. You took a big risk and some people died. I don't know what it is yet, but I'll find out. When I do, your only chance to save your twenty-nine-year-old rear end will be to help me point the story at somebody else and keep you out of it. You'll come around. When you do, give me a call."

Daniels was still gazing at McNaghten's retreating figure when Dahl tossed the cigarettes she'd asked for on the table in front of her.

"Thanks, Ken," she said absently. Picking the pack up by the base, she smacked its top emphatically four times against the palm of her left hand before she started to open it.

"No problem," Dahl said as he seated himself.

"Listen, Ken, I'm sorry about that. I know it looked like a brush-off, but it wasn't. She had something she needed to get off her chest and I felt like I had to let her talk. It was sort of a woman thing."

Extracting a cigarette from the pack, she parked it in one corner of her mouth, where she let it dangle while she searched for her lighter. Having contrived in this way to make herself as repulsive as possible, she still looked dazzlingly beautiful.

"Some woman thing about CAPE-G?" Dahl asked as he opened his menu.

Daniels took a few extra moments to light her cigarette so that she could think about the best way to deal with Dahl's question. Shrugging it off would irritate him. The best way to handle him, she thought, was to give him a peek inside, let him feel like one of those truly initiated into Washington's secrets.

"That crack about CAPE-G was just the hook," she said after she'd blown a stream of smoke toward the ceiling. "The feds think that some of the dues disappear a little too readily. CAPE-G needs someone who can direct the inquiries into constructive channels."

" 'The feds think?' " Dahl actually raised his eyebrows as he asked this question.

Daniels smiled conspiratorially.

"If they were innocent, they wouldn't have to pay my rates," she said.

"In other words, you represent some outfit that steals money from workers?"

"They aren't 'workers,' Ken. They're *government employees.* Most of them never worked a day in their lives."

"You're still talking about stealing from a union, aren't you?"

"CAPE-G isn't a union, it's a civil servants' association."

"What's the difference?"

"A union's job is to transfer wealth from capitalists to workers. CAPE-G's job is to transfer wealth from taxpayers to bureaucrats. Most taxpayers work and most bureaucrats don't. Figure it out."

Grinning in spite of himself, Dahl shook his head. The very complete-ness of her cynicism charmed him. Its matter-of-fact perfection was almost ingenuous, like a virgin's clinically accurate description of kinky sex acts.

"Does it bother you for me to smoke before we eat?" she asked. "I should have asked before I started, but I wasn't thinking."

"The only thing that bothers me about your smoking is that it'll shorten your life," Dahl said.

"Not necessarily. A guy I went out with about eight years ago smoked two packs a day from the time he was fifteen and it didn't shorten his life at all. He died of gunshot wounds long before the cigarettes could kill him."

CHAPTER THIRTY-THREE

▲

Do nothing. Do absolutely nothing. Don't change your behavior in any way."

Arnold Hapner studied his fingernails as Jeff Logan, the criminal lawyer he'd decided to see, offered this pronouncement. He raised his eyes. He looked at the green-bound tomes on the shelf behind Logan. He glanced at the statue of Ben Franklin visible through the window to Logan's left. He gazed at color photographs of Logan's children, romping delightedly through an office where people found out their chances of avoiding hard time.

"I know," Logan said, his voice gentle and almost kind. "You don't like the advice. It's hard to swallow. But it's good advice." He glanced at his watch. "You're paying two hundred forty dollars for it."

"I've seen these media feeding frenzies before," Hapner said. "Like what started today over the Luttwalk execution. One cheesy little two-bit muckraker gets his teeth into it and suddenly they're all ripping at it from every direction. Subpoenas, subcommittees, special prosecutors. . . ." His voice trailed off.

"Mr. Hapner. Arnold. Can I call you Arnold?"

"Sure."

"Arnold, listen to me. Time for a hard truth: you're small potatoes. Special prosecutors don't get appointed for guys like you. Special prosecutors get appointed for marine colonels who decide to conduct their own private foreign policy from the White House basement. Plus,

168

they're out of favor these days. The last one spent humpty-million dollars convicting Ollie North of the bureaucratic equivalent of over-parking. And he couldn't even make that stick on appeal. The only way someone like you gets caught up in that kind of net is if it's part of something a lot bigger."

"Suppose it is?" Hapner asked quietly.

"How big?"

"I don't know. I don't even know what it is for sure. But maybe real big."

"Well," Logan said, "this is all a tad generic. So I'll give you a generic response. Whatever you know, I'd better hear it now, 'cause if something head-grabbing's about to happen we'd better start dealing while we still have something to deal with."

Sighing, Hapner repeated his survey of the visual points of interest in the room.

"When this first came up, I guess I panicked a little," he said. "I called a couple of friends of mine over at the National Committee—real friends, I mean, guys who came from the same place I did, guys I've been through the wars with."

"Okay," Logan said. His expression suggested that this sounded terrible but that there was just an outside chance that a lawyer as brilliant as he could salvage the situation. "How much did you tell them?"

"Not much. I just wanted to find out about this Dahl guy who filed the request, see if anyone knew what he was really after."

"And?"

"One of my guys said—"

"Before you go any further," Logan said, "can we have some names? Or would you rather make it Buddy One and Buddy Two?"

"Let's leave names out of it for now."

"That good, huh? Okay. Buddy One said—what?"

"He said Dahl is fucking the lobbyist for Ohatsu Limited, Ariane Daniels. Ohatsu is a Nip outfit I've been kind of steering to a higher quality consulting operation."

"Gotcha. So Daniels is maybe using Dahl to carry water for Ohatsu. This whole FOIA request might be just to pressure you into playing ball with Daniels's client. How'm I doing?"

"You're right so far."

"I don't see yet where anything big's involved."

"Like I told you," Hapner said, "these guys I talked to go back a long way with me. One of them decided that I needed some insurance. Last night he brought me this."

Removing a white envelope from his inside coat pocket, Hapner handed it across the desk. Logan opened the envelope and removed two pieces of slick photocopier paper. He saw at once that they were enlarged prints of the front and reverse sides of a microfilmed check. The check was drawn on an account of the national committee of the party in power. It was for twenty-five thousand dollars. It was made out to Ohatsu, Ltd.

CHAPTER THIRTY-FOUR

The thing about a shotgun, Hurst thought as he squinted along the Remington 1100's ventilated rib, is that unless your target's absolutely still you really have to lead it. You have to remember the plodding muzzle velocity. He put the red-orange bead at the end of the barrel about four yards beyond the patch where in a glimpse of moonlight a few seconds before he'd seen a dark, crouching shadow slip into the tall grass a football field or so away.

Almost one o'clock in the morning. He stood naked on the deck behind his house, gazing into pale moonlit darkness a distance behind and to the right of the fenced-in area where he kept the dogs he was boarding.

He's good, Hurst thought. Stays downwind of the dogs. Doesn't move unless he's ready to. Wouldn't have had any idea he was there except for a chance look out the window that caught something dark where the moonlight should've picked out a white boundary stone.

He told himself to be patient, even if that meant standing there until dew dripped from his scrotum.

He snatched an image from the corner of his eye—not even a shadow, just a different quality to the darkness. It was already past where Hurst had been aiming. Hurst swung the shotgun barrel, reminded himself to lead the target, jerked the bead over a couple of degrees, started to squeeze the trigger.

The tall grass rippled. The moving darkness disappeared. The Remington boomed, a yellow flash from the muzzle emphatic in the night air. Hurst heard the pellets ripping through the grass, like grease popping on a hot griddle. The brass and plastic shell casing popped from the breach and dropped to the deck. Excited, cacophonous baying rose from the dogs.

"Dammit!" Hurst said softly to himself. "I'm just not cut out for this."

"Dad?" a girlish voice behind and above him called. "Is that you?"

No, he thought irritably, it's Indiana Jones.

"Yes," he said. He kept his tone conversational and his voice unhurried. "Now listen carefully. You listening?"

"Sure, Dad."

"Okay." He licked his lips. "First, leave all the lights off."

"Lights off. Got it. Now?"

Hurst swept his eyes back and forth across the area he'd fired at. He couldn't see a thing.

"Second," he said to his daughter. "Call the sheriff. Tell him we think we've got an intruder out here."

"Sheriff. Got it."

"Third, make sure the doors are all locked, get the two-forty, and don't let it out of your hands till the sheriff gets here. And before that happens throw me a robe or something."

Twenty minutes passed before the patrol car cruised into Hurst's driveway. Hurst hadn't taken his eyes off the tall grass. He'd seen nothing.

"Think you might've nicked him with the shot you took?" the deputy asked after he'd joined Hurst on the deck and gotten Hurst's rundown.

"Nah. Fired too late. He'd already ducked for cover. I was hoping after the shot he'd figure the game was up and make a run for it, but he hasn't bit."

"Well, you stay here and I'll have a look."

The deputy hustled back to his car, which promptly bumped over the edge of the driveway and into Hurst's backyard. Blinding spotlights on either side of the windshield flooded the space for fifty feet in front of the car.

Circling around the fence, the car crawled through the tall grass toward the area Hurst had pointed out. The tough, springy vegetation pressed against the grill and the doors as the cruiser continued its inexorable progress.

The car stopped. With a bit of tire spinning, it backed up twenty feet onto Hurst's lawn, in between the tall grass and the deck. Both headlights and both spotlights bathed a baseball infield's worth of the tall grass with light.

172

His hand resting on the grip of his semiautomatic pistol, the deputy came out of the car and crept toward the lighted area. Drawing the pistol and pointing it upward, he plunged into the waist-high grass. Deliberately, he crisscrossed the territory, pausing occasionally to crouch and examine something.

This continued for a quarter hour. It ended in anticlimax. Reholstering his pistol, the deputy put his hands on his hips and shook his head. Then he hiked back toward the deck.

"There was someone there all right," he said when he was within comfortable talking distance. "No footprints that I could see, but plenty of broken grass and twigs. But you must've scared him off. I can't see a sign of anything out there now."

"I don't see how he could've gotten away without my seeing something," Hurst said.

The deputy shook his head.

"Grass like that, if he knows how to belly-crawl and has enough nerve not to hurry, no one could spot him. Anyway, he's not there now. I'll put a call out to watch for rental cars on the roads around here and I'll cruise by every hour or so, but I don't think you'll have to worry about him. You've shown him you can sling buckshot. I expect you've seen the last of him."

"All right. Thanks for the look."

Hurst strode across the deck and walked down the steps near the driveway. He stood there, in front of the forty-pound sacks of Science Diet and Prescription Diet dog food piled four feet high underneath the deck, while the patrol car made its laborious trip back around the fencing and onto Hurst's driveway. He waved at the departing car.

He was three steps back up to the deck before he thought about the bags of dog food. By then it was too late.

A sharp, stabbing pain seizing his right wrist made him drop the shotgun as he grabbed his numbing right elbow. He felt his arm pulled briskly through the opening between the steps, lost his footing, and sprawled on the stairway, his arm pinned against the side while a powerful hand thrust from beneath the stairs to press the collar of his robe tightly against his throat.

"Don't hurt the girl," he gasped.

"I don't want to hurt anyone," Cunningham said.

CHAPTER THIRTY-FIVE

I knew you were shook when I showed up back here," Cunningham said. "I didn't know just how shook till I heard that buckshot cutting through the prairie back there."

"From the looks of things, I had pretty good reason to be shook," Hurst said. Seated on the top step and leaning against the deck railing, he massaged his right wrist.

"I'd rather have done it over the phone," Cunningham said. "But you wouldn't return my calls this afternoon."

"So you decided to break into my house?"

"I had something a little less ambitious in mind. I couldn't pick a lock in a million years. I was going to wait out here till morning and talk to you when you came out to take care of the dogs."

"How'd you get from where you were to clear over here, and then under the porch, without getting spotted?"

"Once you fired, I figured you'd be looking for me to keep going in the same direction I had been. So I doubled back, kept low and didn't show myself. The dogs picked me up, but you must've figured they were barking at your shot and all the excitement. I barely made it under the porch by the time the sheriff got here."

"You belly-crawled all that way, without making a ripple that I could see? You must be pretty good at it."

"Fella taught me said my life might depend on it someday. I paid attention."

"All right," Hurst said. "You've scared me. You've scared my daughter. You've made me look like a fool, firing guns off all over my backyard in the small hours of the morning—all because I wouldn't return your phone call. What's on your mind?"

"The first time you and I talked, you were about to tell me something. It had to do with your son's murder. Then you pulled back."

"Is that a fact?"

"I'm pretty sure it is."

"Well, if I held back then, why should I do anything different now?"

"Is this the way you wanna live?" Cunningham asked. "Guard duty at midnight, calling the sheriff out anytime you see a shadow, having your daughter sitting inside with a rifle across her lap?"

"Sure as hell isn't the way I'd like to live. But nobody gave me any choice."

"I'm giving you one now."

"Some choice. I don't know which side you're on or what the sides are, for that matter. If I give you what you think I have and you're on the right side of this, then someone else still wants it and I still have to worry about someone coming after me. If I give it to you and it turns out you're on the wrong side, then I've just handed you or the people you work for one helluva good reason to kill me. It just may be that the only thing in the world that's keeping me alive is the fact that I might have that information, and no one can afford to kill me until they're sure."

"That's all over my head—"

"Don't bullshit me, Major. You didn't retire at that rank by being a dummy."

"I understand soldiers and I understand horses and I understand army politics. This high policy stuff isn't my kettle of fish. But what I was gonna say was, the guy I work with told me before I came back out here that you were going to say exactly what you just did say. And he said you might be right."

"That's very reassuring."

"He also said the solution was obvious: don't tell whatever you know to *somebody* else—tell it to *everybody* else. Tell it to the world."

"How'm I supposed to do that?"

"You'd know better than I would. Once you do, though, the good guys have the information and the bad guys have nothing to gain by doing anything nasty to you."

"Hmpf," Hurst said.

"Michaelson also said something else that makes sense to me," Cunningham continued.

"What was that?"

"He said there are four possible explanations for Luttwalk's being killed just before he was going to be executed. One, the army or someone in the government did it to keep his mouth shut at the last minute; two, a foreign corporation that's gotten mixed up in some kind of political problem did it for the same reason; three, you did it for revenge; and four, someone else did it for some other reason that none of us have thought of yet."

"Does this guy get paid to come up with stuff like that?"

Cunningham ignored the interruption.

"He said that he might be wrong, but he figured if I made this pitch to you and you disclosed the information, that'd suggest you were innocent."

"And if you made the pitch and nothing happened, that means I'm guilty?"

"Bingo."

Hurst stood up.

"You could've put that in a letter and I'd have learned it without damn near getting my wrist broken," he said. "I'll see you around."

"Have a good night," Cunningham said.

"What's left of it. Oh, by the way, take it easy going back to wherever you're staying. The sheriff's going to be looking for rental cars around here till after dawn."

"I came on horseback," Cunningham said, and moved off easily toward the tall grass.

Still rubbing his wrist occasionally, Hurst carried his shotgun back toward his house. He made a mental note to telephone Kenneth Dahl as soon as he'd gotten a few hours' sleep.

THE EIGHTH DAY
AFTER
THE EXECUTION

CHAPTER THIRTY-SIX

J eff Logan shook his head as he glanced over the front pages of the *Post* and the *Times.* The pack was in full cry. "Luttwalk Cover-up Hinted." "Official Evasion on Luttwalk Called Troubling." "Congressional Leaders Hint at Hearings." The administration response seemed shrill and defensive.

"This is very bad," he said to himself.

If this thing weren't over by next week, he could see four or five different ways it might play itself out. None of those scenarios did Arnold Hapner any good.

Now was the time for Hapner to deal. Unfortunately, he didn't have anyone to deal with. Logan needed to position his client as a whistle-blower, someone who'd volunteered key information. But he needed to do this before the local reporter, whatsisname, broke anything on Hapner himself. That was the only way he could pass off the Hapner slam as a plant by the bad guys. Having Hapner leak to Congress was a helluva risk, though, and he didn't see any other way to go with it.

He sipped his coffee, hunched over his desk, and began reading the lead *Post* story more carefully. Something in there about a resignation that smelled a little funny. There it was. After studying the three para-

179

graphs for ten seconds he decided that Hapner didn't have to leak the check to anyone in Congress. He could leak it to someone else.

9:35 A.M.

"Who was that?" the young woman with the clipboard asked Dahl as he hung up.

"That was a source."

"Hapner?"

"No. Different story." He drummed his fingers on the desk beside the phone for a moment. "Listen. I need to get to Kansas City sometime in the next few days. There's some horse show called the American Royal starting there this weekend. I need to get to Kansas City before it's over."

"I'm a producer, Ken. I don't do miracles. We're in Washington but we're still a local newscast. I don't think many of our viewers will care very much about a bunch of cowboys showing their horses off a thousand miles from here."

"That's not the story, that's just to see the source." He hesitated for a moment, but when he saw he wasn't going to get anywhere with what he'd just said, he went on. "This is on the Luttwalk story."

"Are you telling me you've got something on that story that every network and the big newspapers have all missed?"

"They missed the bill, didn't they?"

"I'll give you that one," the producer said. "But that was before they were looking for anything."

"So I've got a head-start."

"Maybe," she said as she traded smiles with him. "We'll see. It'll take at least a couple of days."

Dahl made notes to call McNaghten and Daniels. What he'd just heard meant yes, and he and the producer both knew it.

10:40 A.M.

Michaelson shuffled quickly through the pink message slips that had been waiting for him when he returned to his desk at the Brookings Institution. Most of them he discarded. Three caught his attention. He spread them out on his blotter for more leisurely examination.

Someone named Spillner, whose name he didn't recognize but who said he was a reporter for the *Post*, had called just before nine. So had half a dozen other reporters, but Spillner had been sufficiently insistent to persuade the secretary whose services Michaelson shared to take a lengthier than usual message from him:

"Some people are saying some very nasty things things about you and he wants your side of it. If no comment—OK, but still wants to hear your voice."

Hm, Michaelson thought. He crumpled the slip and threw it away.

A lawyer named Logan had called just after nine. It was important. He had something for Michaelson on the Luttwalk matter.

Michaelson tucked that slip under the edge of the blotter.

A gentleman named Matsuyama, finally, had called around 9:30, wondering whether Michaelson would do him the exquisite honor of joining him for lunch today.

Ah, Michaelson thought. He decided to return that one as soon as he'd talked to Logan.

11:10 A.M.

McNaghten turned her answering machine on before she'd even put her purse down. She listened to the messages while she dropped her things, glanced at her mail, found herself a caffeine-free Diet Coke, and otherwise got organized.

Dahl wanted to talk to her. Someone was wondering why a payment was late. Then she got to the one from Daniels.

"I've thought it over and you have a point," the brisk, recorded voice said. "We can meet this afternoon, but it can't be at my office or yours. Give me a call to work something out."

CHAPTER THIRTY-SEVEN

"T he thing I recall most vividly from my early schooling," Matsuyama said as he ladled shrimp Peking over a layer of rice on his plate, "are the stories of the early Christian martyrs."

"I would have thought that an acquired taste," Michaelson said.

"The Sisters of St. Joseph had one of the few outstanding primary schools functioning in postwar Yokohama," Matsuyama said. "The good nuns taught in Japanese, but they made no other concessions to their surroundings."

Nodding slightly, Michaelson nibbled a morsel of moo goo gai pan. They were eating at the Mandarin Orange, a new, assertedly Chinese restaurant near Seward Square.

"What particularly struck me," Matsuyama continued, "was the elaborate justification the Roman authorities developed for putting the Christians to death. They reasoned that the emperor was a god and derived his right to rule from that fact. If the Christians wanted to worship some other god, that was their privilege—but when they insisted on telling people that there *were* no gods besides theirs, they denied the divinity of the emperor and therefore implicitly challenged his right to rule. Hence, they were guilty of treason and subversion, and should be put to death."

"It's not the worst theory used to justify killing people over the past two thousand years, I suppose," Michaelson said.

Without any appearance of haste, Matsuyama concentrated for half a minute on attacking the food before him. When he looked up again, he seemed to have cleared three-quarters of the plate.

"I asked myself, Why did they bother?" Matsuyama said. "After all, the emperors were autocrats. Caligulan Rome had no First Amendment. They could simply have proscribed Christianity as such and executed practicing Christians for disobedience. Why go to the trouble to spin out this convoluted rationalization?"

"A provocative question," Michaelson said. "The only plausible answer would seem to be that they meant it."

"Precisely." Matsuyama beamed. "The Roman pagans weren't just paying lip service to some half-forgotten legal ideal. They attacked Christianity because they were truly convinced that, unlike all the myriad religions they tolerated, Christianity was fatally subverting the Roman society they cherished."

"And they were right," Michaelson said. "Weren't they?"

"Indeed they were. Would it surprise you to learn that I have often asked myself analogous questions about American society?"

"Not in the slightest."

"Of *course* you were going to hang Hidekei Tojo after the war—we would certainly have hanged MacArthur. Why spend three years parading him before courts and lawyers? Why not just stretch his neck as soon as you captured him? Why the legalism?"

"Perhaps, like the Romans, we really believed in the laws we invoked."

"Just so. And do you really believe in the economic dogmas you assert as well?"

"I take it you think the answer is no," Michaelson said.

"I find it impossible to come to any other conclusion. *Naturally* America throws up legal barriers to Japanese cars or electronic consumer goods whenever our competition becomes intolerable. Why pay a swarm of indolent word mongers to develop tortured arguments about how these barriers conform perfectly with America's historic commitment to free trade?"

"I suppose," Michaelson said mildly, "that someone might substitute references to food imports or communications equipment or furniture leather and ask the same question about Japan."

"Exactly," Matsuyama said. He snapped the last syllable off and looked directly at Michaelson, his eyes glinting as if with satisfaction at the quickness of a particularly apt pupil. Michaelson glanced up in mild surprise.

"The parallel is exact, and that is my point," Matsuyama continued. "What divides America and Japan is not their differences but their similarities."

"Definitely a heterodox view."

"But one that I have thought through very carefully. America has much more in common with Japan than it does with, say, Italy or Greece. Japan negotiated its first commercial treaty with the United States under the guns of Commodore Perry's flotilla. It was when Japan used Perry's commendably efficient methods on several of its own neighbors that America objected—objecting not to what was alien but to what was familiar. In assailing Japan America rails against its mirror image."

"Thus far at least," Michaelson objected, "the United States hasn't carried that congruence to the point of limiting imports to raw materials, and imposing an array of open and hidden restrictions on value-added goods—as Japan has."

" 'Congruence' unfortunately overstates the case," Matsuyama demurred. "Those on both sides of the Pacific who assume that Japan has overtaken the U.S. economically simply do not know the numbers. Per capita gross domestic product in Japan is still almost forty percent below that in the U.S."

"Around thirty-seven percent, actually," Michaelson said. "And at least on this side of the Pacific, the concern is with the trend rather than the absolute level."

Smiling, Matsuyama nodded to concede the point.

"Absolute levels nevertheless have important consequences," he insisted. "The sheer economic weight of the U.S. in the world dwarfs that of Japan or any other single country. It puts the U.S. in a category by itself. When America tightens its belt, steelworkers in Korea starve. When the U.S. adopted the Smoot-Hawley Tariff in response to the Depression, it not only failed to solve its own problems but exported its Depression to the rest of the world."

"Your point being that Japan and other responsible countries have a right to say 'never again'?"

"My point is exactly the opposite," Matsuyama said.

"I must not be following the argument as closely as I thought I was."

"Decisions of such significance in a society as open as the U.S. are not going to be affected over the long term by accidents as trivial as which party wins a particular election or what man happens to become president."

"I see," Michaelson said. "In that event, then, Ohatsu would make its electoral choices solely on the basis of customer relations."

"I beg your pardon?" Matsuyama said, with more than the hint of an edge to his voice.

"If the policies will be the same regardless of who wins, Ohatsu as a

184

soundly managed capitalist enterprise would simply support whichever party gave it the biggest orders. Or am I oversimplifying things?"

"Far from simplifying things, you are mystifying me," Matsuyama said. "Ohatsu respects the prevailing customs in the various countries where it trades. In the U.S., we therefore channel money through political action committees to candidates of both major parties. In the Third World it is called 'baksheesh'; in America it is called 'campaign contributions.' But we do not do business with either party. I am puzzled by your comment."

"A lawyer whom I've worked with before told me shortly before I came over here that he had a photocopy of a twenty-five-thousand-dollar check drawn on an account of the national committee of the party in power, and made out to Ohatsu."

"This information astonishes and alarms me. Did your friend by any wild chance give you any particulars about this supposed check?"

In thirty-five years with the United States Foreign Service, Michaelson had never acquired the habit of carrying a pocket notebook. From his inside coat pocket he fetched a page that he'd torn from his desk calendar. He copied information from this leaf onto the paper napkin beside his plate. When he'd finished he handed the napkin to Matsuyama.

"Date, check number, amount, and drawee bank," he said.

Matsuyama studied the data critically for several seconds.

"This is a great puzzle," he said. "I am obliged to you for bringing this to my attention. I intend to look into it promptly."

"I hope your inquiries are successful," Michaelson said.

"If they are as successful as yours apparently have been," Matsuyama said, "I will be well satisfied."

CHAPTER THIRTY-EIGHT

Ginny McNaghten hated Alexandria. Nothing else in metropolitan Washington repelled her as Alexandria did. Sprawling, unplanned, cheap, crowded, tawdry, inconvenient—all things considered, she'd rather have been slogging past the porn shops and live sex shows on New York Avenue.

She was plunging instead into the sterile vastness of Alexandria's Blue Ridge Mall because that was where Ariane Daniels had insisted on meeting. Which figured, McNaghten thought. The chances that Daniels might run into someone there whose opinion she cared about had to be nonexistent.

Stopping just inside the main entrance at a multicolored directory board that looked like a schematic diagram for a gerbil maze, McNaghten determined that she had to walk all the way to the far end of the first level to find the Coffee Trader Sidewalk Café where Daniels was supposed to be waiting for her. On general principles she swore fluently at this information.

"I don't care whether Bernstein kept meeting Deep Throat in a parking ramp," she muttered as she strode off in the indicated direction. "This is ridiculous. There had by God better be a Pulitzer Prize in the middle of all this bullshit, or I'll track that cupcake down and kick her ass up between her shoulders."

At two-ten on a weekday afternoon, only a few customers shared the echoing terrazzo central corridor with McNaghten. A handful of class-cutting teenagers lounging in a smoky group around a fountain, a window-shopper here and there who might be a real estate agent with a slow afternoon or a suburban lawyer loafing her way through a late lunch—that was about it.

McNaghten turned a corner and headed into the most distant wing of the mall's ground floor. She passed some guy who looked like an account executive for a Benihana advertising campaign and wondered briefly why he was interested in the women's overcoats displayed in the window before him. She could see the café perhaps sixty feet ahead. She didn't see Daniels there, and she got ready to curse some more.

"Ginny," she heard then in a strained, almost whispered voice. "Over here."

McNaghten stopped and glanced to her left. Just inside the lip of a side hallway leading to restrooms and a service door Daniels stood stiffly, her face tight and masklike.

"What's bothering you?" McNaghten demanded. "Let's at least sit down and have some coffee."

"Can't risk it," Daniels said. "I thought I saw someone I know go past while I was waiting for you."

McNaghten stepped toward the hallway.

"All right," she said, a complacent shrug in her voice. "You want to talk in the lav or what?"

"Just out of sight," Daniels said. She sounded as if her voice were almost used up and she was trying to save what was left of it.

McNaghten took a stride and a half forward. Then she glimpsed a shuddering movement of someone three feet behind Daniels. She jerked back a step.

"Keep on coming," a masculine voice behind Daniels said. A knife blade appeared along Daniels' right jawline. "Just step back here quietly and she won't get hurt."

"Go ahead and hurt her," McNaghten said evenly. "It's no skin off my nose."

"I mean it," the voice said. "Stay quiet and step back into the hallway."

"My ass," McNaghten hissed.

She pivoted to her left and sprinted down the corridor. Ahead of her, near where the corridor turned, she saw the suede-jacketed man with oriental features who'd been looking at women's overcoats move away from the shop window and toward the center of the passage. McNaghten risked a glance over her right shoulder. Another man was pelting after her and closing fast.

Seizing her purse-strap near its apex, McNaghten swung the bag in menacing loops with her right hand. The man near the turn dropped his hips slightly, hunched his shoulders and braced himself.

"Helllppp!" she yelled just before impact.

She tried to sidestep the man in front of her, but he drove his shoulder into her stomach as she smashed her purse on his back. The bag flew open. Compact, lipstick, pens, keys and wallet rattled across the floor. McNaghten grunted as her back and hips slammed against the floor. The breath exploded from her body.

She jerked her knee up against the face of the man who'd tackled her. The iron grip he'd gotten on her right arm relaxed for a second. Rolling out from under him, she scrambled to her feet.

The man who'd been running after her grabbed her blouse at the neck. She started to fall backward. The man stepped on her lipstick and his foot went out from under him. The blouse ripped. The man who'd tackled her started to get up. He collided with his colleague's other leg. McNaghten felt herself come free.

Pulling herself upright again, she hurtled down the main corridor, stretching her legs out as she pounded through the tastefully muted lighting, weaving past benches, sculptured stabiles, and free-standing pasteboard advertisements, eating up the space that still separated her from the main entrance.

"Poliiiice!" she screeched. "Securrrrrittty!"

She paid for that expenditure of oxygen with a lancing pain down her side and through her gut. After looking up in startled surprise, one window-shopper turned away from the crazy woman yelling nonsense in the middle of Alexandria in broad daylight. Someone else gaped for a moment, then ducked into a shop. The teenagers just scattered.

Her two assailants loped along behind her on either side of the corridor, herding her but not making any particular effort to overtake her.

Good, she thought. She'd beat them to the entrance, dash outside, get to her car—and pound on the window in frustration, because her keys were lying back there somewhere on the mall floor. Better come up with plan B, she thought, as she scurried past the entrance toward the opposite end of the mall.

Now the two men picked up their pace. Reaching an escalator, McNaghten bounded up the steps three at a time. Ten feet past the top gaped the second-floor entrance to the mall's Woodward and Lothrop. It seemed like a trap so she whipped around the escalator well and began running on the second level back in the direction she'd come from on the first. While his colleague hurried up the escalator, the man with Asian features turned back and, looking up at her, ran along the lower corridor on a course parallel to McNaghten's on the upper.

Should've gone into Woodie's, McNaghten thought. She panted as she gulped convulsively for more air. Why *won't* these suburban morons pay attention? The store signs whirled around her in a pastel blur. The thug who'd come up the escalator was now no more than twenty feet behind her. She tried to run faster. Her thighs and belly screamed that her body had nothing more to give.

Something blue loomed up ahead of her. She blinked. Security guard! Overweight man coming forward.

McNaghten slowed.

"What's going on?" he barked.

"Kidnap—" McNaghten gasped, stopping and pointing back at the trailing thug.

"Plainclothes!" the thug yelled. "Shoplifter!" He grabbed her arm.

"Let's see some I.D.," the rent-a-cop demanded.

"Here!" the thug answered.

Releasing McNaghten, he buried his left fist in the guard's diaphragm. The guard seized his middle as his knees buckled. The thug slammed him on the neck and back of the head with his right forearm.

McNaghten bolted away. The guy below had run to the opposite end of the mall and was climbing the escalator there to McNaghten's level.

Now she was trapped. She ducked into a Limited ("Quality for Women with Sophisticated Tastes").

"Can I help you?" an adolescent in a magenta sweater and lemon-custard skirt asked languidly.

"Call—the—police," McNaghten panted. She heard the trailing thug hustle in behind her. She darted to the back of the store, putting dress and lingerie racks between her and him.

"Excuse me?" the adolescent said, her voice cross and puzzled.

"Call—the—police—you—cretin!" McNaghten screamed. She pulled a shapeless dress from the rack in front of her, wadded it up and hurled it through the doorway. When the encoded Shopprotec capsule clamped on the dress passed through the doorway sensors, high-toned *whoop-whoop*s from a cycling siren split the air. "I'm shoplifting!" McNaghten yelled as the siren started. "Call the cops!"

Startled, the thug looked around jerkily at the pulsing alarm. He froze for a moment of panicked indecision, then pelted from the store.

Incredulous at her deliverance, McNaghten took four seconds to catch her breath. The store alarm continued to bellow.

"What did you say about shoplifting?" the adolescent asked.

"Nothing," McNaghten panted. "Call the police. Tell them two men have kidnapped a woman named Ariane Daniels."

The clerk met this instruction with blank, uncomprehending puzzlement. Her sides still splitting with pain, McNaghten gulped as much breath as she could into her lungs and braced herself for one final communicative effort.

"Do it right fucking now, buttercup!" she screamed, leaning over the counter.

The salesgirl jumped for the phone behind her.

THE NINTH DAY AFTER
THE EXECUTION

CHAPTER THIRTY-NINE

9:45 A.M.

C orporal David Gilman,' " Michaelson said over the phone, reading from notes he'd made while going over the list from Estabrook. "Convicted of grand larceny from a PX in violation of several Articles of War."

The sound of riffling pages came faintly over the line for a few seconds.

"Short-termer," Nancy Weintraub said from her telephone in the Joint Congressional Intelligence Oversight Committee staff office. "Toward the end of his first hitch. First and last, I expect."

"Yes," Michaelson said. "Ten years hard labor, dishonorable discharge, forfeiture of all pay and allowances. My word. They're very hard on larceny, aren't they?"

"I imagine there was a time when they shot people for it," Weintraub said.

"Where was Gilman stationed, let's see, last June?"

"Fort McCoy, Wisconsin."

"All right then. Next name. Private Kevin Zech. He seems to have had a violent disagreement with another private over the attentions of a young lady, in the course of which his rival passed away following several blows to his head with a blunt object."

"Just starting his second year in the service," Weintraub said after more riffling. "Stationed at the time at Fort Lewis, Washington. That's state of Washington."

"Fort Lewis, got it," Michaelson said. "How about Staff Sergeant Robert McIntyre? Convicted of embezzlement from the treasury of an enlisted men's club."

"Wow. Veteran. Twelve years. Stationed as of the last update to this roster at Fort Monroe. In Virginia."

"Thank you. Lieutenant Walter Devereaux. That's e-a-u-x. Found guilty of first-degree sexual assault."

"Those are real sweethearts you have on that list," Weintraub said. "What's going on? Someone making a Gulf War version of *The Dirty Dozen?*"

"I understand you have to do something rather aggressively antisocial to get sent to Leavenworth."

"Well, Devereaux apparently lost control of his inhibitions in Ankara, Turkey. That was his last posting."

"As of when?"

"July, according to this. They must take the Speedy Trial Act seriously in the army."

"No doubt," Michaelson said as he concentrated on his notes. He threw out three more names from the list as a blind—but he already had the information he'd called Weintraub to get.

After thanking Weintraub and hanging up the phone, Michaelson settled back in his chair and stared at his black-felt-tip-on-yellow-legal-pad notes without seeing them. Certain that he had the answer, he still checked his impulse to accept the conclusion uncritically. There was at least one other possibility that he supposed he ought to look into.

On his way out of the Brookings Institution suite where he worked he told his secretary that he'd be at Cavalier Books until further notice.

10:28 A.M.

Marjorie Randolph ran her finger down the Events column in *Washingtonian* magazine. She was relieved to come across one event more than a week in the future that looked like it would do nicely.

"God bless the North American Pulp and Paper Institute," she said to herself as she picked up the phone to dial the Canadian Embassy. Trade association events were always easier to finesse than diplomatic receptions. The only thing you absolutely had to have to get into a trade association soiree was a pulse.

She had to go through two layers of phone answerers before she finally reached Leslie Northrup.

"Scheduling," Northrup said.

"This is the Sondra Gottlieb Foundation for the No-Nonsense Treatment of Hired Help."

"Oh," Northrup said, giggling at this allusion to the Canadian ambassador's wife who'd gained short-lived notoriety by publicly slapping her personal secretary. "Hello, Marjorie. Do you need an invitation to something?"

"To tell the truth," Marjorie said, "I need at least two. And that's just for starters."

10:45 A.M.

White letters against a blue background filled the screen on the computer in the stockroom at Cavalier Books. Michaelson was scrolling impatiently through the Luttwalk autopsy report. The first time he'd read it, days before, he'd hurried to the conclusion that confirmed what Lever had already told him, and he'd skipped hastily over the medical jargon in the body of the document. Now he stopped the screen at intervals and lingered over the text.

"What in the world are you doing?" Marjorie asked as she leaned over his shoulder.

"Looking for something that isn't there."

"Are you looking for everything that isn't there, or are you seeking something in particular that isn't there? The arrangements with the Canadian Embassy are under control, by the way."

"Good, thank you," Michaelson answered distractedly.

He halted the text on the screen and studied it in silence for nearly thirty seconds.

"Doesn't that paragraph seem to you to end a bit abruptly?" he asked then.

"I can't understand enough of it to have an intelligent opinion."

"It catalogs the observations about Luttwalk's head and throat."

"I see," Marjorie said. "And what is it that isn't there?"

"Anything about the tongue."

"Perhaps there was nothing worth noting about the tongue."

"In that case I'd expect a comment to just that effect," Michaelson said. "See? It says 'nothing remarkable' or 'no significant observations' about the ears and nose and sinuses and so forth. About the tongue it maintains a rather loud silence."

"So the obvious question becomes, Why?"

"And if we're very lucky, we'll get the answer by giving a Reveal Codes command now. How does one do that on this machine, by the way?"

"Control-Alt F-11," Marjorie said. "What a barbarous dialect these vicious contraptions have us all speaking."

Holding down the Control and Alternate keys with the first two fingers of his left hand, Michaelson punched F-11 at the top of the keyboard with his right index finger. The text already displayed paled slightly as a vivid red horizontal bar filled with white characters appeared across the center of the screen. They each saw it for an eyeblink before the screen popped to black and then burst with white-on-dark-gray garbage: BZ@*#%98#@%, repeating through every line and column.

Shouldering Michaelson a bit feverishly out of the way, Marjorie leaned over the keyboard and pushed Esc/Enter followed by Exit followed by List followed by Reset followed by List again. The result was a flashing, white-boxed reprimand at the bottom of the screen: "Error: Improper I/O Command." The garbage disappeared from the screen, but no manipulation of the keyboard would coax the autopsy report back onto it.

"Richard, please give me a moment alone so that I can say something unladylike," Marjorie said.

"There's no occasion for such an uncharacteristic articulation," Michaelson said. "Though if it would really make you feel better, I hope you won't feel inhibited by my presence."

"Do you mean you actually read the revealed code and remember it?"

"All I saw was backslash-something, d-e-l-period-something, text-at-line-something."

"The key is probably in the somethings. You do realize that, don't you?"

"On the contrary, I think the key is d-e-l-period."

"For 'delete,' you mean?"

"Yes," Michaelson said. "A virus was introduced into the word-processing program for that document. The virus ordered the program to delete whatever the autopsy report said about Luttwalk's tongue unless a specified code were punched in at a particular point during the display. It then ordered the program to purge the entire report, and the virus itself, if the virus command were revealed and not immediately countermanded."

"You've convinced me," Marjorie said. "And I'm terribly impressed and so forth. But the virus did its job. We can't prove a word of it."

"We don't have to. We've already learned the single most important fact in the case so far."

"Namely?"

"That it can't be done. Posner was telling the truth and the Pentagon propeller-heads are right. A virus can't manipulate gross data without leaving tracks that even a blundering technical amateur like me can find with a modicum of luck."

"Forgive my lack of penetration and all that, Richard, but how exactly do you know that?"

"Because if it could be done, those chaps would've done it on this program."

"Well," Marjorie said after a pause. "If you hadn't already submitted your final report and everything you could have included that very intriguing observation. But what will you do with it now?"

"Nothing for at least two days," Michaelson said. "After that, it depends on what happens in Kansas City . . . or doesn't happen."

THE ELEVENTH DAY
AFTER
THE EXECUTION

CHAPTER FORTY

Holding the bridle just firmly enough to let the horse know someone had it, Cunningham stroked the animal's neck and made soothing noises. As he did that he glanced over the gate and scanned the crowd packed in twenty tiers of bleachers around the show-jumping stadium set up on the ground floor of Kemper Arena in Kansas City. Stimulated by the excitement all around it—the bright lights; the huge, noisy audience; the nervous stench of horseflesh and horse sweat—Wendy Gardner's stallion pulled his nose up repeatedly against the bridle.

No way this animal's ready for something like tonight, Cunningham thought reflexively. No way a couple of turns through some hobby-farmer's pasture with a hundred people standing around could prepare a horse for something like he's going to go through tonight. Well, too damn bad.

"Can you still see Hurst?" he asked Wendy.

"Yeah. He's still sitting with his daughter and Dennison in the dress circle."

"See anyone who looks like Dahl?"

"No."

"Fielder's Choice up next," a voice from just above them said.

Cunningham stepped back and swung into the saddle, the tails of a charcoal-gray hunting coat settling naturally over the horse's rump.

"Where in the world did you come up with a name like that?" he asked.

"Sacrifice Fly was taken," Wendy said.

"Well, you'll do fine, Fielder's Choice," he murmured to the horse.

"Bullshit, FC," Wendy said. "You're liable to set show jumping back twenty years."

"Five seconds," the voice said.

"If Dahl shows up, just try to keep an eye on him," Cunningham said. "He'll be the one we'll want."

"Got it," Wendy said. "I understood that the first four times you said it."

"You have quite an attitude, you know that?" Cunningham said, smiling down at the young woman.

"I didn't get spanked enough as a kid," Wendy said dryly. "Now it's too late."

"Go," the voice said.

The chute gate opened and Cunningham coaxed the stallion into the arena. The ripple of excitement through the crowd and the sudden splash of light and color were familiar to Cunningham, but alien to the horse. The animal jerked his head around, calming only a bit as Cunningham stroked his neck and throat. For sixty-two seconds or so, Cunningham had to forget about Hurst, forget about Dahl, and concentrate on making twelve jumps without breaking either of their necks.

He took the horse laboriously over a hay wall and a white rail fence. The stallion started to balk at a false-brick barrier and Cunningham had to lean almost on top of his ears to drag him over it. The horse could have taken the next hay wall in his sleep, but he got jelly-legged and his rear hooves sent the top bales tumbling to the arena deck.

"Hey, that's fine," Cunningham whispered as he brought the mount around for the center series of jumps. "You surprised yourself, now surprise me."

They took the ivy hedge on the strength of this encouragement. The stile and moat shook Fielder's Choice when his hooves splashed. The next rail fence came up much too fast and he balked. Rhythmic applause, intended to be encouraging, came from the crowd. Cunningham swung the horse around, clucked encouragement, and soared with him over that fence on the second try, only to have him flatly refuse the next.

Cunningham pressed his lips tightly together. It would've seemed perfectly natural to everyone in the arena for him to quit after the balk, and he damn sure ought to quit now—but his instincts jerked him in the opposite direction.

"That's okay," he murmured as disgusted groans seasoned the applause. "You're gonna show that smart-ass owner of yours some day."

Circling around, he took Fielder's Choice over the fence he'd refused and then headed him on to the last series of obstacles. The crowd's sympathy had turned to pity. Cunningham's ears burned.

"Come on, FC," he said. "Let's see something."

It clicked. The horse came into synch with him and started gliding through the jumps, hesitating slightly only on the final one. Most of the spectators scowled in stony silence as Cunningham trotted the animal back toward the chute, while only a handful applauded.

The first thing Cunningham saw as he headed down the plank ramp to the sawdust-covered floor in the chute was that Wendy wasn't there. He slipped off the horse and looked anxiously toward the dress circle where he'd last seen Hurst. Dennison was there, but Hurst's seat was empty.

"Where in *hell* did she get to?" he demanded in an angry whisper.

"Clear the chute for the next contestant, please," the voice said. "Please clear the chute."

Cunningham led the horse out of the boxlike enclosure into the concrete, straw-strewn basement hallway that girdled the lower level of the arena. People in western and English riding costumes and handlers leading other horses picked their way through the area. Exasperation mingled with mounting frustration, Cunningham put his hands on his hips and swung his head and shoulders around in a tight, angry circle.

That's when he saw the arrow.

It was a crude brown smear, made a few inches above the floor out of the material most readily to hand under the circumstances. It pointed to Cunningham's right and he followed it, leading the stallion behind him.

He spotted another arrow forty feet farther along, and another sixty feet beyond that. He followed the ugly smears as the noise from the crowd gradually thinned and the hallway forked into a ramp leading away from the show-jumping arena. The last arrow pointed straight up along the side of a large, oblong, darkened portal that led to the dressage auditorium. Tomorrow night it'd be as jammed and alive as the show-jumping arena was now, but at the moment it was quiet, shadowy and remote.

As Cunningham approached, Wendy Gardner stepped out of the darkness and beckoned to him.

"Hurst left as soon as you were on the course and I followed him here," she said. "He's sitting inside, looking like he's waiting for someone."

"Take the horse and get him back to the stall and rubbed down," he said.

"Yes *sir*," Wendy stage-whispered sarcastically.

"You got that right," Cunningham said, grinning over his shoulder.

He crept through the gate into the auditorium itself and crouched beside a stack of pennants on five-foot pinewood staffs that had been unceremoniously dumped here after the parade opening this year's American Royal. The auditorium described an elongated oval, perhaps a hundred yards long on its major axis and seeming even bigger in the darkness. Cunningham's eyes adjusted slowly to the dim light seeping in from outside and above. He could see a gray shape that he gradually recognized as Hurst, sitting quietly on the front row of bleachers that had not yet been demarcated from the show floor by the makeshift barriers leaning against the far wall.

Cunningham's breathing slowed. He realized that his pulse must have been racing ever since the first jump. Nothing to do but wait. He started to feel like maybe this thing was going to work after all. He wondered what Hurst was going to turn over: box full of floppy disks? sheaf of oversized, green-and-white-striped perforated computer paper? reel of tape?

Cunningham focused on Hurst, and it was only Hurst's reaction that told him someone had come in on the opposite side of the auditorium and was approaching the veterinarian. Hurst slowly stood up. Cunningham willed himself to be still.

Dahl stopped about a yard away from Hurst, his features unmistakable even in the muted light.

"Starting to worry you weren't gonna show," Hurst said.

"Took me longer than I thought it would to find the place, actually," Dahl said.

"Here's what you came for."

With one hand Hurst held out something dark and oblong. It looked like it was about two hands long and one hand wide. Dahl took it.

"Thanks," he said. "I'll make good use of it."

"Do you what you want to. I'm washing my hands of it, as of right now."

Let's do it, Cunningham thought. He stood up. Hurst turned away from Dahl. Cunningham stepped forward.

All at once light flooded the auditorium floor. Dahl, Hurst, and Cunningham each looked up, startled.

"Ken?" a strained and uncertain female voice called from across the auditorium.

Dahl's head jerked around.

"Ariane?" he piped.

Cunningham crept forward. He crouched so that the lower tier of bleachers hid him from the other side of the enormous hall. Two hundred eighty feet or so away he saw a white woman with disheveled blond hair, her face disfigured by teary streaks and dirty smears. Thrust into the woman's right ear was the muzzle of a semiautomatic pistol. Attached to the pistol he saw a balding man wearing a brown leather jacket.

"Ken," the woman said, "he says—he says he's going to hurt me unless you bring that over here."

"What's going on?" Dahl demanded.

"I don't *know*," the woman said. "Please, Ken. I'm scared."

"Listen to her, kid," the gunman said. "I want it and I'm gonna have it."

"You'll let her go if I give you this?" Dahl yelled, holding out what Cunningham could now see was a VCR cassette.

"That's right," the man said. "Just walk over here, put it down on the ground, and you and your girl can walk out together. You won't be a chump and she won't be a corpse."

Dahl hesitated.

"Ken," the woman cried, "he's hurting me."

Dahl strode forward. Cunningham jumped up.

"Dahl!" he barked. Dahl spun around at the unfamiliar voice. "Don't be a fool," Cunningham ordered him. "Once he has that tape, you and the woman are both dead. The only way to keep her alive is to keep the tape out of his hands."

"Just keep coming," the man said. "Unless you think she'd look prettier without a face."

Dahl turned back toward Daniels and her captor. He looked over his shoulder at Cunningham. Then, uncertainly, his face stricken, shrugging in resignation, he stepped again toward the gunman.

"No!" Cunningham yelled.

"Now or never," he heard Wendy say behind him. She held the stallion's reins out to him. "Or else we've both come a long way for nothing."

Cunningham grabbed the reins and leaped astride Fielder's Choice.

"Hand me one of those," he ordered brusquely, nodding toward the pennant staffs. Wendy tossed one up to him. By the time he caught it he was spurring the horse toward the auditorium floor.

Less than ten feet from Daniels and the gunman, Dahl whipped around in surprise as Cunningham galloped onto the floor. Dahl dropped the videotape. The gunman forced Daniels to her knees, squatted behind her and straightened his arm to aim the pistol at Cunningham.

Cunningham leaned forward over the horse's neck. Holding the pennant staff near its base, he stretched his right arm behind him at a forty-five degree angle to his shoulder. The stallion hurtled forward, his blood up, white foam speckling his jowls, thundering across the narrowing gap.

It was firepower against nerve, but nothing in the gunman's experience could have prepared him for this encounter. Like footmen for a thousand years, from Balaclava to Hastings, he looked at the charging horseman and saw the face of certain death.

Blue and yellow flame blazed from the pistol's muzzle as the gunman squeezed off two quick shots. The second was very high, but Cunningham felt the first whizz past the stallion's neck and his own thigh.

"If he hurts this horse," Cunningham muttered, "so help me God I'm going to kill him."

Thirty yards away. Blue-yellow flash, concussive roar, and Cunningham felt a bullet rip through the fake right pocket on his riding coat.

Fifteen yards away. He stood up in the stirrups.

The gunman rose as well, pulling Daniels with him. He jerked her to his right, directly in Cunningham's path.

Five yards away. Cunningham flicked the reins. The stallion answered instantly, swerving to the thug's left.

The gunman raised his pistol. Turning in the stirrups as he bolted past, Cunningham thrust savagely down with the staff. He felt it strike flesh and splinter bone as the gunman screeched and his fourth shot went into the ceiling.

It took Cunningham another twenty-five feet to slow the horse enough to come around in a sweeping semicircle. He saw the gunman crumpled on the ground with six inches of the staff buried in his right shoulder near his neck. Daniels, on her knees, white-faced and wide-eyed, held the pistol with both hands.

"No!" Cunningham roared.

But the injunction came much too late. Daniels at point-blank range pumped five rounds into the writhing gunman's face. Then she collapsed, sobbing over and over, "He reached for the gun."

All right, that's done, Cunningham thought. Move on to the next thing.

He clucked the stallion forward until he could swing down and pick up the videotape. Cantering unhurriedly across the auditorium, he handed it to Wendy.

"Go see if you can find the police," he said. "And before you come back, get this to the Worldwide Air Freight courier at the hotel." He paused, took a deep breath, and forced himself to maintain eye contact with her steady, blue-eyed gaze. "Please," he added.

She smiled and put the cassette in her purse.

THE TWELFTH DAY
AFTER
THE EXECUTION

CHAPTER FORTY-ONE

Michaelson studiously avoided looking at his watch. The meeting was supposed to have started twelve minutes before. Impatience cast an irritable pall over the room in the White House basement. No one cared very much about Michaelson's time, or Cunningham's, but Jacobs and Sellinger were self-consciously busy men, jealous of every second.

Jacobs pulled up the receiver from the under-table telephone at his seat.

"Where's Lever?" he asked. "Well if he left his house at 6:30, why isn't he here yet? Morning traffic's light that early. . . . Try his home number again, see if he's checked back there. Maybe he had a flat tire or something."

The room wasn't large, but it seemed vast and sepulchral with only four of them in it. No aides. No notes. No uniforms.

Sellinger and Jacobs looked at their watches at the same time.

"Fuck it," Jacobs said. "We have to get started. Run the thing." He nodded toward a VCR resting underneath a portable television on a two-shelved, wheeled metal stand near the closed end of the inside of the horseshoe table where they were all sitting.

Taking the videotape from Michaelson, Sellinger loaded it and turned the television on. A dark, black-and-white image flickered onto the screen.

The image showed Lever sitting placidly at his desk, one side of his face almost washed out by sunlight streaming through a window to his right. On the other side of the desk sat a very young man in an open-collared shirt and dark slacks. He wore steel-framed glasses under straw-colored hair, and even through the occasionally jiggling, mediocre picture on the small screen, something about the way he held his head and leaned forward as he spoke communicated an infectious intensity.

"Who's that?" Jacobs demanded.

"Terry Hurst," Michaelson murmured.

"Oh shit," Jacobs said.

The sound of Hurst's voice came from the television. The words were fuzzy, and those listening had to strain to make out what he was saying.

"So, uh, bottom line is, we can, that is, we can absolutely, no-shit guarantee—guar-an-tee—the outcome of the next presidential election," Hurst was saying.

"So you've told me and Sellinger, several times before today," Lever commented, nodding. "But you won't tell us how."

"You don't want to know."

"Perhaps not. But if all you're really selling me is smooth talk and sunshine, I most certainly want to know that. I've looked into the concept you've alluded to. I can't find any independent evidence that it's technically feasible."

Hurst passed a moment of TV time in flustered silence. As he glanced away from Lever, his face seemed to pan across the screen. When he spoke again, though, his voice had the same emphatic confidence as before.

"Is that a chance you really think you can take?" he asked quietly. "I don't think we'd be sitting here again if it were."

"There are chances and then there are chances. You're asking for a very great deal of money. Five million dollars a year for four years—"

"It's a small price to pay for the White House."

"We already have the White House," Lever snapped. "And if my colleagues and I do our jobs well enough, we'll still have it after the next election, with or without any help from you."

"The magic word you just said is 'if.' Five million a year takes the 'if' out of it. Consider it a form of insurance."

"Back to the guarantee," Lever sighed. "A guarantee is words. You won't tell me what if anything there is behind your words."

Hurst began to snap an answer, then seemed to stop himself. Another pause ensued as he gazed at the surface of Lever's desk, then at his own fingernails. Outside the television, in the room where four men were watching it, Jacobs's phone buzzed politely. He picked it up, spoke sparingly and quietly into it. Michaelson watched his face, which remained as blank as the government-issue gray surface of the table in front of him. On the screen, Hurst looked back up at Lever and spoke again.

"The guarantee is," he said, "the serious money doesn't start until and unless we've delivered. The people I represent can do it. We know we can do it. But we don't ask you to accept that on faith. Aside from twenty-five thousand a year for development, you don't pay a penny unless we come through."

"But who's to say whether you've come through or not? The whole virtue of what you're trying to sell is that it's undetectable. Undetectable after the fact as well as beforehand. If your plan doesn't work and the election still goes our way, what's to stop you from waltzing in on the Wednesday after the voting and saying, 'Well, we did our part—pay up'?"

"In selected states, a week before the election, I'll give you percentage vote breakdowns that prove out to within two-tenths of a point."

"A week before the election the Wirthlin Group or Yankelovich can do the same thing."

"No way," Hurst insisted, shaking his head.

"You don't really expect me to spend the kind of money you're talking about just because you make dogmatic pronouncements, do you?" Lever asked. "If you won't let me evaluate the service you're offering on its merits, then the only way we can do business is if you prove that you can produce the results you're promising."

"It'll be a little late then, won't it? The way I'm going to prove it is by producing the results."

"I've been thinking about that. If you really can do what you say you can do in a presidential election, then you should be able to do it in any statewide election. Right?"

Hurst nodded.

"As long as the state has more than eight million people in it and tabulates votes by computer, and as long as there's at least a twenty-five percent turnout in the election," he said.

"Very well then. The other party will be having a number of primaries, well in advance of the general election, in states that meet those criteria. Since that party isn't burdened with either incumbency or aggressive leadership, those primaries will be hotly contested."

"I can see this coming," Hurst said, smiling and shaking his head. "Right down Broadway."

"I'll pick the state," Lever continued. "I'll pick the candidate. You produce the numbers. Then we can get down to business."

"Deal," Hurst said without hesitation. "Two conditions. One: we need at least three months' advance notice. Two: we have to have the twenty-five thousand a year for development."

"Even twenty-five thousand a year is a great deal of money if it turns out you can't deliver."

"You can justify the expenditure two ways," Hurst said. "First, you'll get value for value. The work we do will be worth that much to you even if we flop on the principal objective. Second, the project has to go, it has to get financed, and if we don't get the money from you we'll have to get it somewhere else."

"Your position doesn't come as a complete surprise," Lever said, smiling. He picked up a white business envelope from his desk and handed it to Hurst. "That's year one. Be very sure about the value-for-value part before you come back for year two."

The picture turned to snow. Sellinger flipped the television off.

"Has Lever shown up yet?" he asked.

"In a manner of speaking," Jacobs answered.

"Meaning what?"

"That was the call I got."

"I was afraid it was something like this," Michaelson muttered.

"Bridge abutment on the beltway at eighty miles an hour," Jacobs continued in a flat, hollow voice. "No seatbelt." Michaelson paled. Sellinger winced. "The weather was clear and the highway smooth and dry, as the insurance lawyers say."

Shrugging after the group shared a moment of shocked silence, Sellinger started to speak.

"Mr. Sellinger," Michaelson said in low, even tones, "if you say what I think you're about to say, I'm going to do my level best to kick your teeth in."

"All right, can the crap," Jacobs said as Sellinger's mouth clamped tightly shut. "I've been in worse scrapes, but I sure as hell can't remember when. We've got a shitload of work to do and we don't have a helluva lot of time to do it. We've gotten to the bottom of one can of worms and all that's done is open up another one."

"We haven't gotten to the bottom of anything," Michaelson said.

"What do you mean?"

"I mean that while we're busily answering the difficult questions we're ignoring the obvious ones. And the obvious ones are more important."

"That's very constructive," Jacobs snapped. "That's a very positive contribution to the process we're all engaged in. You have any suggestions?"

"As a matter of fact," Michaelson said, "I have."

ONE WEEK LATER

CHAPTER FORTY-TWO

wo pinkish red dabs of stray lipstick marred the bottoms of Ariane Daniels's even, sparkling front teeth. They were the only blemishes Marjorie could see on Daniels's otherwise flawless appearance. Less than two weeks after Ginny McNaghten had seen her in Alexandria with a knife at her throat and front-paged her dramatic kidnapping and Dahl had seen her in Kansas City with a pistol in her ear, she moved with elegant poise beside Dahl, every golden hair in place, her face radiating vitality and self-assurance.

She stood now with Dahl at the far end of a twenty-by-twenty-foot room that the Canadian Embassy visitors' guide with delicate understatement called a foyer. She munched on the North American Pulp and Paper Institute's British Columbia salmon hors d'oeuvres, sipped that organization's golden ale, and nodded at a soldier in dress uniform ten feet away. Every man who entered the room looked at her within five seconds. As knots of people eddied around her, she brushed Dahl's bicep and turned in his direction, deflecting the warm, glowing attention toward him.

"She seems to have made a remarkably rapid recovery from her ordeal," Marjorie said.

"Perhaps emptying a pistol into her assailant was the ideal catharsis," Michaelson said.

"Mr. Michaelson?" a voice behind them broke in.

Michaelson turned slightly. The man who'd spoken had thinning black hair and was almost as tall as Michaelson. The European cut of his navy blue suit emphasized the breadth of his shoulders and the tautness of his midsection.

"Brooke Murdoch, attaché for science and technology affairs," the man said.

Michaelson shook his hand.

"Delighted to make your acquaintance. Allow me to introduce Marjorie Randolph, proprietress of Cavalier Books, the foremost establishment of its kind in Washington."

"How do you do?" Murdoch said to Marjorie.

"You know," Michaelson said, "the science and technology affairs attachés I encountered in the U.S. Foreign Service were all spooks. They were smitten with the title for some reason and it got to be their favorite cover. It's quite a pleasure to meet a real one. I suppose acid rain must be one of your most pressing briefs?"

Murdoch offered Marjorie and Michaelson a tight, dry smile and held it for an extra second.

" 'The tales of Tory heritage,' " he recited then, quoting Canada's poet laureate, " 'Are full of lies and blanks. / But what else is there / To show that we're not Yanks?' "

"What a diplomat," Marjorie said to Michaelson. "He's got you there."

"I hope we can discuss acid rain later on. At the moment, there's a gentleman who's asked particularly to meet you. If you have a few minutes, perhaps I could take you to him now."

"By all means," Michaelson said. He tilted his head toward the soldier. "You don't mind if Lieutenant Devereaux joins us, do you?"

"Not at all."

Murdoch led the other two through an inconspicuous door on the opposite side of the foyer from Daniels and Dahl. Without making a production out of it, Devereaux followed about eight seconds behind. A short hallway took them to a narrow flight of stairs. At the top of the stairs a few strides down a much more generous hall brought them to a high-ceilinged room paneled in dark wood. Large oil paintings that seemed to depict Canada from Thunder Bay to Newfoundland dominated the walls. A short, solid-looking man who gave every impression of being absorbed in a view of the Citadel as seen from the Plains of Abraham stood with his back to them. Corky Baldwin stood beside him.

"GOJ gave us to understand they would be pleased to have Ohatsu's lawyer present for this meeting," Murdoch whispered. "GOJ" is diplomatic jargon for "Government of Japan." "I trust there's no objection?"

"None at all," Michaelson shrugged. "It's their party."

The shorter man and Baldwin turned toward the group at the door, which Devereaux had by now joined. Leading Michaelson and Marjorie forward, Murdoch took care of the introductions. The shorter man's name was Jenji Isuru. His eyes were dark brown, his face smooth-shaven. His less than inscrutable expression said that time was money and he wasn't interested in wasting either one.

"Mr. Michaelson, I have something for you."

A flicker of surprise marred Baldwin's face as Isuru pulled an oversized, mustard-colored envelope from the inside breast pocket of his coat. The envelope was thickly stuffed and seemed a bit battered.

"Thank you," Michaelson said, accepting the packet.

"I was led to believe this was just going to be a chat," Baldwin said. "Am I allowed to ask what the paperwork is?"

"It is a summary of an independent CPA's very rigorous audit of the books of Ohatsu Limited," Isuru said, "for a period covering the last three years."

Michaelson began to slit the envelope open.

"An audit establishing, I assume, that the check in question never passed through any Ohatsu account," he said.

"Correct. Among other things. The complete audit report is voluminous, but is available for examination by an American firm, if that is desired."

"It's not my call," Michaelson said, "but I doubt very much that it will be desired. Mature governments only lie about important things."

"What check are you talking about?" Baldwin asked.

Scanning the first page of the summary, Michaelson ignored the question.

"This is extremely helpful, Mr. Isuru," he said. "Thank you very much."

"You are welcome. I wonder if I might ask a return favor."

"Certainly."

"I should like to see the videotape that was retrieved under such dramatic circumstances in Kansas City."

"I don't see any reason why not," Michaelson said. Marjorie took a large cassette from her purse and handed it to Michaelson. "This is only a copy, of course, but it's clear enough. Is there equipment conveniently available somewhere?"

"Naturally," Murdoch said, sliding open a scarcely visible door cut into the paneling. "As we approach the twenty-first century, how could any self-respecting embassy expect to function without a full panoply of electronic toys in every room? Sony, of course," he said then, gesturing toward the VCR and the television behind the panel.

Murdoch took the cassette from Michaelson and quickly produced a steady, dark, black-and-white image on the screen that the sliding door had revealed. The group in the room watched a replay of what Sellinger, Jacobs, Cunningham, and Michaelson had seen in the White House basement.

"It is curious the way the mind associates things," Isuru said as the screen went dark. "As I watched that, I thought of the famous photograph of General MacArthur wading ashore when the Americans retook the Philippines. The caption said that he was coming in with the first wave of marines. But the picture was taken from the front and the Pacific Ocean was behind him. I couldn't help wondering which wave the photographer had come in with."

"The association seems quite apt," Michaelson said. "As we watch the Lever-Hurst vignette, the intriguing question is, Who was holding the camera?"

"It's obvious, isn't it?" Baldwin interjected. "It was a sting. The camera was hidden. Just like Abscam and Mayor Berry. We lawyers call it *modus operandi*. The FBI uses the same method of operation over and over again, just like the bad guys do."

"FBI?" Murdoch wondered skeptically. "No one asked me, but it scarcely seems plausible that the principal police agency of the executive branch of the American government would have entrapped a senior White House official."

"Oh, it's *possible* that something like that happened," Michaelson said. "Just like it's possible that two experienced special ops personnel from the army, or the CIA, or the Japanese secret service, panicked when they thought they were under fire and let themselves be chased away from Dahl's apartment by a rank amateur whom they exponentially outgunned. It's possible that a veterinarian in Topeka duped a longtime associate into a criminal effort to exact essentially symbolic revenge on his son's killer. It's possible that the army arranged through invidious machinations to keep Luttwalk's mouth shut about the computerized vote-counting project, even though the army's role was innocent and protected by a paper wall without a single chink. It's possible that the Japanese government undertook some type of adventure of the same variety, even though the risks were grave and long-term and the potential benefits dubious and short-term. All of those things are *possible*. But none of them is likely, is it?"

"Okay," Baldwin shrugged. "Then who was holding the camera?"

"Ariane Daniels."

"That's preposterous."

"Why?" Michaelson demanded. "She was Ohatsu's Washington consultant. She had access to the prototype of an experimental television camera that could have produced that tape. She pitched supposed software security services to Sellinger, on the claim that she could guarantee victory in the next presidential election."

"That's bullshit sales talk that no one with his head screwed on straight would take seriously," Baldwin said.

"On the contrary, Sellinger and the army took it seriously enough to spend several million dollars trying to find out whether she could carry out the veiled threat she was making. Which, it turned out, she could."

"What're you talking about?" Baldwin snorted. "You don't mean you actually buy that crap, do you?"

"Your comment misses the point. Ms. Daniels's implication was that her client had found a way to manipulate computerized vote counting. Neither Ohatsu nor anyone else had found any such thing. But once she had Lever on videotape handing that check in that context to Hurst, she had what she needed to make the threat just as good as gold. In an election where protectionism and resentment of foreign competition promise to be major issues, all she'd have to do is leak that tape to the networks in the middle of October and she could indeed guarantee victory in the election—to the other side."

"The tape's not that conclusive," Baldwin said.

"Quite conclusive enough for her purposes, I think," Michaelson said. "Especially when it turns out that there's a top-secret military project that associates 'software security services' with manipulating vote counting, and someone exposes a documented under-the-table payment that Ohatsu denies because Ohatsu never received it. It's enough to make Watergate look like smoking in the boys' room. Ariane Daniels wasn't bluffing. The threat to leak the tape would've gotten her anything in Lever's power to give."

"Why would she try something like that?"

"Because it's a ticket to the top of her field. From five hundred thousand gross a year to ten million. From one of three dozen consultants who know their stuff to the woman no one can say no to."

"Nonsense," Baldwin scoffed. "There's not a chance in hell something like that could've worked."

"On the contrary, once Lever bit there wasn't a reason in the world that it wouldn't have worked—except that Terry Hurst was appalled when he realized the enormity of what he'd gotten involved in."

"He must've realized that sometime after that tape got made," Baldwin said.

"Exactly. When the tape was made he thought he was participating in a clever scam—bluffing twenty-five thousand dollars a year out of politicians who might've suspected they were buying blue sky and hot air but who couldn't take the chance that Hurst might actually be able to deliver, and who then couldn't complain when he didn't. When he realized what was really going on, though, he was stunned. A little old-fashioned Washington confidence game is one thing, but subverting the Constitution is something else. He got a copy of the tape and was going to spoil everything. So he had to die. Unfortunately, his kidnapping and murder were improvised and something went wrong. Luttwalk was captured and had to be kept quiet somehow. That was where you came in."

"I thought Ohatsu wanted me to defend him and I didn't care why," Baldwin shrugged. "Daniels was the key contact with Ohatsu. If she wanted to disguise the billing I didn't have any objection. Billings dictate compensation. The management guys at my firm don't ask how, they just ask how much."

"I think it was even more cynical than that," Michaelson said. "I think that since she paid the piper, she called the tune. When she told you to sell Luttwalk out, you did it."

"Sell Luttwalk out how?" Baldwin demanded. "I defended that low-life scumbag all the way to the Supreme Court. I was fighting for his worthless hide right up to the morning he was executed. Maybe I didn't do it for free, but I did it. You find a lawyer who looks at the record and says he could've done a better job and you've found yourself a liar."

"I'm certain you're right. But you didn't do the one thing that might have saved Luttwalk's life. You didn't advise the FBI that he was willing to tell what he knew to avoid the death penalty. And you told Luttwalk that you'd passed on his offer and been turned down."

"That's a very serious accusation," Baldwin said. "What do you have to back it up?"

"Nothing whatever."

"Then you'd better start watching what you say."

"At one time, though, the army had an audio tape of your last conference with Luttwalk. Unfortunately, the tape was erased."

"I'm not surprised," Baldwin said. "Taping that conference would be illegal as hell."

"So would passing thiopental sodium to Luttwalk and telling him it would counteract the soporific he was supposed to get, so that he'd be awake right up to the execution."

"How am I supposed to have accomplished that?" Baldwin asked, bemused.

"There's only one way you could've accomplished it. You rubbed it in paste form on your own fingers and then wiped it off on his forearm during the farewell handshake. During your last chat with him you told him to transfer it to his own fingers and put it under his tongue. That's what he did, and that's why the soporific he got thirty minutes before he was supposed to be executed amounted to an overdose that killed him."

"And why would he want to be awake right up to the execution?"

"So that he could make one last offer himself to save his life by telling what he knew, in case you hadn't delivered by then. As he could have. The FBI was there, ready to take him up on it."

"So why wouldn't he have made that offer before they put him on the gurney?"

"Because you told him, falsely, that the president would be issuing a stay of execution fifteen minutes before he was to be put to death. You told him you had the whole thing wired, but it was going to be delayed to give it maximum political effect. You knew he wouldn't want to play the stool-pigeon card except as a last resort. That meant you were safe until just before the execution was supposed to happen—and you saw to it that by then he was dead."

"You have a first-rate imagination."

"What I have is the fruits of a conversation with Lieutenant Devereaux here."

"Who's he supposed to be?"

"He's an army officer who six weeks ago was supposedly convicted by a court martial of raping a civilian living near Fort Hood, in Texas. This was a remarkable feat, inasmuch as Lieutenant Devereaux was stationed in Ankara, Turkey, at the time of the incident in question. He was nevertheless sent to the disciplinary barracks at Fort Leavenworth, and once there was assigned to a work crew that was used rather often to take care of chores at Leavenworth Federal Penitentiary."

"You're saying he was operating undercover and he's the one who supposedly recorded the conversation?" Baldwin asked.

"Yes," Michaelson answered. "And he has an excellent memory."

"Thus illustrating the profound wisdom of the common law's aversion to hearsay evidence," Baldwin said. "I categorically deny each and every word of that cock-and-bull story. Not a syllable of it's true—and you couldn't prove it even if it were."

"About the last part you're absolutely right," Michaelson conceded mildly. "There's no surviving physical evidence, the tape's gone, and Lieutenant Devereaux's recollection is inadmissible. We know that it happened exactly as I described it, but we can't prove a word of it."

"Then perhaps you could shut up about it."

"What we can prove is the interconnection among Ariane Daniels, Luttwalk, Hurst, and the vote-counting scam. The videotape establishes

Hurst's involvement in the scam. Luttwalk killed Hurst. Ms. Daniels's role in getting you paid to defend Luttwalk is documented—as is the fact that shortly after she learned Dahl had that documentation burglars tried to steal it from him. That case looks much more promising."

"Good luck and God bless you. Not that I give a damn, but sometime while you're presenting all that to the jury you might think about how you're going to explain why the bad guys kidnapped her when things started getting warm."

"She wasn't kidnapped," Michaelson said. "The kidnappers couldn't have counted on getting her unnoticed out of the Blue Ridge Mall against her will. They certainly couldn't have taken her halfway across the country and into a crowded auditorium under duress without risking some attention."

Baldwin shrugged.

"I almost hope I get the case," he said. "I wouldn't mind putting that one to twelve good men and true."

"I don't claim any expertise in the area," Michaelson said, "but I don't think a key witness for the prosecution would be eligible to serve as defense counsel."

"What are you talking about?"

"You're going to turn state's evidence, Mr. Baldwin. You're going to talk."

"You're dreaming."

"I'm realistic. You didn't let me finish cataloging my doubts about the supposed kidnapping. You see, I also don't think a man whose right collarbone had just been broken reached for a gun with his right hand. I think Daniels staged her kidnapping in an effort to keep the videotape from falling into anyone else's hands. I think when the scheme failed, due to Major Cunningham's heroism, she killed her confederate to keep him quiet—just like she had Luttwalk kill Hurst and you kill Luttwalk."

Baldwin started to talk, then thought better of it.

"Think it over carefully," Michaelson said. "Ms. Daniels had two accomplices at the Blue Ridge Mall, and it's probable that Luttwalk had the same two when he kidnapped Hurst. One of them rather messily died in Kansas City, but the other one's still alive and, with Ginny McNaghten's description, much more likely to be captured than he was before."

"So what?"

"All of this will soon be explained to Ms. Daniels as it is being explained right now to you. Her only choices are to cut her own deal or to dig in and hang tough. If she decides to make a deal, her testimony will be fatal to you. If she decides to hang tough, your testimony could be fatal to her. In the recent past, three people whose silence she desired ended up dead. Unless you decide to come across quickly, you're liable to become the fourth. As you said, it's what you lawyers call *modus operandi.*"

Baldwin's lips paled. He broke eye contact with Michaelson, tried to reestablish it, failed, and looked down again. Then, looking around at Murdoch, he drew himself up to his full height.

"Good evening," he said with massive dignity.

He turned and stalked out of the room, his pace quickening as he neared the door.

At the top of the main staircase he paused and composed himself. Five deep breaths, in through the nose, out through the mouth. He found a smile and put it on. He waited until he felt some color come back to his face. He started down the stairs.

"Bullshit," he told himself.

At the bottom of the stairs he snared a glass of champagne from a shimmering silver tray that a liveried waiter brought by. He spotted two colleagues and began to weave his way toward them.

"Is the woman in your book beautiful or brilliant?" he heard a female voice ask as he passed a conversational group.

"Both—like all the women I deal with."

This must be real life, Baldwin thought. Nobody could make shit like that up.

He made it to his colleagues. They greeted him warmly. They were talking about something called COBRA. Baldwin wondered if it was a new weapons system. It turned out to be a law that had something to do with employee health benefits. Within three minutes Baldwin was feeling warm and confident again.

He looked around for some more champagne. Ariane Daniels's violet eyes were staring straight at him from less than a yard away. She looked serious. Not worried. Just serious.

He didn't feel warm anymore. He felt chilly, starting with a cold, wet spot in the base of his stomach.

"We have to talk," she said.

"I'll give you a call first thing tomorrow."

"Tonight."

"Tonight?"

"Not here." She smiled at him, full wattage, dazzling. "Why don't I ditch Barbie's boyfriend and you can take me for a drive."

" 'Barbie's boyfriend'?"

"Ken Dahl," she said, smiling and punching Baldwin playfully. "Let's go be grown-ups. 'Cause we have to talk. I mean it."

"Sure," Baldwin said. He tried a smile, decided he didn't think much of it. "I drove over in a brown Mercedes. I'll meet you outside in"—he glanced at his watch—"ten minutes."

"Perfect."

Smile, flash, dazzle, and she turned away.

"It's the prisoners' dilemma," Baldwin said to Daniels as they drove over the Key Bridge. "And all we have to do is be smart enough not to fall for it. As long as we both keep our mouths shut, they've got nothing on me and not much on you."

He kept one eye on her as he drove. He told himself that she'd have to be crazy to try to kill him. There'd be no way to avoid a murder rap if she did. A dozen people knew they'd left the Canadian Embassy together.

"You're absolutely right," Daniels said. "If you don't testify against me, I can handle whatever else they have on my end. And I'm the only one who can prove you killed Luttwalk."

"Which you can't prove without putting your own neck in a noose."

"I know that," Daniels said.

How might she do it? he wondered. Shoot him and claim self-defense? He saw one of her hands holding a cigarette, the other lying placidly in her lap. Fake a suicide? Knock him out, drive him to a garage and leave him in the car with the engine running? She'd need to grow some muscles before she tried anything like that.

"It may get rough," Baldwin warned. "They can make some noise about the vote-counting business. But the bottom line is—"

"The bottom line is, my lawyer will be highly motivated," Daniels said. "Won't you?"

"You know you can count on that. I came through for you on Luttwalk and—"

"You came through for both of us. You're the one who found Luttwalk and the rest of the muscle. Luttwalk could've started them down a trail that would've led to you as well as me."

"Fair enough. The point is, I took care of it. I kept his mouth shut and then I took him out."

"Yes, you did."

"I came through for you on that, and I'll come through for you on this. All—"

Baldwin stopped talking as he saw the red and blue lights flashing on the grill of the black, unmarked car thirty feet behind him. Automatically, he checked his speedometer, which told him he was only nine miles over the posted limit. Then he realized what was happening.

"You're wired!" he screamed at Daniels. "You made a deal!"

Baldwin pounded the leather-wrapped steering wheel with the heel of his right hand. The unmarked car pulled alongside his Mercedes. A second set of flashing red and blue lights showed up in his rearview mirror. Sirens began wailing.

"Goddamn bitch!" he yelled.

For one exhilarating second he stood on the accelerator. The Mercedes's powerful engine yanked the car forward.

The instant the first rush had passed, he realized he didn't have the nerve, that none of it made any difference any more. Numb, he dropped his foot from the accelerator and let the car slow as it coasted. When it had finally stopped, he lay his head on the steering wheel and whispered, "How could I have been so goddamn stupid?"

CHAPTER FORTY-THREE

The flag's snap as the two marines pulled it taut seemed as loud as the rifle shots a minute or so before. With stiff, precise movements they folded the banner horizontally, then folded it again. That done, the marine at the far end began walking toward his colleague, flipping the folded flag over on itself in triangular sections as he did so, each movement as ritualized and mannered as the intricate steps in a Japanese tea ceremony. When he had finished, the flag was a tight, neatly packed bundle, with only the white stars on the blue field showing.

A solemn man in a navy blue civilian suit took the flag from the marines and walked past the mound of freshly turned dirt and the gold-on-chocolate-brown marker that said when Nathaniel Lever had been born and when he had died and what branch of the armed forces he had served with. He handed the flag to a white-haired woman whose face was set in masklike hardness. He spoke a few words to her in low tones.

The woman accepted the flag, nodded, looked down, turned away, tucked the flag under her left arm. The man, who had bent slightly to speak to the woman, straightened and stood still, head up. He knew exactly what to do. He'd been through the ceremony before. More than once.

After a few uncertain steps through damp, manicured grass, the woman found a chalk-white concrete walkway. Her pace quickened slightly as she began to move along it, seemingly oblivious to the small crowd trailing behind her.

"Can we offer you a ride, Deborah?" Marjorie asked 140 seconds later as the party stepped from the walkway onto a gray asphalt parking lot.

"No, thank you." The woman stopped and turned around. She was clutching the flag as if it were her first-born child. She nodded toward a limousine with a driver standing at attention beside it. "They sent a car for me."

"Please call if there's anything we can do."

"I will."

The woman started toward the limousine, then turned back. She looked over Marjorie's shoulder, searching out Michaelson behind her.

"He left an envelope with your name on it," she said.

"I thought he might."

"Do you want me to send it to you?"

"No," Michaelson said. "I know what's inside. If I'm ever asked under oath whether I've read it I'm going to say no, and I'd prefer for that to be the truth."

The woman nodded. She gestured minimally with her head toward a man and a woman standing ten yards away.

"Is that the reporter over there, the one who's been writing all the stories about this?"

"Yes," Michaelson said. "Ginny McNaghten."

"She's been very—*fair* to Nat. Sellinger calls it excellent spin. I'd like to thank her."

"I'll handle that for you, if you like. Ms. McNaghten is being well compensated for her fairness. She'll continue to be compensated as long as she continues to be fair—and she knows it."

"Perhaps that's best. Thank you, Richard. Thank you very much."

The woman moved again toward the limousine, and this time she didn't turn back.

"Great visuals," McNaghten said to Dahl as she gazed at the vignette and imagined the words being spoken. "Too bad you don't have a crew here."

"I would have, but I'm live at five on a congressional aide being arraigned downtown. Did you know it's three-to-one on Connecticut Avenue that Ariane Daniels'll never hear the steel door slam? They say black judges can't bring themselves to send white women to prison unless there's absolutely no choice."

"Take the bet," McNaghten said, shaking her head. "She's implicated in four murders. She may've turned state's evidence but she won't have to worry about accessorizing her wardrobe for five to seven years."

"Maybe," Dahl shrugged. "At least if they catch the second accomplice."

"If I were he, I'd turn myself in. Beats being shot resisting arrest."

"That'll cinch the case against Baldwin, anyway."

"The case against Baldwin's a slam dunk," McNaghten said. "He'll cop a plea to avoid the death penalty, get twenty to life times four concurrent, find Jesus in prison, and turn a nice buck as a TV evangelist after he gets out in about thirteen years."

"You're a hard-bitten cynic, Ginny."

"I don't know about that. Except for Terry Hurst, he wasn't responsible for killing anyone that I really expect to miss. What bothers me more, to tell you the truth, is Ariane Daniels setting up shop five to seven years from now as a Washington consultant to some prison reform group's fund-raising organization. I'll bet she calls it the St. Dismis League."

"Five to seven," Dahl said. "I guess that's life in the big city."

"Keep making cracks like that and you'll never get a Nieman Fellowship."

"Wouldn't want one. What would a pretty boy like me do at Harvard except get whistled at?"

"You can be an electronic journalist even at Harvard. There's plenty of tragedy in Cambridge."

"I'm not sure this was tragedy," Dahl said. "The Constitution was saved, justice was sort of done, and we each got a story."

"What about Nat Lever?"

"He lived to be sixty-eight and as far as I'm concerned he died for his country. You could do a lot worse."

McNaghten turned to Dahl and gazed at him for a long moment in frank appraisal.

"You know something?" she said. "You might wanna give me a call in a couple of weeks. The way things are going I'm gonna need some help—and once you get slapped around a little bit and have a few doors slammed in your face and someone teaches you how to get the lead in the first 'graph, you might actually make a halfway decent excuse for a reporter."